The Turning Hour

THE TURNING HOUR

a novel
by
Shelley Fraser Mickle

Library of Congress Cataloging-in-Publication Data:

Mickle, Shelley Fraser.
The turning hour : a novel / by Shelley Fraser Mickle.
p. cm.
ISBN 0-913515-22-1 (alk. paper)
1. Mothers and daughters--Fiction. 2. Suicidal behavior--Fiction. 3. Teenage girls--
Fiction. I. Title
PS 3563.I353 T87 2001
813'.54--dc21
2001002095

Designed by Lissa Monroe.
Cover art painted especially for this book by Karl Franklin.
Manufactured by Vaughan Printing in the United States of America.

RIVER CITY publishes high-quality books of fiction, nonfiction, poetry, and art by
a variety of distinguished authors and artists. Our imprints include River City,
Starrhill, Sycamore, and Black Belt. Visit our web site at www.rivercitypublishing.com
and visit the author's website at www.shelleymickle.com.

Acknowledgments

This book could not have been born without the aid and support of many:

Marilyn McLean helped me to *pretend* to think like a lawyer. Mary Ann Coxe who, when I told her I'd used up many of my own family stories in other novels and essays, generously said, "Oh, here, take some of mine," then proceeded to tell me some of the funniest family anecdotes I have ever heard! Thanks, too, to the Spies Family, who loaned me their wonderful tale of "The Run-Away Party."

My son Paul, without hesitation, always said, "Sure, I can tell you that," as he filled in one of my blanks with the words of his generation. My daughter Blake always said to include the voice of the mother, because daughters can't ever get enough of finding out what it is that is making their mothers so loopy at one time or another. My husband Parker who, after twenty years as a pediatric neurosurgeon, carefully and kindly walked me through the medical details that the story required.

Dr. Candace Valenstein provided me with details and insights into the treatment and issues dealing with teen suicide. Her guidance and support have been beyond measure.

Special applause is due my agent, Sam Pinkus, who has the tenacity of a hard-shell crab and the kindness of a shade tree in Florida.

And too, thanks to these friends: John and Eve Cech, Candy Fossum, Elise Kroell Griffin, Gloria Bronte Lane, and Dale Eldridge-Kaye, whose friendship is always the unsinkable ship. And to Wayne

Greenhaw who is as steady as the seasons.

Perpetual thanks to those at River City Publishing—Tina Tatum, Amilee Sedberry, and Jim Davis—who saw the good in this story and refused to walk away from it.

May the power and comfort bloom.

—Shelley Mickle
September, 2001

There's a certain Slant of light,
Winter Afternoons—
That oppresses, like the Heft
Of Cathedral Tunes—

When it comes, the Landscape listens—
Shadows—hold their breath—
When it goes, 'tis like the Distance
On the look of Death—

—Emily Dickinson
"There's a Certain Slant of Light"

Just as despair can come to one only from other human beings,
hope, too, can be given to one only by other human beings.

—Elie Wiesel, Nobel lecture, 1986

Dedication

For Louis Rubin, and

With thanks to the woman on the beach who,
during that afternoon in the fall of 1995,
gave me the bones of a beautiful story,
then encouraged me to do with it as I might, and

To Dr. Candace Valenstein, who guided me
while I told it, as if it were my own.

<u>Part I</u>

<u>ONE</u>

Bergin

I'm still inclined to lie about this. Because the lowdown is, the truth didn't set anybody free. And I wasn't after attention or revenge, as most people will think. At least I know that's what goes through someone's mind when they hear that a girl has tried to do a mean two-step with Saint Peter. Or to buy the farm. Or to cash in her chips, if you know what I mean. No. *Words* had more to do with this.

Words.

And if there had been any on the piece of paper that I saw that day at lunch when I was sitting on the side steps of the school, it didn't matter. It was a wide scrap of paper. A single torn slip of paper that danced up on the wind and floated. Then was carried off to somewhere I could not see. I took it for a sign. Not a word had been spoken out loud or even in my head. But that single piece of paper spoke to me, telling me that it was okay. That this was to be how it would be. So in a few hours I was standing in my father's kitchen alone, knowing how I would do this.

It was a Monday, 3:32. No one was expected home earlier than 5:30. And even *that* depended on the traffic. I couldn't keep my mind on any one thing. I could look at something, hold on to something.

But it wasn't really there. Not the white tile floor, or the big Sub-Zero fridge that I used to think was so god-o-mighty fine. Or the vase of flowers that sat by the sink like *Architectural Digest* was, at any second, on its way to drop by. I was not anywhere close to being where you would call *Here*. And yet my heart was beating faster than any heart around. A last-hurrah beat, I guess it was thinking. A swan song of a beat. And my stomach? Well, it had caved in on itself. I could feel the sides of it touching themselves, sucked back like a mouth with no teeth. At any minute I thought I was going to be sick.

It was the first week in December. The whole city was getting into its Christmas thing. At least as much as some place in Florida can look like it's getting into a Christmas thing. No white. *Nothing* white. Just green, still green. It'd never look like anything you'd see on the front of a Christmas card. So far, there were camellias, some outside lights, already a few yard reindeer. The ground was like chewed gum from a recent rain. I'd begged out of soccer practice with a headache. "I really have to go home," I'd told Carol Ann, the coach. "I've never had a migraine before. But this may be one. My mother has them. Can these be inherited?"

"Sweetie, anything can be inherited," Carol Ann had said, laughing. "Especially money and headaches."

Carol Ann is built like a bulldog with a Pocahontas hairdo that she holds in place with a beaded headband. She isn't the usual coach type. Our team was added only in the last year, and Carol Ann had been recruited from Modern Dance. "Go ahead, go home, take a day off. You deserve it," Carol Ann had said.

But my head didn't really hurt. If anything, it was my eyes that bothered me. If I could only make them stop, keep them closed for a while. From the kitchen window, I could see my green Celica sitting in the drive. My biology book would still be on the front seat open to the diagram of the Krebs cycle, because I'd been looking over it at every red light. My notes would be open too. *Adenosine triphosphate* written out in large black ink on one page alone, hyphens between the syllables because I was the only girl—person really—in the whole class, if not the whole school, who insisted on using the full name for ATP. It had been my claim to fame lately. It was the one thing I could count on to hold me in place for the three whole seconds it took to roll the seven syllables off my tongue. And always whoever was in the room, even Mr. Whitstruck, King of Biology himself, would stop in their tracks and turn and marvel.

Marvel, yes. Drop-dead marvelous it was. More than once I had heard "My God." Or an out-and-out astonished "Shit," since it was not what anyone expected coming from someone five feet three, blonde as corn, captain of the cheerleaders who defected to the soccer team without being sure if I was right-footed or left. Didn't even know all the rules, either. Carol Ann was starting to suspect, too. But I had become a star. Even at that, too. It hadn't been hard, not when you don't mind about bouncing the ball off your head. Or diving out of the goal to stop a drive, since breaking your neck or outright killing yourself isn't what you're really eager to avoid. Lately, though, not even the seven syllables of *adenosine triphosphate* had been anything I could count on. Nothing was any longer listed or boxed. No sooner would I get the full name of ATP out than my thoughts would once again go cartwheeling off, shredded like lettuce for a salad.

I didn't study how to kill myself, either.

I had some ideas about it from a story I once read in a magazine. And a month before, a girl on the far side of town had tried it, and been successful at it, and had been written up in the newspaper for having done it all the way. The hard-copy details had been spelled out. The point being that I knew that high places and guns and heavy drugs weren't really necessary. No. I just went down the hall from the kitchen into my father's bathroom in his big new house, opened up his medicine cabinet and took out all I knew I would need. It was a three dollar and fifty-nine cent bottle of aspirin. Microcoated and buffered. Really, this was going to be very simple.

I went back to the kitchen. The cat was sliding a tuna can around on the floor, and the tinny sound must have jiggled loose that rhyme—*Hey diddle diddle, the cat and the fiddle.* Because it started hip-hopping through my mind. And I didn't stop the can. And I didn't stop the cat. And *whoa*, I knew better than to even try with my head. So I just watched for a while. He was a gray cat, fat and striped. He'd been brought home by my stepbrother, Dylan, who, to be funny, had named him Liposuction. So I washed out the fat-sucker's water bowl. Took a glass for myself and filled it with water from the tap. The only trouble I had was lining up the little arrows to get the top off.

The taste of them, two by two on my tongue, didn't register, either. I walked all the way down the hall, popping them like M&M's, washing them down with swallows. This thing about killing yourself, or dying by your own hand as I now like to think of it—borrowing a phrase from Shakespeare taught in Mrs. Kinnard's A.P. English class— When the time comes, you no longer feel the hand. No bed, either, as I lay down on it. Or at least I couldn't feel it. Or the sheets. Or light over me. Or the rain that was starting outside the window across the room.

How long should this take, I was wondering? An hour? Thirty minutes? Certainly half an hour would be enough to get this dying really going.

I'd decided not to leave a note. I really didn't have enough time. I couldn't have gotten everything on one page, anyway. And how could I have chosen the words? I figured, too, it'd be just my luck to misspell something.

So it was turning out that I was going about this dying the same way I danced, rising up all at once on the wave of some music and going off with it as though the notes were my body and I was them. The music had been there for some time, though. Licking around the corners of my thoughts. Driving down the side streets of my mind. It was about like the sounds of the ice cream truck that, as a little kid, I used to run to wait for, its tinny-like tunes winding their way to me through the neighborhood. And it was not so much that I was in love with the music I was dancing to, or the feel of the darkness I was moving off with. It was just that I did not know how to turn away from it. Like a dance partner, toe-tapping and waiting for my hand, it was simply something I could not say no to.

And after all, this dying was turning out to be really quite something. Magic and strange, with more the feel to it of a cat stalking something in high grass than a how-to manual read real close. What was really funny, too, was that playing in my mind like the final credits of a film was the diagram of the Krebs cycle. *Adenosine triphosphate.* If my tongue could have moved, I would have laughed. For what a side-splitter, really, that the molecule with the energy for life should be the last thing I could concentrate on. But it was *So long, old Krebs cycle.* And *damn*, because I could have made an A on that.

As the dish ran away with the spoon.

THAT'S WHAT everybody would love to hear about. Everybody is still so interested in *why* I did it. And *how*. As though someone like me, who has been where I have, is kin to a saint. Or a freak. Somebody who has seen things and been places no one else has. And yet, at the same time, a lot of people seem afraid of me. Afraid to know what I know, I guess.

It doesn't really matter, though, not now. Not anymore. Because what interests me now. What I don't just want to know but have to know. Need to know. *Desperate* to know, if you really want to get

17

down to the skin and bones of this, is—now that I am still here. And well, *Duh*, that's pretty obvious. And everyone thinks that I am fine, doing okay really. After all, I saved two goals in last week's game. I've always been good at faking it.

But how do I get back?

TWO

Leslie

Thinking about those first few days after Bergin swallowed the pills, I see my shoes, right there at the foot of the bed, my shoes. I would come home from the hospital where I would sit beside Bergin (why, *why* running through my mind like the drip from a broken faucet—*and why had there been no clues? How could I, her own mother, not have known?*) and I would lie down fully dressed, the toes of my shoes—black heels, plain pumps, or brown loafers, tennies even—like splayed fenceposts on top of the bedspread. If I slept, I don't remember. It certainly wasn't sleep as I had known it. My body was a mannequin that I inhabited from eight to two, that I then laid down on the bed to be refueled.

When Bergin decided to take her life, she took mine, too; but then, I guess that was partly the point. Before then we were certainly as severed and distant as two clocks keeping time in separate rooms. I attributed our difficulties to her being sixteen and my being pre-menopausal. (Lord knows—as everybody knows—hormones make the most dangerous minefield in the free world!)

But as the facts unraveled, as Bergin began to let go of them, and I began to enter Bergin's mind, see things the way she saw them—I saw myself. Our history was so messy, so unresolved. There are always multitudes of leftovers when you love someone and then leave that love, as I left Doug, Bergin's father.

The afternoon that Bergin decided to do what she did, I was in court. I've been a public defender for the last six years, and at 3:30 on the day that Bergin was trying to die (no sense mincing words), I was sitting at the defendant's table looking over my notes for the closing argument in the trial of *Richard Murphy vs. Lawson County School District.* He'd been accused of stealing tools out of a school bus, and more than likely he had. But it wasn't my job to concern myself with that; I was here to apply the law, and the most I was hoping for was planting reasonable doubt in the jury's mind.

All afternoon I'd been thinking about Bergin while making a list of things I needed to get or to get done. She was moving back in with us. By the weekend she would be swelling the number in our house to five. Before she got home, I wanted to clean the carpet in her room, get the dog hair off her bedspread (one of the dogs had practically taken up permanent residence in Bergin's room after she left), stock the fridge with diet drinks and cookie dough—Bergin's favorites. I planned to stop off at Walgreens on the way home to look for a Pictionary game. Board games are about the only way I know how to blend Kirk and Maggie, my two younger children who are twins, and Jack, their father, together with Bergin, at least for an hour or two after dinner. I absolutely refuse to let any of them go off on their separate ways every night to a computer, or to a TV, or to their rooms, where it seems Bergin can talk on the phone for hours.

All this I started in the last two years, or at least since Bergin turned sixteen and began trying so desperately, yet normally (I knew it was to be expected, but still that didn't make it any less difficult), to pull away from all of us. Five months earlier, Bergin had moved out to go live with her father. Much to my satisfaction, if not delight, she'd finally seen that he wasn't all she'd cracked him up to be. It wasn't all peachy keen and hallelujah time living with him. Now I was sure that Bergin was coming back as the daughter she had once been: obedient, close, adorable, adored—my best friend. (I was trying hard not to gloat.)

My Getting-Ready-for-Bergin list was right beside my notes for my closing argument, and Richard Murphy, otherwise known as Hoot, glanced over and watched me write down *Wheat Thins, Reduced Fat,* while the prosecutor went on with his version of events. Hoot was dressed in a borrowed suit, his hair slicked back with some kind of grooming gel that made me almost laugh. I smiled at him and patted his hand. His nails were long enough to pass for a classical guitarist's, and he smelled of mothballs and wintergreen breath mints. I'd known him for at least eight years now, and this time I was insistent that, if I won his case, he would go straight to the de-tox unit of the county hospital, then on to A.A. I was going to drive him there myself.

"What's he doing now?" Hoot whispered.

"Presenting his evidence," I whispered back. "But don't worry, it's all just circumstantial evidence."

The prosecutor was holding up the report that showed Hoot's fin-gerprints all over the bus. Of course they were all over the bus. It was Hoot's job to clean those buses, which would be easy for me to point out when my time came.

The prosecutor was verbally painting a nighttime scene in which Hoot climbed over the chain-link fence, going after tools the way he might desire a woman. Personally I doubted Hoot could climb over anything or "do" anything man-woman-wise. But high drama is the main ingredient for closing arguments, and I was sitting on my own. My fingers were resting on the edges of my typed notes. The day before I'd gotten a new manicure, a high gloss polish called Biscayne Sunset. I was thinking I was looking pretty foxy, at least if you looked

21

at my fingers only. (Let's just say, physical beauty is not my forte. It is Bergin who has inherited that, who is magnificent in ways I can never be.)

"What's *circumstantial* mean?" Hoot whispered.

"It means they don't have any real proof—they're just trying to make you look bad," I whispered back. "You watch. When my turn comes, I'll make it not count."

Confidence—at least in the courtroom—I never run short of. I was my father's daughter here, for sure. Judge Bergin, as everyone called him (even waitresses in restaurants and gas-station men), had been on the Supreme Court in Florida for fifteen years. He was elected; that's the way those things worked back then.

When I married, I couldn't bear to throw my maiden name away. Leery, too, of turning it into one of those hyphenated jobs when I married Doug, I instead gave it to our child.

Bergin Gwendolyn Talbot
7 lbs. 3 oz., 20 inches
January 12, 1981, 4:12 P.M.
(a semi-natural birth—3 Demerol, an epidural, and four martinis.)
Doug thinks she is the greatest thing since sliced bread and light beer.

That's the way I sent out her birth announcement.

I used to prop her up in front of the TV every afternoon and aim her toward *Sesame Street*, or wrestling, just anything that had a lot of color and movement. Then I could have a moment to myself. Bergin walked at nine months, climbed the woodwork at two, the refrigerator six months later. I had trouble keeping up. And then some days I had to go to bed with a migraine. By the time she was three, I paid her a dime for every PBS program she sat through. When she turned four, she was rich and reading on her own.

I wonder if it could be that I passed on my father-love to Bergin the same way I bequeathed to her the color and texture of her hair, the way our ears are so closely placed on our heads as if apricots have been laid on our profiles, and her eyes, almost grape-green? I so totally adored my father that Bergin must have just assumed this is what every father was to be: idolized, longed for, missed.

She was four the summer I drove home to Tallahassee, the state capital, where I grew up and where my father still lived. The court had a recess every July 17th for a month. That month was ours—mine and my father's and Bergin's. My mother had died three years before Bergin was born.

The house sat at the top of a hill on a double lot. It was big and brick, its trim pale yellow. My father met us as we pulled up into the drive. He was wearing khaki pants and a white shirt with the sleeves rolled up. He was fifty-eight then, ramrod-straight like the dusty gray-haired cowboys in the movies of my childhood. He grabbed up Bergin and swung her around, narrowly missing her feet on the side-view mirror on the car. No reserved, restrained lawyer at this time. Judge of nothing when it came to giving himself away. He didn't take a minute for consultation or consideration when it came to me and Bergin, who grew to look so much like him they could have been five-decade-apart gender-switched twins.

"There was a man in our town," my dad began quoting to Bergin, "and he was wondrous wise." My dad memorized nursery rhymes the way he ate beer nuts, nonstop and with little effort. (But then, there's no trick to it when you have a photographic memory.) "He jumped into a bramble bush," he went on, while jostling Bergin in his arms. "And scratched out both his eyes." Now he and Bergin had their lips rolled down like crying clowns. "But when he saw his eyes were out," he nodded to Bergin and she chimed in with him in a verbal duet, "with all his might and main, He jumped into another bush, And scratched 'em in again." With the last word, my dad began tickling Bergin in her ribs, and as she squirmed and squealed he set her down in the grass. They ran up the lawn then, holding hands. Yes, he was fifty-eight that summer, going on four.

Of all those visits, only a few details remain: Afternoons in the backyard, Tallahassee heat like a left-on oven, a kiddie pool blown up with a bike pump. My dad could sit beside us with the patience of Job, or of a pioneer woman. I swear I've never seen anything like it—his ability to find in himself an enjoyment of the little bitty details that we women seem to need to thread our lives with: recipes, distinctions and variations of fabrics, who said what to whom that pissed off whomever. He gave up golf and *Wall Street Week* with Louis Rukeyser for as long as we were there.

(And yet I never told him anything about the trouble Doug and I were in.)

I think I must have been four, myself, or a little older, when I realized my mom was not a real mom. She slept too much, spent too much time cooking supper and swirling wine into a variation of sauces. She craved ironing and spent hours with the ironing board set up in front of the TV, a wine glass on the end of it beside the sprinkling bottle. My mother was tall, her hair light brown that each night she swirled into circles under bobby pins, then combed out into tight waves. She could be a wonderful raconteur when she could remember a plot. And she loved a party more than her own life, at least the first hour of a wingding. Even after Dad hired Letty to keep house and do the laundry, Mother insisted on ironing. When she ran out of Dad's shirts and my dresses (always cotton because cotton needed ironing), she started on our underwear and sheets. I swear, I've never been so wrinkle-free since.

On my fifth birthday, we had a party to put all parties to shame. The whole house was full of kids. A clown was hired, and a pony to give rides in the backyard. My dad worked all the time then, it

24

seemed. He came home for the last few minutes of that party, and that's when he must have sized up what was really going on. Letty was running the party by then. Mom was in the back bedroom passed out, which we passed off as a migraine. My dad and Letty cleaned up, and I remember their silence. It was the silence that was the hard work of mental digestion, I now know—the time needed to absorb the facts.

The next day my mother felt so guilty for missing my party, she went out and bought me a duck, not a stuffed one, but a real one. It was a baby duck, left over from Easter at the pet store. I named him Daffy, which showed I wasn't given to much originality back then. But I had just turned five, so what did I know? I put Daffy in a big black kettle that ordinarily we grew geraniums in by the back door. I filled it with water and sat down for a while to watch him swim.

For four days, Daffy swam. He swam and swam and swam and then just keeled over. I found him one morning before breakfast, floating sideways. I scooped him up and sat down on the doorstep cradling his little body in my lap, his wet down soaking the cotton of my skirt so thoroughly I was unfit to go to school. I was crying and ashamed and mad and puzzled, and that's how my dad found me. How did I know a duck couldn't swim forever? He didn't yet have the oil on his feathers to have been a long-distance swimmer, anyway. I'd given him no place to crawl out, no beach or shore for rest. Damn. But I wasn't given to cuss words back then. I just cried.

My father rushed into my mother's bedroom. She was still asleep, as usual. He rummaged around in her dressing table—all that stuff then was as foreign to him as a third-world language, but he came up with a hair dryer. He ran back out to me and to Daffy and pulled us into the kitchen where he plugged in the dryer. With me in his lap and Daffy in mine, he flipped and flopped that duck over and dried him out, as thoroughly as we never could my mother. The care Daffy received could have outdone a hundred-dollar coiffure in a salon on

Park Avenue. I was all smiles when Daffy sat up, looked around, wobbled a bit, but was clearly revived. After that, my Dad rivaled Jesus, at least in my eyes.

That's when I can count back and see that he changed, learning to fill in where filling-in was needed. I didn't mind having a mother then who couldn't do everything a mother should. Of course, there was a hole, a slit in the cloth of whatever childhood should be. But it became to me more like the feel of a torn seam, a place where you know you can be exposed, be embarrassed over, but that you also know that, with a little careful and discreet posturing, you can get by. The whole of the garment was never in danger.

There were all these other times when he turned tragedy to comedy: The fifth-grade graduation when my mother didn't see or read or remember the note that said to send me to school in all white. There I stood in the wings of the stage in an azalea-pink dress and clashing red shoes. God, how I loved those shoes! Patent leather with no straps. I called him on a pay phone by the gym, using up a dime from my lunch money. He was in court, a public defender then, like I am now. I told his secretary it was an emergency like no other. I said I would die before noon or be forced to leave town on the next Greyhound bus if she didn't get my father on the phone, pronto. She took down my number, and I stood there by the pay phone and waited for him to call back, as I knew he would.

I still don't know to this day how he got that judge to declare a recess; but in what seemed about two minutes flat, my father called me back, learned the problem, then asked, "What size?" After a quick gallop through Belk's department store, he delivered to me a white organdy pinafore and white sandals, which he helped me to put on in the back seat of his car. Then he made me a ponytail, a hallelujah straight-as-a-whisk-broom, but still lovely, ponytail bound with a rubber band off the newspaper on the floor of his car. He went then to sit down in the audience. So what did it matter that the dress was too short-waisted and that my toes hung out over the edge of my sandals? I was called up to receive the award for the highest reading score in the fifth grade. From that day on, I made sure I read all my school notes myself. I learned to keep my own scheduling notebook, to carry a purse, and to have travelers' checks at all time. Mad money, my father called it, so I would never be farther than a cab ride or phone call from him.

Some things he felt compelled to leave up to Letty, though, who, when I turned twelve, taught me that periods weren't just the punctuation at the end of a string of words. They would be the sign that I could have my own child, she said. She called it "dropping roses" and told me that when the time came we would secretly celebrate. A year later, my mother popped a bottle of champagne in what she said was the celebration of my uterus shucking its lining. It was my mother who was great at celebrations. It was Letty who taught me how to think about being a woman. But it was my father whom, every day, I counted on.

I know, too, this is strange, but have you ever heard of anything so lovely (at least if you're female?): He painted my nails the night of my senior prom.

He did it again the morning of my wedding.

And get this: I am no beauty. A face as long as a summer squash, a nose coming down the center of it like a sand dune. My teeth, though they are very white, are as wide as peanuts. Yet I have never felt a lack of what beauty could bring me. I have other attributes that I cash in on: funny and smart, I also have nice hair—the color of it, anyway—and I am never at a loss for words. I am able to assess myself with honesty, without a whit of self-consciousness or shame, for, after all, my father was my mirror. I will never be mistaken for beautiful, and maybe I grieve over that as I do my mother. She died right after

27

my freshman year in college. Forever afterward we kept pictures of her all around the house. The amazing thing was, I didn't hate her. I never regretted who she was. I never felt damaged or deprived. My father turned us into the character of that nursery rhyme, the man who, when he saw his eyes were out, scratched 'em in again. He relegated my mother into being the circumstantial evidence in my life. He dismissed the harm she could have done. Her problem just didn't matter in the whole scope of things.

THAT AFTERNOON in the courtroom, when my turn came, I stood up in front of Hoot and the judge and the jury and let loose the voice and rhythm that my father gave me. I pointed out that Hoot had been cleaning those buses part-time for five months; he had plenty of time to get fingerprints all over them. Furthermore, even though he was found to have some of the stolen tools in his possession, no one saw him take them. They could have been planted in his tool box, or mislaid there. There was plenty of room for reasonable doubt.

The jury was out for forty-three minutes. It was nearly 5:20 when they pronounced Hoot innocent. He turned to me and said, "Whoopee! You done good."

I pressed down on his arm and looked him straight in the eye. "Not nearly so good as you're going to," I reminded him; "I'm not letting you out of my sight."

Tess, our office secretary, slipped me a note. *Call home.* It could wait, I decided. More than likely it was Kirk or Maggie, one of them squealing on the other, or begging for me to pick up a pizza. Probably they didn't like what Lydia, our housekeeper, was fixing for supper. Besides, Jack always came home a few hours every afternoon to be with them, then he'd go back to the hospital where he is the assistant to the CEO. Jack is my father reincarnated, only with a little wider job description. (He's my lover too.)

It was raining when Hoot and I walked out of the courthouse. Hoot sat like a zombie in the front seat of my car. He'd replaced the hangdog look of the courtroom with the hangdog dread of being driven to the hospital. Yeah, I was a busybody and completely unorthodox. I made him buckle up, too.

"Ain't we even gonna take a minute to celebrate?" He twisted around, looking at my profile. The windshield wipers thumped a dust-free arc in front of us.

"No sauce on this deal, Hoot. This is the best chance you're gonna get," I said.

"I know it is. I 'preciate it." He looked away from me then and silently stared through the windshield for the rest of the way.

In the admitting office, while Hoot was being checked in, I picked up a phone to call home. (I'm too cheap for a cellular. Don't like to hook my life to constant interruptions, anyway.) While it was ringing, an ambulance pulled around to the emergency entrance, its lights whirling and making kite-tail-like streaks in the rain. I could see it through a window. I watched it, aware of it, but not thinking anything about it, really. Yet, Bergin was in it. That's what, as soon as Jack picked up the telephone, he began telling me. Bergin was being brought here, being *rushed* here to the hospital. I could barely understand what he was telling me.

There had been an accident, he said, and yet, not really an accident. *What was he saying? What was he trying* not *to say?*

Most of it, finally, I pieced together. Bergin had swallowed some pills. She had been found comatose and barely breathing. She'd been found in time, though—*found in time*; Jack kept saying that. She was in critical condition, but it didn't appear there was any permanent lung or brain damage. They'd put in a tube to breathe for her. And Jack would be there as soon as he could.

As I hung up the phone receiver, I realized that I myself had forgotten to breathe. I put my hands on my chest and pushed in and out. Instinctively, I turned to see Bergin being rushed into the E.R. door, and as I ran to follow her, I saw Doug step out of his car and run across the wet pavement.

DON'T ASK me about sorrow. Don't ask me what I know of my guilt or of my father's grief. How lonely and frustrated he must have felt all those years in his marriage, and why we never talked about that before he died.

Don't ask me why I spend so much time taking people like Hoot to de-tox centers and defending them when they are barely defensible. Or why with my mother, it was easier to keep her secret than to confront her and be tough.

Because this is what I want to know—*have* to know, have to find out somehow and soon: *Where is my father in Bergin now? Where is his resilience?*

THREE

Bergin

What happened was—it rained. And because of that, Dylan came home, dropped off from his car pool when *his* soccer practice was canceled. And he found me.

That's crazy funny now, when you consider this—Dylan has a stomach as weak as his mind. Can't even eat lasagna. Says the white cheese in the middle reminds him of flesh. Pudgy, down low, belly flesh. And the sight of me was . . . well, that was the first thing they said I had to know.

By then I'd been moved to a private room. They get you out of intensive care after a few days because they're afraid you'll bolt from there. And they pretty much lose interest in you there, anyway, once they see you're gonna live. So they put me where they could lock the doors behind me. Then on the fifth day a nurse came into my room and said, "Come with me." I was going to meet Dr. Cone, she said. And that, from then on, Dr. Cone was going to be my head doctor. No pun intended, I guess, because the nurse didn't laugh. So here I go, walking down the hall in one of those paper gowns held together in the back with string bows, because they'd taken away my clothes. Said

I had to earn them back. Said undressed was the only way they could trust me. Yet they wouldn't even let me take a shower alone.

So here I was, being led into this room to meet Dr. Cone. It was a small room. Scandinavian teak furniture in it, and you know how its arms and legs look a little bowed? Every chair in there had a brown tweed seat. And what really blew me away was that sitting right there in one of the chairs was Dylan, his hands resting on the chair arms like they were nailed. His face was the color of the white cheese in lasagna, too, I swear. And someday I'm going to tell him that. But I was in that green gown with the ventilation in the back, so it's not like I had a whole lot to lord over him.

"Have a seat," Dr. Cone said, standing up and pointing to the tweed seat of the chair beside Dylan. She was the tallest woman I think I had ever seen. Six feet, at least. She was thin and black, with her hair not exactly gray, and not exactly black. But a lot of both going on. It was pulled into a knot like a fist at the back of her neck. As she sat down, she said—her voice husky and smoky, like someone's two days out from laryngitis, her nose a little square at the end, but her face rather pretty, in fact kinda nice, like a sculpture in wet clay, not bad for someone older even than my mother—she said, "Dylan was kind enough to come in to help us today." She looked from me to him. Then him to me. Her lips rounded the sounds of her words, as if licking them. Under her white clinical coat, her blouse was lime green; under the desk, her shoes were brown lizardskin, shiny and expensive, that was clear. The overhead light was skimming off the rimless lenses of her glasses as if they were ice.

Her eyes were drinking me. I looked away. But I was still clueless about what she was talking about. She had made it sound as if Dylan was in there waiting to empty the wastebaskets or something like that.

And Dylan himself? He had a solid lip-hold on silence.

At the time, Dylan was having a love affair with his roller blades. Usually he'd have on Janco jeans, big enough for two, and so long that when he skated you couldn't see his feet. The idea was to look like he had no feet. He wanted you to think he glided everywhere. Sticking a flame to a firecracker string or up a paper rocket's kazoo gave him the greatest thrill in life. He was as much in love with the sound of something blowing up as he was in the sound of his own voice imitating something blowing up. And for as long as I'd been living in the same house with him, I'd never seen him sit at a table without drumming on it. But now he was sitting no more than a foot from Dr. Cone's desk in pressed khakis and a pinstriped shirt. And with his arms on the chair like fish, filleted and ready to fry.

"Who brought you here this morning, Dylan?" Dr. Cone asked him, looking only at him. There was a whole row of dried-up plants on her window sill.

"My mom dropped me off."

"Is she waiting?"

"Not really. She's down in the gift shop looking at stuff."

I thought, *Good ol' Vicky La Tour.* Talbot now. My father's second wife. She could win a gold medal in a Shopping Event, if they had one. Which meant we didn't need to hurry here a bit, though I wanted to. Dylan's face is so much like his mother's, it can freak you out. Some people say he looks like a cherub. Cheeks so clean he seems sweet. Sweet, my ass. Dylan can make seedlings just up out of the ground want to turn around and go back. He glanced at me. Then he looked back at the side of Dr. Cone's desk.

I put my whole mind on trying to find a word to describe the color of Dr. Cone's hair. It started out like melted nickels, then ended like metal stirred with coal. And slicked back in a style so severe she could have been a freaky-tall over-the-hill ballerina. Yet the style, I have to admit, looked okay. Good, in fact. At least on her. And with polished nails, a shade of coral like the inside of a shell, so when the darkness of her skin ended at the tips of her hands, it seemed her fingers were held in sunlight. The plastic name tag above the pocket on her white coat said Dr. Harriet Cone. Through the ice-lenses of her glasses, she was looking at me while, at the same time, feeling around on her shoulder. Having trouble with one of her shoulder pads, that was clear. She maneuvered her thumb up under the top of her blouse. Which looked to be silk, or a substitute, the lime green of a new apple. She twisted her lips a little. Some kind of coral-brown lipstick, too. On either side of her mouth were two lines like parentheses. And her skin looked thick as hell. But I couldn't have told you anything about the color or shape of her eyes. Because I wasn't looking.

Dylan cleared his throat and looked out the window. He was fourteen then, already taller than me by half a foot. There wasn't the sign of one whisker on his whole face. And he had a mouthful of braces that looked like the razor wire at a state penitentiary. His hair, the color of a manila folder, was moussed straight up.

As though instinctively, my eyes started following Dr. Cone's hand as she began feeling all up and down her sleeve, trying to locate her shoulder pad. The whole time she was hunting, she was talking, and I started hating when the lines on her mouth didn't move. Because the silence then was like being under water. And Dylan sure wasn't about to add anything to the conversation. Let's just say he has the social skills of a wart hog.

But he was getting real interested in the shoulder pad hunt, too, watching Dr. Cone's hand feeling around on her sleeve. And then she reached all the way inside of her blouse and rooted around for a while.

"Dylan is the one who found you," she was saying when she looked at me and let her eyes land on mine for a good little while. "And it's important that you know how what you did affected others.

34

Can you tell us, Dylan?" She then looked from me to him. And I looked at Dylan like the good student I am.

Dylan on the spot is like hoping a rock will sing. Words die in his throat, and he forgets to breathe. We were both watching and waiting for him to say something when I glanced back at Dr. Cone and saw the tip of her shoulder pad peeking out from her cuff. "Yeah, well, she was in her room," Dylan finally said.

"And?"

"That's where I first saw her."

"Start from before that, Dylan. From the beginning, if you can." The pad was halfway out of the cuff now, and she looked down and saw it. And without one word being said about it, began to fish it back up her sleeve.

Dylan was going back and forth from her face to the shoulder pad, too. "Yeah, well, I came in because of the rain. And then I messed around in the kitchen for a while."

I knew what Dylan couldn't say, or wouldn't think about saying, about how he was scuffing up the floors and making a mess. Because he never takes off his cleats, no matter how much anybody yells at him to. And the house has all this white tile in it and blonde wood and floor-to-ceiling glass that fingerprints can dot in a heartbeat—all of it designed by my father. And my dad likes for the whole house to stay fit enough to be pictured in a magazine. Any time. Any day. So, dripping wet, Dylan probably stopped off at the fridge for a shot of Gatorade or a mound of Rocky Road, then sat down to watch a little MTV—the Backstreet Boys or Sublime—something lame, before going to his room. Along the way, he no doubt popped his hand on my door because he'd seen my car in the drive. And, since I'd moved in, he'd started badgering me to take him here, take him there, or to borrow this CD or that. He couldn't ever walk past me and not do something.

"And then I found her." His voice wasn't too steady, I have to admit.

"You went down the hall, you mean. And then you went into her room. How did she look when you first saw her?" Dr. Cone was looking at Dylan, and her hand was maneuvering the pad up her sleeve. Her voice was hard-candy sweet, like a math teacher's when she gets you at the board. And in its huskiness, it owned the air. Every once in while she'd look over at me to make sure I was getting the full effect.

"Not good," Dylan said.

"How not good?"

"She was blue."

"Cyanotic. Almost all the oxygen from her blood was gone."

"I guess."

"And what else?"

"She had thrown up and was breathing funny."

Dr. Cone looked at me. "Which means that her body had rejected what she had done to it. She was nearly devoid of oxygen. She was unconscious, and her eyes were rolled halfway back. She had aspirated her *vomitus*—which means inhaled her own vomit—and she was close to being dead. In fact, Dylan, if you hadn't found her, in the next thirty minutes she would have died. The biggest risk was destroying her lungs with the vomitus, which can burn lung tissue irreparably, leading to A.R.D.S., Acute Respiratory Depression Syndrome. In turn, this could have destroyed her brain. You had a very dangerous situation there."

"Yeah, she was disgusting," Dylan said.

I couldn't help myself; I laughed.

They both looked at me. I guess I came off as crazier than they'd been thinking I was. But it was just that word Dylan had used. *Disgusting*. Because for a long time I'd already been thinking I was that.

THE FIRST time I met Dylan, he was seven. I was one month from eleven, and my dad and his mom had just gotten together. Probably literally, too. I mean, I had a sneaking suspicion even then. As much as eleven-year-olds know about such things. That they were doing the big trick. Because every time they were together with me and Dylan, they would send us off to do something. Play a stupid video game or to buy an ice cream or to play one of those silly games where, for a quarter, you get to drop a mechanical arm down into a pile of stuffed animals and try to come up with one. For over a year and a half, Dylan and I had a direct line to an endless supply of quarters. And every time we went back for one, so as to play some machine or other, Dad and Miss Vicky LaTour would be kissing or rubbing their feet together, or touching some part of themselves to the other like they were those sticks Campfire Girls teach you to start a fire with. Their whole life seemed to be foreplay.

Looking back, that was one thing I'm pretty sure that probably had a lot to do with making me as crazy as I am. Because there was this *rumbling* under everything, under every minute and every movement like you could feel the earth shift on its plates all day long. And I didn't know anything about what it meant except for what my mother had told me over the years. Which was enough that I was aware of this hidden power, this energy that runs things that can lead to the making of another human being. But you couldn't see it. It was a secret or invisible; I wasn't sure which. But it was like the power in telephone wires and e-mail and TV. Yeah. And that's how I thought about it. About sex. That it was under everything, mixing with everything, everything pushing toward the one stand-still minute of the big trick. And yet no one mentioned it. I was nearly eleven years old though, three years from my own rumbling.

And besides, I had other things on my mind. I had seen something happen between my mother and father. Love get smashed, or lost, then die. Murdered, I guess you might say. Or at least part of me had seen that—filmed that, in a sense—since I was zero to six while it was going on. So what I saw has to be stored somewhere inside this brain. Filed away. Sitting on a mind disk, if that's how you want to think about it. And now at eleven, I was supposedly watching it rise up and catch fire in the shape of Miss Vicky LaTour. Who for some strange reason couldn't leave my father's feet alone. I swear that woman could play footsie more than anything you'd ever see in the monkey house at the zoo.

In December of that year, my father asked her to marry him. Which I got to witness on a canoe trip down the Santa Fe River. That's a real family-like thing to do. Dads get in their boats with their daughters. And the sons get in the boats with their mothers. You know, so the muscle power distribution is about even. Only in our case, I was older and about five times stronger than Dylan. So it wouldn't have been fair for my dad and me to be in the same canoe. So here I was paddling down the river with Miss Vicky LaTour, who was in a red sweater and tight jeans and high-heeled cowboy boots, for Christ's sake. Miss Vicky LaTour studies fashion magazines like my dad studies the stock market. She is an interior designer. And you ought to see the interiors she designs. She likes that Victorian look—you know, a little of this and a little of that, absolutely everywhere. Which now in my father's super-modern house gets cut down to one cabinet stock full of doilies and *humble* figurines, or whatever she calls them. Anyway, they're a bunch of little dolls that all look like they herd sheep. And she makes up in talk for what the rest of us lack. Especially my dad. Who is for the most part so quiet, it's as if he thinks words cost money. And not only is Miss Vicky LaTour a nervous talker, she's infected with an overuse of asking you if you know what she means.

Which gets to be contagious, if you also know what I mean. And she was saying now, "I wasn't real sure how to dress this morning when I got up—seeing as how it can heat up and cool off about five times each day. You know what I mean?"

"Um humm."

In December, north Florida is about like March anywhere else.

"And I wanted to have enough time to make deviled eggs, because your dad says you like them and they take a good long while to make—digging out the yolks and putting in mayonnaise and pickles and all. So I got up at 6 A.M. Have you ever had them like that?"

I was dying to tell her I didn't give a wart hog's care in hell how she deviled her eggs. But instead I said, "Yeah." It would just about kill my dad if I wasn't nice. So what was my choice?

I FEEL A little sorry now for Miss Vicky LaTour, telling this like this. If you know what I mean. Trashing her so bad. She was scared I wouldn't like her. And there was no way I was ever going to like her. Which is a shame when you think about how she got up at 6 A.M. to devil eggs, hoping her brand of deviling would do it. But the eggs did- n't stand a chance when you consider that I, and I alone, had long ago decided that it would be me, and me alone, who would be all the fam- ily my father would ever need. So where did that leave poor red-cow- boy-booted Miss Vicky LaTour?

If she hadn't come into our life, though, it still would have blown up sooner or later. It was just that Dylan came with her. And Dylan made all the difference.

I guess I ought to back up here and put in some facts. Because if you saw me and my dad, it would be so obvious that we are related. The sparkly part of which is that, athletically, there is probably very little we can't do. My father was a big-shot football player in college.

A remarkable one, to tell the god's truth. Because he is only five-eleven and weighs, oh, I don't know, back then about 160. He was a quarterback at Duke for two years in a row. Yeah, pretty remarkable, even though I know they're not much known for football. But still. Now he is an architect with this quiet artistic side. And he weighs a whole lot more. His shoulders are the size of grapefruits. And his neck is like a post. If you ask my opinion, though, all that athleticism is going to pot.

He can draw about anything. But he does buildings. Draws buildings and oversees them being built. And even though we live in this little Florida city, he designs shopping centers and big buildings for cities all around. We live here because of my mother. Her father was a state Supreme Court judge, and she wanted to move somewhere to be near him. She also wanted to go to law school herself, which to hear her tell it was the secret she sat on like it was a desire to rob a bank. And in the long run it robbed her marriage, or so she will tell you if you ask. So the three of us split when I was six.

Starting two years after that, I've spent, for the most part, *all* of my Saturdays with my father. We'd play Putt-Putt or go to a movie and then out to eat. In all these years I have learned to play Putt-Putt like a female blonde-haired honky Tiger Woods. And I can play that moviegoers' game by naming every actor who has ever been on the same screen with Kevin Bacon better than anyone you'll ever know. I've seen that *Flipper* movie twenty-two times. I can sing all the songs in *Annie*—not on tune, but I can. In fact, *Annie* is my dad's favorite kid flick.

Long ago he should have bought stock in Blockbuster.

I look like my dad, too—which pleases my mom to no end. No, I'm serious. Because he is pretty and she is not—though I know you're not supposed to call a man pretty. But he and I both *are*—at least if you ask any stranger on the street who happens to be looking at us. I

40

don't have his color hair, but his skin and face shape and shape of his body, considering I am a girl, are mine. I have banana-shaped legs, though. I am a little knock-kneed, to tell the truth. And I still have a little bit of an overbite because I think they took the braces off too soon. But overall I am the packaging that seems to please the most. I have been elected homecoming queen twice—once in the ninth grade and then again last year. About two years ago I had a movie agent come up to me on the beach—I was fifteen and in a red bikini, and I guess the rumblings were getting pretty loud by then, except this agent was a woman and not a man, not the kind of man who'd started watching everything I do, almost everywhere I go, and now it seems there are eyes on me all the time, like I am money—and she asked if I'd like to try out for a movie. Not really, I said.

I wonder now, though, if the movie she had in mind would have had Kevin Bacon in it?

My mother and I—well, you can tell we are related, and she tells me all the time that having me is like having the flip side of herself in a fairy tale. Yep, I got the best of both my mother and my father. And it's not nearly so much fun as you would think. I wanted to be on the swim team when I was eight. I could already outswim my mom then by a length and a half. The coach at the university saw me in the pool when I was taking a swimming lesson and said I had the makings of what might eventually qualify for a scholarship. And would I like to swim on a team and maybe even train for the Olympics? My mom answered for me, said a quick *no* and *no thanks*, that academics were going to be my route, she was sure. She told me later that she didn't want me to swim—not competitively—because I'd get those great big shoulders, and mine were already predisposed for that, seeing as how I was built like my dad. So don't tell me my mom doesn't understand the power of what she never had.

SO HERE I was, paddling Miss Vicky LaTour down the Santa Fe River on the steam of a smaller version of my father's shoulders. He passed us, though. Dylan, being seven, was just about trailing his paddle like a spoon. He had on a sweatshirt with Michael Jordan slam-dunking across it. He was just a sweet little innocent kid then. His feet were the biggest thing on him. Sitting down, he was only about two feet taller than the sides of the canoe. And he talked a lot then, but then most seven-year-olds do. I guess it was just Miss Vicky LaTour that it never wore off of.

Dylan's father is a restaurant owner over in Palm Key. Which is a little less than an hour's drive from where the rest of us live. Dylan goes to see him about every month and for three weeks in the summer. I often wondered if Miss Vicky LaTour drove Dylan's father crazy like she did us—or at least me.

That day the sun shone on the water, lighting up the river grass underneath so it was like long waving beards or Christmas evergreens draped over a mantel. Beautiful and magical, if you stopped to think about it. You could look down into the water and see fish. It seemed they were preserved under there like the water was glass. And I thought about how I'd gone canoeing here once with my mother and her father. And he had pulled a button off his shirt and let it slip from his fingers into the water. And we had watched it sink to the bottom where it sat like a pearl with the current doing a shimmy dance across it. That's how clear the water was. And still was.

And now in a canoe with Miss Vicky, I watched the leaves fall into the river and the circles rippling out from them. And then the leaves floated like tiny paper boats, rusty brown and golden, that we paddled through. But I don't remember a thing of what Miss Vicky LaTour was talking about. But then I rarely do. Probably she was pointing out trees and birds and fish like she was a guide on a TV animal show.

Only she wouldn't have known their real names, only that it was a big tree or a brown bird or a god-o-mighty huge fish.

Suddenly we realized my father was not in front of us. We couldn't see his canoe anywhere. "Now where has he gotten to?" Miss Vicky LaTour asked.

I was thinking he was just way, way ahead. Miss Vicky was hardly paddling at all, which meant that it was me, a nearly eleven-year-old, who was the only motor we had. And the current was fast, and so my dad could have steamed way off from us. And I said something about that, pointing it out. Miss Vicky LaTour yelled out my father's name, *Doug, Doug.* Which fell on the river and against the trees on the bank in a silence that was scary. I kept my paddle quiet while we listened to see if he would answer. But nothing. Nothing. Not a thing came back. The wind was cold and hissed through the trees, to then be still like a cat asleep. There were the far-off cries of picnickers having a fine time. But other than that, we could hear nothing.

As we got close to where a spring came into the river, you could see minnows darting near the bank. By now Miss Vicky had me paddling like a missionary with cannibals on our rear. "How could we lose them?" she kept asking over and over. But she didn't really want to hear my opinion. Because she never could stop answering herself. "They were right in front. They have to be right around this bend— you know what I mean? Because where else could they be?"

Nary a word needed to pass through my lips, if you also know what I mean. Besides, I was practically doing all the paddling and didn't have any breath to talk with.

The trees on the bank were so tall, it felt like we were in a cave or in a tunnel. The river was narrow. Then it opened on one side into the mouth of a creek. And just as I was going to paddle into it on a hunch, I heard my father. He was somewhere above us. The sound of him was muffled but loud. And he had a teasing tone that I'd never heard before. Which is just another sign of the power of sex—how it can change even a full-grown man's voice. "Miss Vicky LaTour and Bergin Talbot. Stop where you are and look up."

We did. He and Dylan were up in this tree, standing on a platform-like thing that had obviously once been part of a tree house. It was clear that somebody at some time had lived there and had left their child's tree house. And it was ramshackled and probably about as sturdy as a loose tooth. But my dad and Dylan were standing on part of it. And my dad was holding onto the back of Dylan's belt with one hand, while with his other he was holding one of those bullhorn things that people use at a football game. Up until then he must have been hiding it in his ice chest. Miss Vicky LaTour burst out in giggles. And a couple of other canoes were now coming up on us. We were all in this thing now—paddling backward to hold us in place. And every one of us was looking up.

"Miss Vicky LaTour," my father yelled through his bullhorn.

"Yes?"

She was up on her knees in the canoe now, as though to get closer to my dad. Then she swiveled around for a second toward me. "Can you keep the canoe still, Bergin, honey?"

Fat chance with this current. But instead I said sweetly, "I'll try."

Miss Vicky must have known my father was up to something unusual and needed her help to bring it off. "Doug. My God—I can't believe you're up there. Be careful. Don't step on anything rotten. But we're listening. We can hear you. It's hard to keep our canoe still, if you know what I mean. So go ahead quick. Go ahead, because we can hear you just fine."

My Dad really needed two hands on that bullhorn.

"I want you to know . . ." he yelled.

"Yes. Yes!" Then to me, "Bergin, honey, can't you get this damn canoe back up under him?"

"It's pretty hard with this current," I said. I was having to paddle us in little circles now, keeping us constantly turning.

"You're the light of my life," my dad broadcast. "The one thing I know I can't live without, if you know what I mean."

Behind us, there were three canoes now with about six people and a couple of kids in them, paddling backwards to keep from crashing into us. They could have passed us. But I guess my dad and Miss Vicky were getting pretty interesting, too.

"Yes, Doug. I know. *I know* what you mean," she said.

And then he asked, "So will you marry me?"

I did a fishtail with the paddle. And the canoe swung around. Miss Vicky LaTour nearly fell out. But I swear I didn't do it on purpose. Dylan stepped on a bad board, lurched forward. And with my dad holding onto his belt loop, unbalanced both of them. The bullhorn fell out of my father's hand and flew in the air like a bird, dive-bombing toward Miss Vicky LaTour's head. It bopped her on the topknot, then splashed into the river. A heron flew up squawking. And we were once again headed downstream on the current.

I glanced back to see my dad and Dylan standing side by side, holding onto each other in the dilapidated tree house, watching us, as we steamed off down the river. The canoers behind us steamed off, too, clapping and calling out, as they floated under my dad. And one of them called out, "Way to go!" while a whole canoeload of them starting singing "For He's a Jolly Good Fellow."

All the while, Miss Vicky LaTour was yelling back over her shoulder, as she held her hands over her swelling goose egg, "Yes! Yes!"

SO THAT'S how we got bound into three families—my dad and me and Dylan and Miss Vicky LaTour in one. And on the other side of town, my mom and me and her new husband, Jack, and the twins

45

they made between them. And an hour's drive away, Dylan and his dad, Carl LaTour, in Palm Key. Separate but equal, close but not close. And me and Dylan, the badminton cocks between. If you also know what I mean.

WHEN I WOKE up in the emergency room, the first thing my eyes opened onto was the brightness of the ceiling. There were so many lights on me, I couldn't see. There was a tube in my throat. And another one in my arm. And in my ankle. Monitors were blinking and clicking behind my head. A machine was doing my breathing. And a doctor was leaning over me. Nurses were moving things from here to there and touching me. They'd turned me back. They'd kept me here.

But that was their choice, not mine.

Now I looked at Dr. Cone sitting there beside Dylan in her office. She offered him a bowl of wrapped peppermints like the kind that restaurants hand out after you eat something with a lot of garlic in it. She told him he could leave.

He took a mint, then got up and walked out after a quick glance back at me. His face was blank. And he was moving in long swoops with his hands in his pockets.

Maybe it was because she set the candy bowl down and didn't offer me one. Or because I didn't think I could sit there one second longer in a green gown made of paper. Or that I was getting pissed off as hell about having to be somewhere that I never wanted to be. And never even intended to be. And with someone who made me nervous and who, it was clear, had about as much chance of knowing me as an ant crossing the Florida Turnpike and living to tell about it. So I looked straight back and said, dead serious, "Next time I won't fail."

She stood up and walked to the window. She picked up the leaves of one of those nearly dead plants and picked a bug or something off it. Her shoulder pad was now back up into its rightful place. She touched it with the tip of her left fingers as though to see if it was going to behave. She looked at me so steadily, I guess that's what made the shape and color of her eyes register. Through the ice-lenses of her glasses I could see they were more than the usual round. They were perfectly round. Like cake pans or wheels. Quarters. Or fifty cent pieces. Eye circles of the darkest brown with a fleck of yellow in the white of her right one, as if a painter had, by accident, dripped paint there.

"First, though," she said, "don't you want to get your clothes back?"

She had a point.

FOUR

Leslie

I can't remember a time when I did not know Doug Talbot. There were only four miles of Tallahassee hills between us from the ages of zero to fourteen. Even though we did not go to the same school in those early years, on Sundays we both sat in the same mildewy basement room of the United Methodist church learning about Mary, Joseph, Judas, and Hell. Most often Mrs. Lockabee taught us. She was a banker's wife who wore mink stoles as soon as the thermometer dropped. She was Latin, originally from Peru, and fixed her hair in a long page-boy that was the same brown color as the pulpit. I can still recall her voice, jazzy and halting like a Latin band heavy with syncopated castanets. Doug would sit in the room in nut-brown penny loafers, dark pants with a white shirt and a tie (even when he was five!), and build paper airplanes out of his Sunday School coloring book. His hair was never more than a two-inch raven-colored bowl that caressed his head like feathers.

Only when Mrs. Lockabee stepped out of the room to get our snack of graham crackers and grape juice would he let fly his double winged B-52's and needle-nose jets decorated with colored Josephs and Abrahams. If Mrs. Lockabee caught sight of the last swoop of paper, or of the flash of Doug as he ran to retrieve them, she would stop and admonish, "Oh, let's—uh—not do that, my darlin' Doug." It was true—Doug was just so darn cute, not to mention so generally well behaved, that no one could out and out yell at him. (He won the citizenship award from the Rotary Club four years in a row. I won it five.) And he would turn and look at Mrs. Lockabee, his eyes round as pennies, true blue, while holding his paper airplanes, then quietly walk back to his seat. No apology. Nothing. Doug was solid in his silences, stone-quiet like a sphinx.

That's why he wanted me, I believe. Born with a lawyer's tongue and the desire to rule, I could out-clackety-clack even Mrs. Lockabee, except that my accent was milked-down Southern white. With me, Doug had a front man.

The year we were twelve and on the verge of going to Hell during puberty, Mrs. Lockabee decided to stay on with us as the Methodist Youth Director. She brought in an oscillating fan to show us how the devil worked. "Watch—uh—this," she said, plugging it in and making us sit close. We were hunched on cold metal chairs in a circle as it blew across our faces, flipping up our bangs and drying out our eyeballs. "You see," she said, standing over us, "you just never know when Satan's force will blow smack dab on you and bear down." We sat there watching the black metal face of the fan that, I swear to god, looked so much like an evil mask that it still gives me the willies when I think about it. Even though Mrs. Lockabee's visual aid struck me as out-and-out silly, it still gave me the fight-or-flight syndrome. I hadn't done anything that would qualify me for certain damnation, yet. But I knew I was capable. "Now the trick is," Mrs. Lockabee went on, "you have to learn how to sit still and be strong until Satan passes by."

Actually I was highly pissed that my new Flip hairdo was getting blown to kingdom come. I clamped my palms on the sides of my head like ear muffs. (I guess I'd had a crush on Doug all my life, for I can't remember ever not trying to get him to notice me.) By then, he'd given up his paper airplanes. He had moved on to filling his religious educational materials with doodles. He could copy anything: Dick Tracy, Charlie Brown, Mrs. Lockabee's profile. But I guess the opportunity was just too good to be missed. For quickly he folded two sharp-winged jets out of pages six and seven of the *Guiding Light for Methodist Youth* and let the Devil launch them. "Heavens to Betsie!" Mrs. Lockabee cried as the jets swooped and soared across the room, down then up, then down again as the oscillation caught them. For what seemed like a good three minutes they curved around in a delightful dance. Devil-may-care, I guess you could call it.

"Doug has just shown us how to fly off from the Devil's evil. Yes, he has. I swear to goodness. He has, uh, made angels!"

When we were in high school, Mrs. Lockabee retired from teaching. I think I wore her out. Fascinated with Hell and Mary and the virgin birth and Judas, I cross-examined Mrs. Lockabee as if she had murdered Jesus herself. I couldn't understand why something good in the world couldn't last. I was fascinated with Judas, that snitch. How would it be to live with that guilt? How could it be that you could go on, knowing you had taken a perfect good from the world?

It wasn't until our junior year in high school that Doug and I began to date. We'd been going to the same school then since the ninth grade, but it was only when I was nominated to run for student council president that I made the first overture. It was a Monday afternoon, I remember. Fourth period study hall. I was sitting in the library at one of those big wooden tables. Doug sat across from me. There were only four days left to plan my campaign. The room smelled like chewed wooden pencils and skin on the verge of sweat. There was no air conditioning in the school back then, and the tall wooden windows were all pushed up to as high as they could go, letting in bright sun, pollen, and horny bird song. (I'm sure all of us were praying that our deodorants wouldn't give out.)

It was 1975; the most popular song was the Captain and Tennille's "Love Will Keep Us Together," and folks in the Watergate mess were heading off to prison. Across from me, Doug was drawing doodles in his chemistry book. Every once in a while I felt him glance in my direction. I would fan my face with my hand and whisper, "Whew, it's hot." And he'd smile. He thought I was funny. Rearing back in his chair and grinning lopsided, it was as though he were waiting for my next entertainment.

He still had his hair cut the same way. Still looked the same as he had when he was five, but he was tall now, or at least tall enough. He has one of those faces whose features are perfectly in balance, short straight nose, lips straight and calm, his light-complexioned cheeks blistery red from being recently shaved. He'd been the starting quarterback for the Tallahassee Devils all that season. And in the spring he played baseball. It seemed he was gone from classes for games more than he was in them. But he still made the honor roll. It was funny, because if you asked anyone if they knew Doug Talbot, they would say *yeah*, and then *not really.* He was like a billboard you drove by everyday: well known, every inch memorized, its message clear and constant, yet existing at a distance.

Do you have time to help me with some posters?
I could stand to have you draw on a couple of big ones for
the cafeteria, if you don't mind.

I slipped the note over to him. He read it, then we passed it back and forth:

When?

This afternoon. 4:30. My house.
Okay.
Do you know where I live?
Yes.
Do you need a ride?
No.

Like I said, he has always been a man of few words. But when the bell rang and I stood up to collect my things, I glanced over at him and saw that in the margin of his chemistry book was my profile. All along, it was me he'd been doodling. And with a profile like mine, I knew it had to be eternal love. (Or at the very least, the study for a helluva poster.)

He called me that next week. "Wanna go see *Jaws?*" I recited the meat of at least three printed reviews, and all the way through he kept saying, "Yeah? yeah?" and then, "I hear it can scare the bejesus outta ya." So five days later we went to get our bejesuses removed, which gave me the opportunity to scream and shriek and grab onto him in the dark in at least a half dozen acceptable instances. All of which he seemed to love.

The posters in the cafeteria did not carry my profile. They were full-length front portraits of me in my cheerleading outfit. He made my legs long, tan, and firm, better than in real life.

I won.

By the end of May, Doug and I were an item. By senior year, we were two standouts who weren't afraid to take hold of anything and lead it. People thought we belonged together, and that made us believe it even more. We were like an old married couple already. We didn't even make love. (Doug said he had to save himself for the Tallahassee Devils, and I didn't have a mole's idea in Hell of how to discreetly get my hands on birth control pills, even though I was tempted to ask

Letty for advice. I was just so terrified of getting pregnant and disgracing my father. So we sat on our libidos like they were beasts in a bag. We experimented in a low burn of petting in the front seat of Doug's crimson Chevelle on a side road near the city golf course.) We didn't fight. And we didn't spend much time apart. We kept that for later.

Our senior year we went to see *Rocky*, watched *Roots* on TV at my house, and attended the Halloween Costume Dance as the Odd Couple. Me as Gertrude Stein. Doug as Hitler.

That next fall we both went off to Duke. He played football; I ran a sorority and the newspaper and the Humanities Club and made Phi Beta Kappa. The second year there, we let the beast out of the bag, so to speak. And once we had, we couldn't get it back. We made love in the back seat of his car on a dirt road beside a farmer's watermelon field more times than I could count. I loved the feel of his chest pressing down on me, solid and firm, and the size of his arms that the whole of my hand could not reach around. Most often Lionel Richie would be singing "Three Times a Lady" on the radio, or the Gibbs brothers would come on with "How Deep Is Your Love." (Deep enough to get us in trouble, it turned out, and enough to prove to anybody that I was not 100 percent a lady.)

But I don't think it was just that we were making up for lost time; it was as much that we were trying to convince ourselves there really was more between us than the reputations of two people who could set the world on fire any day of the week. By then I was on birth control pills, but the April of my senior year also on penicillin for a recent strep throat. And back then, no one knew that one could cancel out the other. A month after graduation we married, and seven months later Bergin was born.

Ask me about love. Ask me anything you want to know about love. And yet, it seemed I didn't know anything about the depth of it until Bergin, or about joy. The sight of her after those first few minutes when she left my body was the clear, simple, full meaning of that. My body might have been relieved of carrying her, but I was newly stretched wide by a sure and incessant love. It felt that for the first time I understood what the world was really about, how we all, no matter who or where, fit together. Doug was no different. We even discussed our new knowledge, and I had never known him to be so effusive. He held Bergin in the delivery room, studying her closely, then at arm's length, exploring every inch of her. He rubbed the thick base of his thumb across her cheek, then kissed her. "I didn't know it would be like this," he said. "I had no idea." He cradled her for a second longer.

All through Bergin's babyhood, it seemed that any number of times I would find him silently studying parts of her, holding in his hand her tiny feet, rubbing her individual toes, her fingers. To him every bit of her was a precious mystery. He even drew her, and more than once, putting down on white paper in black ink the intricacies of her ear, the creases in her thighs, the growing length of her fingers.

It was not that these feelings left. No, never. Or that Doug and I changed in how we thought of ourselves as family. It was a whole lot of things that undid us. And I guess if I really want to get technical, I could say it was my own blasted placenta that got the whole mess going.

Apparently postpartum depression has stumped mankind since the days of Hippocrates, for he wrote a good bit about it in 700 B.C. Mrs. Hippocrates must have been giving him a pretty hard time too, since he described all the symptoms in detail. Messed-up hormones is the first thing to blame. And I would have done a thorough research job on the whole subject, if, at the time, I hadn't been so tired.

It wasn't until a decade later that I learned that what is missing after giving birth is a hormone called CRH. Usually the hypothalamus secretes it. But in a pregnant woman, the placenta takes over. In fact, in the last three months before the baby is born, the placenta releases three times the normal amount of CRH. And then after the big event, sometimes the hypothalamus gets lazy in getting back to work. Often it can be downright shifty and no-account. In my case, a bum.

Damn placenta left me high and dry.

We were living in Virginia then. Doug was at the university's school of architecture, and I spent the days in our four-room apartment. Letty had come to help me those first few weeks. She had driven up with my dad soon after Bergin's birth, but then my father went home. He called everyday, but it was an accepted fact that taking care of babies was women's business. So it was up to Letty and me to learn about Bergin. I remember on the day Letty left, I stood in the drive, holding Bergin in a mass of blankets as it snowed, watching Doug back out of the driveway in his crimson Chevelle to take Letty to the bus station. Letty was afraid of flying and afraid of snow, and was eager to get back to Tallahassee where she would have only my dad to housekeep for. I don't think I have ever felt so alone in my whole life as when I watched Doug and Letty drive away.

The next week, Doug's mother came for ten days. She was a short woman with a tight perm and a box of recipes for making baby food from scratch. She had grown up on a farm, had raised five kids, and could can and cook and quilt till the cows come home. She was as strong-willed as I was, and her smile was so much like Doug's, I thought of it as a blueprint. She would dress Bergin one way; I would come along and dress her another.

She insisted on coaching me in breast feeding, and told me that drinking beer would make me so full of milk that Bergin would grow as fat as a hog and be forever content, too. She wanted me to tank up on Budweiser and whole milk, and give up coffee and chocolate, and stop worrying about losing all the weight I had gained. I sat there in the living room on our olive-green couch, oozing fat over the cushions like Jabba the Hutt in that *Star Wars* film. Doug's mother, or Mrs. Talbot as I called her, would watch her watch and time me while Bergin screamed like a dog caught in wire. "Not yet. Don't feed her yet. You've got fifteen more minutes to go." Breast feeding more often than every three hours would spoil Bergin and decrease my breast milk, she was sure. When Bergin had her first colic attack, Mrs. Talbot concocted what she called a Sugar Tit—a bottle made of whiskey, water, and sugar, heavy on the sugar.

It was me who needed the Sugar Tit. But between it and the beer, neither Bergin nor I should have been feeling any pain.

No sooner had Doug driven his mother out of the driveway headed to the airport, than I plunked down on the couch with a Bud Light in one hand and Bergin at my breast with the other and turned on *Days of Our Lives*. From then on I let Bergin chug-a-lug just whenever she wanted, which turned out to be pretty much at every commercial.

It was like I had a serious illness or had committed a crime and was under house arrest. I was housebound, watching the snow fall outside and cars slide down the hill in front of our apartment. Every night Doug came home, ate the dinner I fixed him, and half listened while I ran on and on with what had made up my day. Sometimes the only person I had seen was the washing machine repairman or the landlord, who had to frequently tend to our furnace. Doug would sit with Bergin in his lap while he watched the TV news and a football game. He would then go into his study and draw on his drafting table until midnight. I would feel him slip into the cold sheets beside me an hour or so before it would be time for me to get up and feed Bergin. I was trying hard to be the perfect wife, the perfect mother. It was just that I couldn't get the hang of the homework.

I grieved for my lost body. I was praying daily for just a little hint of a returning waist. I felt selfish and stupid and ashamed of my complaints. I didn't let them out loud often; they just showed up in the scraping sound of my house shoes, in the wasp nest of my disheveled hair, in my poking and cussing at the elastic in the pants I had to wear—size 12 and holding. I wanted sex and yet didn't. I thought about it all the time, but didn't do anything about it. Doug assumed I'd lost all interest in him. Certainly every minute Bergin was asleep, I was, too.

By now my mother had been gone for three years, dying in the hospital of cirrhosis of the liver after my freshman college year. And I think, in the first six months of Bergin's life, I grieved for my mother for the first time. I gave her more thought than I ever had in my whole life. I knew for the first time how really easy it would be to iron through the afternoons with a glass of wine in my hand. Or a beer on the dryer as I folded diapers for the umpteenth time. I threw out all the alcohol I had in the house and would only buy beer for when Doug wanted to watch a ball game. I whirled enough baby food in the blender to stuff a life-sized doll, while Bergin screamed with colic in the wind-up swing where I kept her a lot of the time. During colic attacks, that wind-up swing was my savior, my Sugar Tit substitute, or else the top of the washing machine when I put it on Spin.

My days were like a symphony fast-forwarded: sweet lyrical moments in which I could see myself in Bergin's tiny face and feel swollen with the pride of having her, then dark percussion-driven sections in which I could not feel my life at all. Whatever I did—mopping, diapers, food-blending, cooking, scrubbing the tub—there was no record of me. It would all need to be done all over again the next day or sooner. My actions dissipated as quickly as if the music coming from a radio had been turned off. And the thing none of the books tells you is that this malady is catching. Even when the body gets back in tune, days stay out of whack. If Bergin's birth gave it to me, I gave it to Doug. And neither of us had sense enough to look at anything but ourselves.

I hadn't been bred to dissolve my life like a pill in the requirements of Doug's, or of Bergin's. I needed to make an A in something. I wanted to last. I, I, not attached to anyone, but I as *me*. And yet I believed in what I was doing. I wanted to be Bergin's mother. I wanted to please Doug by being Bergin's mother. That's where he wanted me—there in that part of his life, just as his mother had been in his family's life—constant, dedicated, what the hell if all signs of her disappeared? I felt crazy and selfish. I breathed as if I were drowning. I craved to be the head of anything, and remembered a line by T. S. Eliot expressing his fear that his life was being measured out in coffee spoons. I longed to be invited to any meeting where I had not washed the spoons.

September, 1981, Bergin was on the verge of walking. She held on to the top of the TV and sugar-footed from one side of the screen to the other, grinning her two new front teeth at me. Around the bend of her body, I watched Sandra Day O'Connor being confirmed as a Supreme Court Justice.

The winter of 1982 was one of the worst on record. I would take Bergin out in her stroller, slide on the ice, then hurry back in to run warm water over her mittened fingers, while she screamed on the verge of frostbite. In the spring, I joined women's groups that promoted charities. I decided to become valuable to whatever community we settled in, when and if we settled. I fought my feelings that I seemed frivolous. I missed too many meetings to be of much use. I didn't want to ask my father for babysitting money. Doug and I wanted to make it on our own. And he was losing patience with me.

"Why is it so hard for you?" he was looking at me at the dinner table, while beside us Bergin was smearing applesauce on her highchair tray. "Every woman in the history of the world has done this."

"I know."

He meant the whole shebang—the mother and wife thing—not the dinner, though my pork chop, potatoes, and peas supper could have been the proof of the pudding, so to speak. For the kitchen looked like it had been booked for a wrestling match: dirty pans stacked in the sink, spoons with sauce on them dotting the stove, corn husks dangling out of a paper sack, trailing their silks on the floor. "I'm just not good at this," I said, on the edge of tears. But more than once he had made fun of me for breaking down and crying. Poor Doug, he didn't know how to relate to anyone in trouble except as a football coach: try harder, move faster, take it, and be tough. Tears made him nervous.

My distress made him feel weak. I wanted to be consoled. I wanted him to wrap his arms around me and tell me that yes, mine was one of the hardest jobs on this earth and I deserved one hundred million dollars in salary per year, or every month. Or, that money could never measure what I did. Or, damn it, to really get it right—money was the only measure of worth that anyone paid attention to, so therefore suck it up and take my rewards thirty years down the road when I might be a grandmother without one kid in jail. I wanted him to help me because we were in this together, not because I was the weak one he had to rescue. We counted on the fact that Bergin couldn't yet talk. We hadn't counted on the fact that she, like any living thing, could read anger.

My frustration and loneliness oozed out and ran onto Doug. And he blamed himself. *He* was not enough. *He* was not who I wanted. *He* would never be able to give me the life I wanted. Why couldn't I be like his mother? She had never had any trouble. She'd raised five kids without going crazy. (Privately I had my doubts.)

It was my problem, and he interpreted it by thinking he was the source. I made him feel as frustrated as I was. And even though over the years things changed somewhat, and I changed somewhat, the habit of discontent and blame lived under everything we put on top of it, until it was a festering sore we could not heal. We went on that way for another five years, until, finally, I called it quits.

THAT NIGHT when I took Hoot to the county hospital and just happened to be there when Bergin was brought in, I watched in surprise and shock as Doug ran across the wet pavement. Yet I instantly recognized him, as if wherever my life takes me, it is only to be expected that he will be there, too. The whirling lights of the ambulance threw red streaks across him, and he ran through the doors of the E.R. just as I hung up the phone from listening to Jack tell me what I struggled to believe. When Jack had told me that Bergin had been found unconscious, he hadn't mentioned the words *dying, nearly dead*. But now, the quickness of the movements of the people attending to her told me that.

Jack had told me he would be there as soon as he could. He was on his way. I kept trying to focus on that.

I stood by Doug in the waiting area, both of us too stunned to speak, only trying to digest the magnitude of what was being told to us: the procedure of *gavage* that would pump Bergin's stomach, the blood tests to determine which drug she had taken, the endotracheal tube that would continue to breathe for her—and that, as yet, no permanent brain or lung damage could be detected.

I had to remind myself to breathe, to try to take in air and stay calm. Then the lawyer in me took over. I had to see her, be the first one to question her, to puzzle this out. I could not believe this child, my child, had tried to take the life I had given her.

A second after we were told she had been brought back to consciousness, I was standing there beside her, watching the machines count the beat of her heart, take breaths for her, replace the life fluids that had been drained. Doug was one step behind me. Bergin's eyes were partly closed. Her lips were so blue around the tube that went down her throat that I put my hand over my mouth in shock. A pencil was dangling from her fingers. A nurse removed it, and at the same time touched my arm as she showed me and Doug the words that Bergin, during that brief moment she was conscious, had written on a slip of paper: *I want Jack.*

By then Jack was walking into the E.R., and as I rushed to get him to Bergin, she had fallen back into a half state of consciousness, too removed from words to write or to talk, since the tube allowed no spoken words. It was strange and funny and touching that Bergin should ask for Jack. She'd never been close to him; in fact, for all the five years we had lived together as a family, she had pushed him away as strongly as he had leaned toward her. But this was his world, this hospital, the place where he worked and knew how to arrange things, and now when Bergin was in her darkest hour, he was the one she was turning to.

THE NEXT day I was in the Intensive Care Unit, sitting beside her. At noon, Doug was there, too. He was standing; I was sitting. And Jack came walking in to be with us. He had on a dark blue suit, a red tie with yellow circles, knotted a little off center. Jack is stocky, his hair coppery red. His mouth turns up like something is silently tickling him, and his eyes are rimmed with lashes so light they are like threads bleached by sun.

"How's it going?" he said. He was the only one of us who still seemed to be himself.

"She looks so peaceful," I whispered. We watched her sleep, the machines hooked to her, keeping watch.

"Has she been like this the whole time?" Doug asked me, looking strained. The lining of his eyes was red like he hadn't slept. None of us had.

"Mostly." Even I, now, was short on words. The truth was, all morning, Bergin had been coming in and out of sleep, and whenever she was awake she would look at me and ask for water—the breathing tube removed now—or I would question if she was too hot or too cold, or in need of anything. And then once when I was alone and no one could see me, and when I could not stand it any longer, my frustration and an odd mixture of sorrow and anger made me take hold of her arm and force her awake. "Bergin, what's wrong? Why did you do this? You know you can tell me. Why?"

But "I want Jack," was all she had said, and turned away.

Now with all three of us standing over her, Jack said, "It's going to take a while. But she's going to be fine. You have to believe me on this. And no, I don't have any clues yet." He was addressing the way I was looking at him. For, of course, the first thing I wanted to know was had Bergin told him or anybody anything about why she had done this. The need to know was like a mad heartbeat.

"We'll learn everything sooner or later." Jack came to stand behind me, pat my arm, and, for a long brief moment, hold my shoulders. "And it's going to be okay. Remember that." As he spoke, I turned my head back to look at him, gratitude oozing out of me as if it were liquid. I wanted to keep his words with me like a chant. "I'll be back later," he said. " I have a meeting I've got to get to. Don't let her throw a party in here." He laughed and walked away. Doug and I looked at each other and smiled. For, once when Bergin was in middle school and Jack and I were out of town—and while Lydia, who was staying with the kids that weekend, had taken the twins to a movie—Bergin had opened our house up for an impromptu party that had gotten out of hand. Police had been called. Doug had been called. Bergin had called him herself when she'd gotten so scared, the police cars driving up in the yard, catching her standing on a picnic table in the backyard yelling, "Everyone who does not know my name, *leave*. Leave right now." And all the kids there, the whole horde of them, had started chanting, "Bergin, Bergin, Bergin."

Doug now looked at me. "Do you have any idea?"

"No. Not really. I can't imagine what was going through her mind. And why didn't we know?"

"What did you talk about last Friday? You all stayed out together for a pretty long time."

I heard accusation in his voice. This wasn't information-gathering; this was becoming a hunt. It was me who recently had been like a visitor in Bergin's life. I was the one who saw her one day a week since she'd moved in with Doug. It was me who could throw the rhythm of the week out of whack. "What makes you think I said something that upset her? What about you? What time have you spent with her lately? Did you see any clues?"

He looked away. Neither of us would speak anymore now. That was our pattern. And yet we both continued on in that silence, continued watching Bergin, continued being there while she slept. I had the strangest feeling that now, right now, these moments in which I understood nothing, was the time that I would look back on with a strange skewed sense of envy. For I didn't yet know anything that could be called the truth, and the truth couldn't help but change me in ways I could not imagine. I looked over at Doug. His head was lowered and he was studying Bergin's closed eyes. The tips of his fingers rested on the edge of her bed, her fingers only a few inches from him, but he did not reach to touch her. (That is Doug, too. He is as reserved with his gestures as he is with his words.) We glanced at each other, and in our faces I could read our minds. If we learned what we feared, how would we live? How could we go on, if we found out that we had been part of very nearly taking from the world this perfect good that, out of our youthful love, we had placed here?

FIVE

Bergin

E very time I woke up in the hospital, I was never alone. It was like the Atlanta airport around my bed. There was always someone there, sitting or standing. One time, in what seemed like the middle of the night, it was my mother. And another time my dad. He was sitting there under the window with some book or magazine in his lap. Something flat and white. Every time, something flat and white. And if someone came, he would quickly close it up and tuck it away. Like it was an account book or something connected with money. And if it wasn't Mom or Dad or Jack, it was some farty nurse with Ben Franklin glasses sitting in a chair reading a magazine and glancing at me over the top of it. Even in the dead of night. Frankly, I didn't care what they did with my body. They could watch it and poke it and drip things into it as much as they liked. The real me hadn't stuck around. It was a stuffed doll in a green gown I'd left on the bed.

On the second day in the ICU, Jack brought in my breakfast. Or that's what they called it. Hot tea and toast and a new pitcher of ice water. "I hear you've been wanting to see me," he said and stood by my head.

"Oh, really? I don't remember." Because of the tube that'd been jammed down my throat, my voice was hoarse. Whenever I swallowed, it was like fire. Vaguely I could recall, in what felt like a fast-forward frame in a dream, someone putting a pencil in my hand and letting me write whatever I wanted. *Jack* had come out of my fingers. Not out of my head. I was as surprised as he was.

"Yeah. Well, you did." He pulled a folded piece of paper out of his pocket and held it up for me to see. *I want Jack* was scribbled across it. The J was capitalized, and the T was crossed. Frankly, I was impressed with how well I'd done. But still, the fact that I'd done it was pure mystery.

"I guess I figured you knew how to get me out of here," I said, without looking at him.

"Yeah, maybe."

"You run this place, don't you?"

"Only in a manner of speaking. I mostly make sure everyone gets paid." For a moment neither of us spoke.

"I guess this is costing a whopper."

"Insurance will cover it." He rolled a table over to my bed. "You don't need to worry about any of that. Even if it doesn't handle all of it, I'll take care of it."

For a moment we just looked at each other. His tie was knotted crooked, and he had a red patch on his cheek. He has this real thin skin that can get all splotchy after he shaves. Sometimes I tell Jack he reminds me of Bozo the Clown, that all he needs is a strip of white around his mouth. And when he eats powdery donuts, he even gets that.

"What got into you, Starlight with a Crown?" he asked. That's what he likes to call me, Starlight, after a song he once wrote when he was about sixteen and still sings. It doesn't even make sense—a crown on starlight?—but he says it doesn't matter; at sixteen it did.

"I had a headache," I answered.

"Just wanted to make sure you cured it, right?"

"Yeah."

He smiled. Jack likes to try to get on your wavelength and play with it like a fish he intends to keep. "You have to be careful with headaches." He held out the tea on my breakfast tray. "You like it with milk and sugar, right?"

"But I don't want any now."

"Well, I'll just fix it like you like it, in case you do."

I watched him pouring and stirring and buttering the toast. I swear, sometimes I think Jack is a woman in a pinstripe suit. He does all the cooking at home. Or at least plans all the menus and sets Lydia, our housekeeper, to work on getting them started before he gets home for good. And I sure wish he knew how to ask for a decent haircut.

He set the tea down on the table that slid across the bed over my lap. "What I always like to do with my headaches," he said, "is to give them to someone else. They're hell alone."

"Well, it's gone now," I said.

"At least for a little while." He sat down and watched me look at my toast.

There wasn't anything said between us for at least a good ten minutes. To tell you the truth, that was crazy funny. Because the room was buzzing with nurses and a whole string of people poking and prodding four other patients in the room. There was this sound of machines blinking and ticking, hooked up to bodies that all looked about half dead. But Jack just sat there. Right in the middle of all that hullabaloo, he was as still as a stone. We were like two dumb cows parked head to tail under the shade, swatting flies off each other, not thinking we had to be saying anything. Just cuttin' out from the herd, for a while, if you know what I mean. Maybe that's why I'd asked for Jack. Maybe I

69

knew he wouldn't need me to say anything. He could leave me alone in the talk department.

"I'll check back in later," he said. "And if you haven't eaten that toast by then, I want it. Blackberry jelly, too. Save me some."

He walked out. The back flap in his suit was flipped up. And one of his shoelaces was half-tied.

I REMEMBER when we first moved here. *Here* meaning Florida. And *Here* meaning in town. Not the farm my mother and Jack built when they married, because my mother got this wild idea when she was pregnant with the twins—I was twelve then—that we ought to grow up with animals. So she moved us all out fifteen miles from town. And there we have a cow, two horses, three peacocks, a dog, and a pot-bellied pig named Spam. *Eeeeiii, eeii, ohhh.*

No, I'm talking about where we lived when I was six. Back when my mother and I had just moved here. We rented a house with four rooms two blocks from the university's law school. I didn't know anybody. But that was okay. All right, really. Nothing much bothered me anyway because I had this thing. This thing that was like a secret that I could call on just whenever I needed to. I hate to even try to nail it down. Certainly I will never say it out loud. It is one of those things that can't really be put into words, and also looking back now, I see how dorky it really was. Because what I was banking on, putting all my hope in, downright coming close to worshiping—I guess you could say—was a round circle that I could draw inside of my head. And it would spread and flow like a warm pond running over and all through me. A Federal Express solidness and calm.

I felt it for the first time when my father put me and my mother on a plane to fly here. He was standing at the window of the waiting room. I was going up the steps into the plane, and I could see a thin

70

line, like what a spider weaves, running from me to him. I could sit in the plane seat and wind the line up on my arm, clear and invisible. It would lengthen out, too, to wherever he would be. We would no longer live in the same house. *But my father loved me.*

And whenever I wanted to remember who I was, I drew this circle behind my eyes. I stared at it until whatever I didn't want to look at, or to hear, or to pay attention to, dissolved. *Because my father loved me.* He was not beside me. *But he loved me.* He thought about me all the time. If he could, he'd have me with him. I was in his head every minute, just all the time. And for a while I got this crazy thought that whenever I moved my arm, the invisible line, still stuck to him, would move his. I could see him. I could feel him. We were like puppets in the same show, 635 miles apart. He saw everything I did. And he cared. The thought was like a charm or a rabbit's foot—yeah, a *juju,* like what I read about that some African tribes believed in. I could rub my mind across it at just any old time.

I used it when I made an F on a spelling test in the second grade. And I used it when Noah Fastbender called me a whore on the playground, and neither of us knew what a whore was except that it was dirty ugly. *But my father loved me.* You'd think over the years the juju thing would get grown up into something more like what someone my age—seventeen now—believed in. I guess in some ways it has. But for my whole long silly life I've been calling on something that no one can put a finger on, yet can be named anything, since there is no one good word for it. I guess it's a lot like stuff that anybody anywhere can believe in. A sticky ball, in a sense. A sticky ball in the center of an everyday, every minute, that everything moves to. That holds you together, solid and central inside of your mind that helps to make everything in your whole life—even everything that happens to you— make sense. But anyway, I can sure say this. I'd given the Daddy Juju a wingding of a workout by the time my mom married Jack. And I hit middle school.

Oh, lovely nuts I was, even back then.

I was living inside of my own fairy tale.

BEFORE THAT, though. Back to when I went to first grade at the public school, and my mother went to law school. If she had a late class I went over to the Bateses' house, two streets over, and stayed with my best friend, Simpson.

Simpson Bates and I paired off in first grade. She didn't know anybody, either. We found ourselves standing in the back of the first grade room like two mismatched shoes nobody was picking. We followed each other around at recess and hung upside down side-by-side on the monkey bars. Then joined hands and sashayed to the lunchroom before we even knew each other's name. Which, when we did learn, made us seem like two parts of the same crossword puzzle. Names you'd never find on any pre-made key rings.

Simpson has always reminded me of one of those pipe-cleaner dolls. Arms and legs long enough, it seems, to tie in knots, bows even. Her hair is licorice straight, and her eyes are globes that leave a little too much room for her eyeballs. So when she opens them wide, they roll around in white like a Cheerio in milk. Her lips are full and wide, and her skin seems, all the time, tan. I remember how her fingers could slip between mine like cool ropes of modeling clay. We weren't allowed to walk to each other's houses alone since our mothers feared a crazy person might steal us on the way. So often I would ride home with Simpson after school in her mother's car. And on weekends, when my mother was studying, I practically lived at the Bateses' house.

For her tenth birthday, Simpson's father gave her an inner tube. I don't mean just a common, everyday inner tube. I'm talking about a god-o-mighty inner tube with a mesh-like hammock in the middle hole where you could sit and get pulled by a boat. Her father got the whole shebang, too—a fire-engine red motorboat and a big cooler stocked with Cokes, and a tape player with speakers up front by the steering wheel where he blasted out the big songs of that year, "Baby Baby," and "I've Been Thinking About You." I can even still hear Gloria Estefan hitting the high notes in "Coming Out of the Dark" all the way across Cowpen Lake. In fact, when you get right down to it, Simpson's parents gave her the best party for turning ten that I've ever seen in my whole messed-up life.

And it looks like I'm still going to be counting.

They rented a van and took fifteen kids out to the lake. And Mr. Bates, who reminded me of Ichabod Crane in my reading book, built a bonfire on the sand and sent us into the woods to hunt sticks. He sharpened the ends of whatever we brought back, then speared a weenie on each one while Mrs. Bates painted the insides of buns with mustard. We roasted our dogs and rode that inner tube across the lake, one at a time, over and over. Until the cicadas and crickets in the thick palmettos on the banks sang so loud they were like the static of a hundred broken TV's. All the while, Mr. and Mrs. Bates sat in the front of the boat, him driving, her helping—and looking back at us, laughing, watching out for us. We went back to the bonfire, put mosquito spray all over us until we smelled like an oily gang of all-girl thieves. And Mr. Bates told us stories that made us shiver and lick tears of fear in the dark.

All through that whole party, all through that whole time, I was Simpson's best friend. Yet it seemed there were a dozen best friends surrounding her. And whenever I looked at Mr. Bates driving the boat—the whole time I was riding in the donut hole of that inner tube—I would see him glance back at me, checking on me. Yet I was on the edge of feeling loose, like at any minute I would fly up off the tube and disappear. I was in the middle of the party, and at the same time on the edge. It was like staring at Christmas gifts under a tree, all of them for me, that I did not know how to open. It was not the fact of a *party* that was getting to me. I'd had plenty of god-o-mighty parties. I've been partied out, in a sense. It was just that Simpson's party was so damn *whole*. I rubbed my mind across the Daddy Juju and didn't give a black-burned weenie's ass for what anybody had that I didn't. I rode that tube more than any other kid, rock solid in its center.

When I got home, my mother was in the kitchen running a law school paper off on the computer's old tractor-feed printer, which was set up on a table in the middle of the floor. It was clacking and whooshing, and the legs of the table were shaking, as the papers piled up. "I'm going to be a professional water skier," I announced. "I'm going down to Cypress Gardens and ride on somebody's shoulders. And then I'm going to learn how to jump over things."

"Oh?"

"Yeah. And so I think it's probably time for us to get a boat so I can practice. Maybe Grandpa can drive it, except for the times when Dad is here."

"What about college?"

"I've changed my mind."

"I thought you wanted to be a doctor. I thought you were thinking about that?"

"Naw. I'd rather ski."

"Well, all right then, Miss Cypress Gardens." She hugged me in one hand while she collated her paper in the other.

I called my dad that night and asked him for a boat. He said he'd think about it. But more than that, he told me something that was better than any damn fire-engine-red ski-pulling boat. He'd been offered a job teaching at the university. And he was going to take it, he said. He was moving to be where we were, he said. He was going to be moving down real soon. We were going to be together, after all.

Power ball. That's what that round circle in my head was, after that. One single god-o-mighty radiating power ball!

So that's how my dad moved here. And yeah, I can think of it as mainly for me. But it turned out to be just like that saying, killing two birds with one stone. Because he'd also just met Miss Vicky LaTour at a house-building conference. And she already lived here. So it was for us two birds—me and Miss Vicky. Both of us flying around my dad, crying out like blackjack players. *Hit me! Hit me!*

I guess we were both just about dying to be the bull's-eye.

LATE THAT midmorning in the ICU, I woke up with "Starlight with a Crown" being sung in a high tenor into my right ear.

> *O-ver the earth, High, Oh High*
> *Over Us. Do youuuuuu, see me lovin' you.*
> *Ooooooohh Baby, If I could*
> *I'd Give To Youuuuuu*
> *Starlight with a Crrrrrrown.*

I couldn't believe Jack was singing, right there in the ICU in front of everybody. And *that.* That silly stupid song that made no sense whatsoever. The tune faintly resembled "Home on the Range" with a rock beat. And worse, he thinks he can sing. When he was sixteen he was the lead in a garage band. He won't tell me the truth, but I'm pretty sure the band never got out of the garage. He wrote a lot of songs back then, he says, but this is the only one he remembers all the words to. Which, when he admits that, my mom yells out, "Praise Jesus!" Which also only makes him sing louder. But it was his youth, he explains. And when he sings "Starlight with a Crown," his youth comes back. And not just the memories of it, either. Frankly, I wish he could hold it down to just memories, because when he cuts loose and dances, it is like he is afflicted with a disease you can look up in a book. In fact, almost every minute he is awake, he can embarrass me out of my mind. Or at least *further* out of my mind. Long ago I stopped bringing anybody home. "Thanks for saving me the toast," he said.

I'd drunk a little of the tea. But my throat was way too sore for toast.

"You want me to tell your mother anything?" He spilled jelly on his tie but didn't notice.

"Yeah, I want some clothes. Some jeans and a shirt. And can you get me out of here?"

"Anything else?"

"No."

"Fine. Jeans and a shirt and . . . I've been told you have more to do with getting out of here than any of us do."

I held my eyes open for a little bit longer. *Okay. So, all right, fine.* I would have thought up a whole string of words to let go. But I was too tired. I just wanted to be left alone. "I have to go to sleep now," I said, and dozed off with his tinny little funny voice doing a duet with the ticking of my body machines.

Yes, ooooohh yes, oooooohh Baby,
If I could, I wouuuuuuld
Starlight with a Crownnnnnn.

But inside my head, I had my own tunes. "Baby, Baby" and "Coming out of the Dark." I was looking everywhere for that damn god-o-mighty power ball.

THREE DAYS later I was moved to a private room. It was in the crazy ward. Every door was locked and the nurses wore keys. It was just like jail, only I had my own private toilet. Yet every time I went to it, I had to have someone with me. That's when I found out what Jack meant when he said getting out of there was up to me. They had this "ladder"—this thing on poster board they hung up on the wall. And there I was on it, my name. *Bergin* in black magic marker. Up at seven, *check*, go to the ward school, *check*, go to therapy, *check*, go to group therapy, *check*. And when there were enough checks, I'd get my clothes back. I'd get to sit out on the patio. Then take a shower alone. Talk on the phone. Listen to music. Eat without someone watching me as if any minute I was going to stick a fork down my throat. Or theirs. In fact, I had a long way to go before they'd even give me a fork.

By the end of the second week, I was pretty solid on the ladder. I'd been to group therapy, where I was pretty good at chewing the fat with whoever else was there spilling the beans, or pretending to. I'd had that meeting with Dr. Cone and Dylan, where I learned how disgusting I looked when I was dying. And I'd also earned the patio.

When I walked out on it, I saw that even though it was pretty— banana-like trees with big leaves everywhere and blooming plants where the December sun would keep them going—there was no way out. The tall stucco walls of the hospital surrounded it on every side. The only way to escape was straight up. It was a manmade canyon. There were benches all around, as though you could sit down and wait for a bus. In fact, it was just like that. Like a park with seats all around. There were about half a dozen patients in there, and other people dressed real nice—visitors, I guessed.

A nurse in a white jumpsuit was stringing twinkly Christmas lights on the trees. Her face reminded me of someone who is in the middle of swallowing a yawn—the chin pulled down and the jowls stretched and the lips sort of pulled into a V, if you know what I mean. And she was built like a mailbox, curbside type, which meant she had absolutely no business being in that jumpsuit. It made her look like a Dallas Cowboy crossdressed. A little bit of the cloth in the back was pretty darn close to being caught you know where, too. I knew her name because I'd already had a few run-ins with her, like when I'd tried to close my own bathroom door, for Christ's sake. And when I'd wanted something besides a spoon to eat salad with. Mrs. Stewart. Mrs. Dottie Stewart.

I sat down on one of the benches and watched her picking around in the trees. The warm sun came through the paper robe I had on. I felt almost hypnotized by the meticulous way Miss Dottie went about getting those lights on the leaves. Then the strangest thing happened. The door to the hospital canyon opened. And Simpson came walking out. She looked around a second. Then came straight toward me. "Hey," she said, sitting down on a bench cattycornered to me.

I said, "Hey," back. Then we just sat looking at each other. Simpson and I didn't even go to the same high school now. She must have heard about me—and that I was here—from someone she knew at *my* school. And what was really making all this super strange and downright awkward, other than the fact of what you might call my unspeakable situation, was that Simpson and I hadn't been friends since middle school.

The truth is, Simpson hadn't made it out of middle school. I'm not talking about grade-wise. No. Simpson is smart as hell. It's just that everything was getting divided up back then. And you had to choose. There were the surfers, the grunge kids, or the wiggers, who were white kids into rap and acting black—which was right on the edge of offending almost everybody, black and white, which I guess was the point. And the preppie kids who were like me, who wanted to please and pass and to get to stand up in front of everybody and their whole family all in one place at the same time for awards. And Simpson hadn't made it through middle school because she'd been ousted by the cool group. So in most ways that count, you couldn't see her if you walked into the city high school. You'd have to ask for her. She was invisible, even though she worked hard at not being.

That day, Simpson had on farmer's overalls. Fit for a big farmer, too. By now Simpson is a hair under six feet. And she had on black boots with high heels and an orange long-sleeved T-shirt under the overalls' bib. All grunge. And a green and purple butterfly was painted on her left cheek.

"How's it going?" she asked.

"Not too bad."

"How's the food?"

"Not great."

"Want me to slip you in something?"

"I doubt you could."

Making all this doubly strange was that over the last two weeks, I'd gotten a bouquet of balloons from the cheerleader squad I'd defected from. And Carol Ann and the soccer team had sent me a signed poster-sized card that said *Thinking of you*. And *Hope to see you back real soon*. That seemed to me pretty close to being one of those get-well cards that make your illness sound like a homeless person passing through. But I guess they don't make cards for someone like me. Because what are you going to say, *Welcome back*? And now Simpson was the one who had the guts to appear in the flesh.

"Give me your hand," Simpson said, reaching for it. "I bet you didn't know I read palms now."

She rolled my hand over in hers. All of her nails were painted blue with sprinkly stars on them, and each of her fingers had a ring on it. Even her right thumb. I let her do with my hand whatever she wanted to. The coolness of her fingers was still like touching ropes of modeling clay, smooth and damp. "Yeah," she said and put her index finger on my palm. "I got into this the middle of last year. You know, I've always had this thing, this sixth sense, like I always felt I could read a body's heat waves and brain waves, and especially talk to animals, remember?"

I smiled. "I guess I don't."

"Think back. My cat Pepper, the law school, fourth grade."

I did recall the summer Simpson was convinced her cat was sending messages from the dead. We had set a booth up on the sidewalk outside of the law school with Pepper in a cage, and anybody who was willing to plunk down a quarter could let Pepper pass on to Simpson whatever messages she had. The trouble was, Pepper could only talk to cats, not people. And not too many people were hot on hearing from their dead cats. Otherwise, Simpson might be right now rich and on a cruise to Acapulco.

At the sound of us remembering and laughing, Nurse Dottie Stewart looked over at me. In a minute, she turned back to decorating the trees, and Simpson said, "Now I'm into hands."

She touched the base of my ring finger. "Oh, my God, your Mount of Apollo is huge!" She moved then to the skin right under my pinkie. "And your Mount of Mercury sucks, to tell you the truth, and that surprises me."

"Why?"

Simpson looked from my hand to my face. Her irises floated in the white of her eyes for a second. Then she squinted. "If the Mount of Mercury is undersized and flat, it can mean you have difficulty with relationships and an inability to express affection." She looked back at my palm. "But, hey, see these short straight lines crisscrossing the mount?"

"These?" I touched them.

"Yeah. Now, *they* make sense."

"They do?"

"Yeah, you see, these are Samaritan lines. Doctors and people like that usually have them. And I've always thought of you as wanting to become a doctor, a pediatrician—remember?"

"I've lost my taste for children."

"Well, a veterinarian then."

I laughed. "How about a psychiatrist? By home-schooling." I glanced away from Simpson and saw Nurse Stewart looking at me again. I turned back to Simpson. She had earrings on that went like bolts of lightning across her lobes. "What about my Mount of Apollo?" I reminded her. "You said it was huge. Is that bad?"

"Well, it's not good."

"Go ahead, tell me."

Simpson touched the base of my ring finger again. "The truth is, if your Mount of Apollo is well formed—neither too large nor too small—you are charming and an enthusiastic lover. But if it's very prominent, like yours is, it means you can be prone to extravagance. Everything has to be your way. And chances are you'll be aggressive in bed."

"Oh?"

"Yeah." She looked at me and her eyes swirled in their white. Then her right eyebrow shot up.

"S'not so bad," I said.

"No, but look at your fingers." She pointed.

"What about them?"

"Well, they're not really what I'd call *spatulate*. They're mostly psychic—long and narrow with pointed fingers and glossy skin. These fingertips belong to diehard romantics. They're idealistic, especially in relationships, and depend on intuition and spiritual impressions to guide them. In fact, they live in a world of imagination and need a partner who is steady and strong to keep them grounded. On the plus side, people with psychic hands are sensitive and trusting. They are motivated by deep feelings. Yet they lack common sense and are easily crushed if a romance does not work out." Our eyes met.

Then the door to the hospital opened. We both turned to watch a tall skinny man, who looked like he could stand a good worming, push a book cart through the door. He had on the green clothes of a patient, and his face had been so recently shaved it was blanched with scrapes. His whole face seemed to come to a point under clear-framed glasses. "Mornin'," he said as he rolled his cart to us. "Care for a book, or a game, or a puzzle?"

His fingernails were long enough to stab. It was as if he were an airline stewardess coming down the aisle with a cart of drinks, just about like we were all on a trip to the bottom of craziness. In fact, his hands were shaking so much, it was clear he was hurting from the lack of a drink. Or maybe he was just the most nervous person in the whole universe. "Maybe so," I said and started thumbing through the books on the top shelf of his cart. Simpson picked up one too.

"How about a puzzle?" He squatted down beside the bottom shelf of his cart and started pulling out boxes. "What about one of these?" He held toward me a sack full of those little plastic number squares. The ones where you can try to figure out how to get the numbers to slide into sequence. I was thinking about reaching in to get one.

"Just sign this card," he said, "and I'll make a list of what all you take off the cart." As he held the card, it fluttered in his hand. I wrote *Bergin Talbot* on it and handed it back. He looked down at it. "Talbot," he said. "You any kin to Mrs. Leslie Talbot, the lawyer?"

"She's my mother."

He laughed. "Small world, ain't it? Your mother's helped me out of trouble a whole handful of times." He stood up then and laughed again. "I guess she's kept me out of jail more times than I can count. She even put me in here." He held out his fluttering hand for me to shake it. At the mention of *jail* and being *here* in the same breath, we both laughed. "I'm Richard Murphy," he said, "but people call me Hoot—like in 'don't give a Hoot.'" When he grinned, his teeth were the yellow of onions.

He held out the sack of puzzles again. But just after my fingers closed around one, Nurse Stewart dropped her string of lights and came running over to me. In fact, she was all over me, pressing her hand down on mine, over the puzzle, as she took it away. "You can't have one of these. You can't have anything off this cart."

She handed the puzzle back to Hoot and told him to move along.

When she turned back to me, she said, "Everything here has to be earned." She looked straight into my eyes, clearly trying to make her look come off as heavy punctuation. For a few long seconds we just stared at each other.

I wanted to tell her how fat her ass looked in that jumpsuit. But we were, all of us—me and Simpson and Hoot—frozen. Too stunned to say or do anything, really. As she walked away, shooing Hoot along with her hands, I sat back in silence. Simpson picked up my left hand and started looking down at my palm again. I was too fascinated to speak, because it seemed so strange, so odd really, to feel mad and embarrassed and ashamed. All at the same time, but in that order. And I could also see absolutely everything about where Nurse Stewart and that damn ladder system were coming from. *Life was a privilege,* they were trying to say. So okay. All right. I could play along.

But I didn't have to buy it.

"Now, as for your Mount of Luna." Simpson said, pressing down on the fat part below my thumb. "You're not in so much trouble here."

SIX

Leslie

Dr. Cone had said she wanted to see the whole family for a therapy session. Whether she realized it or not, I interpreted her request literally, and that meant we'd equal a whole SWAT team, because I had made sure that Doug and Dylan and Vicky would be there; and Carl, Dylan's father, was supposed to be driving over from Palm Key. (I'm not sure why I wanted him there, but he was connected to us, so why the heck not?) And me, Jack, and the twins. I was desperate for clues. I wanted to put pressure on Bergin. I wanted answers, *now*. This was all taking too long.

So, on the morning we were expected to be in Dr. Cone's office, I was herding Maggie and Kirk into the van. The day before, I'd told their pre-kindergarten teacher they would be missing this morning at school. Jack was already at the hospital and would come straight from his office for the session. All I was in charge of was getting our menagerie fed and watered (and keeping the peacock crap off our shoes while we walked across the yard to the van). We were supposed to be there by 9:30. It was 8:45 already.

The peacocks, Sonny and Cher, were pecking around their corn bowl by the garage. "Why's Bergin still there?" Maggie wanted to know. Maggie's the oldest of the twins by three minutes, and—I guess just like all the women descended from my father—quick to take the lead with a death grip and hold it. Frequently Jack calls her Little Bo Peep, meaning we are her sheep.

"She's still sick," I said, backing out the van.

The traffic leading onto the highway toward town was heavy and quick. It made me nervous to have to go that fast, 55 or 60, on narrow country roads. But so many people live out where there is elbow room, and where the real estate prices are lower, that there are a lot of us commuting now. Kirk was walking a Power Ranger figure up the window in the backseat where I had buckled him and Maggie in, tight as ticks.

"Well, when's Bergin going to be well?" I could feel Maggie looking at me earnestly.

"I don't know," I said. "That's what we're trying to find out."

"So give her some Tylenol."

"I will, Darlin', I will."

I was going to have to drive even more like a maniac to make the meeting now. Putting a hump in the traffic were garbage trucks, school buses, cattle on the way to market.

"I'm hungry," Kirk said.

I passed back over the seats a box of Cheerios, dry and unopened. I knew he would need them. He'd skipped the oatmeal I'd cooked at 6:00.

All the way there, in fact every minute I was awake and then some, playing in my mind were questions as pressing as in any murder trial that I'd ever prepared for: What had pushed Bergin to this? Was it the pressure of her senior year? Was it making out the applications to colleges, the January deadlines? Harvard, Yale, Wellesley, Stanford, Duke. It was a heavy list. She'd stayed up nights working on her essay, trying to make it smooth and authentic, about how doing volunteer work in a rural clinic near our farm had led her to want to be a physician, a family practitioner. That was where she'd been headed—her dream, supposedly.

Or had it been Luke, the boyfriend she had broken up with right before Thanksgiving? The whole time she'd been going out with him had been so volatile, so fraught with the threat of explosions, angry words, tension. Our relationship seemed like leaking gasoline fumes, all the time, every minute. Why shouldn't she accept a curfew? What did it matter that no one else in her crowd had one? I had standards. I had expectations. Bergin had a future few kids in her school understood. My father didn't bequeath to her his photographic memory just to be hidden and denied. I had to protect her and her future. As her mother, it was my job.

But somehow the fact of whatever happened between her and Luke didn't seem enough, not for this, not for this total rearrangement of all of our lives. There was a part of me that wanted to shake Bergin, a part that was angry, and too ugly to let loose, or to look at closely. The main verdict was that if I only knew why she had done this, I could fix it. I could fix anything, though what would be the chances now that Bergin would finish the applications, be able to go off to college, be on her own? What were the chances of anything usual or good happening now? What did it matter?

I turned into the hospital parking lot. Dr. Cone had said she'd put Bergin on an antidepressant, Zoloft. I was placing my hope on the miracle of that drug. I wanted my daughter back. She was alive, yes, and thank God and Dylan for that. But I wanted her as she had been, and *now*. I wanted all of her back.

WHEN WE walked into Dr. Cone's office, there were Doug and Dylan and Vicky, sitting in side-by-side chairs like the three monkeys,

Hear no evil, See no evil, Speak no evil. Figuratively, of course. In fact, they looked recently scrubbed and well watered with coffee. And they had been punctual, as usual. We all nodded and said good morning, and Kirk offered up his box of Cheerios to each one of them. Dylan took a handful with a smile. Dylan's jeans were so big they looked like they were hanging on by a prayer. I glanced at Doug and Vicky, looking for signs they had argued over this. Doug wasn't one to go in for Janco jeans or hair moussed straight up, at least not for someone to be seen with him in public. But being Vicky's child, Dylan was probably off limits for Doug most of the time. I sat down next to Vicky and gave Maggie a coloring book and crayons out of my saddlebag purse.

"Nice weather, isn't it?" Dr. Cone threw out. She was wearing a blue silk blouse under her white clinical coat, and a navy skirt with matching low-heeled shoes. She is so tall and straight and polished. I wanted to know more about her, but all I knew—and was allowed to know, because her professionalism kept all personal knowledge of her at a distance—were what the framed degrees on the wall told me: Johns Hopkins Medical School. Residency at Massachusetts General. Board-certified in psychiatry. Anything else I knew, I knew through Jack. "She's good," he had said. "I asked around. She's well respected in her field, one of the best. So don't worry. Bergin's in good hands."

I took a deep breath and peeled the paper off a crayon where Maggie was telling me to, then picked a Cheerio off of Kirk's collar. As we waited for the others to arrive, we made small talk, and while each of us were admitting how little of our Christmas shopping we'd done, Jack walked in. Two minutes after that, Carl LaTour came through the door looking a bit sheepish and unsure. He had on khaki pants and a white shirt with a crewneck sweater. Carl is thin and tall, and his hair is totally white. He stays tanned year round. His eyes are surrounded with squint lines, like an old fisherman, which he is, part of the time. Since a recent net-fishing ban, he'd been cultivating clams in an acre off the Gulf that he'd leased, and he was counting on the clams being on his restaurant's menu. "Mornin'," he said, smiling, and took a seat next to Jack. Then a nurse escorted Bergin in.

Dr. Cone didn't try to cushion Bergin's entrance. Bergin just walked into the most palpable silence, all of us looking at her, then glancing away as soon as we could, then glancing back. It was Maggie who broke the ice, running to Bergin and taking her hand, handing her a crayon and showing her the coloring book. Bergin had on jeans I had brought her earlier, and a T-shirt, and Birkenstock sandals. Her hair was combed, but she looked detached and stiff. I wanted to pull her into my lap. I wanted to hold her as if she were two or four, as I still did Kirk and Maggie. Her pain was so evident, it was like that of an animal struck by a car, who was now peeking out from the bushes where it had retreated to lick its wounds.

"Have a seat, Bergin," Dr. Cone said. Bergin sat in one of the teak chairs, and Maggie squeezed in beside her, throwing her legs over one of Bergin's thighs.

"I'm trying to get to know your family, Bergin," Dr. Cone said. "I see it includes a fair number of people."

Bergin nodded. The atmosphere Dr. Cone set up was no better nor worse than a judge in a courtroom. But then in the next few minutes, she worked to make it change. I saw that. I was aware of where she was going. "What do you do together?" She threw out the question and looked across all our faces. I could see how she watched to see who would answer first.

"We canoe together and go to Shoney's for breakfast and feed all the animals and give the dogs a bath. And that flea stuff stinks." It was Maggie answering, of course. "But not all of us. Just us four," Maggie added, pointing to Jack and me and Kirk and herself. She turned around and patted Bergin's cheek. "Are you coming home with us today? Why are you here? Will you do a French braid in my hair?"

"Bergin will go home, Maggie, when she's better, " Dr. Cone said.

We then talked about Carl's drive over from Palm Key, and Doug's job, and Dylan's skating, and my caseload and hours at work, and then *bam!* Dr. Cone looked straight at Bergin and asked, "What was going on, Bergin, that you attempted this?"

We all looked at Bergin. We couldn't help it. It was what we all wanted to know, dying to know; and yet the question, sitting in the air all by itself, seemed strange and stark and frightening.

"It's been a hard year," Bergin said.

Maggie twisted Bergin's ponytail around in her fingers. "Come here, Maggie, come sit beside me." Dr. Cone pulled a chair up next to her and set out some white stationery and an ink pen. "Draw me a picture of your house," Dr. Cone said. "Draw me the farm Bergin has told me that you live on."

"Okay. But I have to warn you about Spam."

"Who is Spam, Bergin? Who is Maggie talking about?"

"He's the . . ." Maggie offered.

"Shhh . . ." Dr. Cone put her index finger against Maggie's lips. "Let's let Bergin tell us. Let this question be hers."

Maggie looked at Bergin and twisted her lips loose from Dr. Cone's finger. "Okay. Go ahead, Bergin. Tell her. Tell her who Spam is."

"He's our pig," Bergin said.

Everybody in the room laughed.

Maggie elaborated. "And he's rooted up all the bushes in our front yard, so our place looks like white trash live there." Maggie was working on her picture now. "That's what Mama says, and Daddy says he's going to rake the yard but he doesn't, and the peacocks go to the bathroom all over it, so we have to scrape off our shoes every time we go anywhere." She held up her foot, so the sole of her shoe was on display to Dr. Cone.

"Thank you, Maggie," Dr. Cone said. "Thank you for painting a picture of where you live." Everyone was laughing, or at least chuckling now, and I was embarrassed but relieved at how the atmosphere was changing, and then Dr. Cone looked at Bergin again and asked point blank, "What made the year so hard?"

There was a long stretch of silence. "I don't know." Bergin looked down and picked a loose thread on the seam of her jeans.

"Was it something that happened? Was it something that didn't happen? What can you tell us?" Dr. Cone wasn't letting up now.

I couldn't help myself—I was leaning toward Bergin and waiting, waiting, so hungry for words, for her explanation. I felt suspended. My whole body was aching to draw the words out of her. She glanced at me. She looked down at her jeans and twisted the thread some more.

"I didn't get chosen for the student government thing," she said, glancing up, "and then Luke broke up with me, and then . . ." She sighed deeply as though she were tired of all of us now. "And I've got to get into college. You know about that, don't you, Dr. Cone? You went to college once upon a time, didn't you?"

"And what else?" Dr. Cone pushed.

"That's it; that's all. My boyfriend dumped me, and I didn't get chosen to go to the state government thing, and Christmas was coming, and I couldn't think of a darn thing to ask Santa for."

Dr. Cone sat back and turned her attention to Carl. "We appreciate your driving over to be with us, Mr. LaTour. And Dylan, I thank you for giving up your morning at school. What are you missing, by the way?" She smiled. And Dylan looked up smiling, too.

"Latin," he said. "First-period Latin, and then math."

"In fact," Dr. Cone added, looking at Dylan and then at all of us, one after the other. "I know how hard this is for each of you. And it takes great courage to come in here and be willing to deal with an issue like this." Then she looked at Bergin. "We all know, too, how much pain you are in. And you are very brave to begin to share it. In fact, let's have another session next week. Same time, same place. Is that okay?"

Maggie thrust her ink-pen drawing of our farm into Dr. Cone's face. "See Spam. See the holes he's made. Mama says she's going to cook him for dinner. But we all know Mama can't cook."

Bergin threw her head back and laughed, and while looking at Dr. Cone said, "That's sure the truth." She got up and left, and the rest of us trickled out into the hall. I watched Bergin being let back in to the locked ward by a nurse.

Jack touched me, putting his arms around my shoulders. "It's going to be fine," he whispered into my ear. Everyone else was gone now. The rest of our family menagerie was getting into the elevator at the other end of the hall. "I promise you," Jack kept whispering. "It's all going to be fine."

Maggie sat down on his right shoe, and Kirk sat down on his left, face forward toward his knee, with their arms wrapped around his calves. He walked them that way to the elevator, and then he arbitrated between them while they fought over who would get to push the Down button.

As I went back to the car, I couldn't get out of my mind the sight of Bergin walking back to the locked ward. I kept seeing that over and over, and I kept hearing her voice as she said every time she was asked why she had done this, "It's been a hard year, hard year, hard year . . . Luke and college and . . ."

But if there's one thing I know from all my years as a defense attorney, it is a lie when I hear it. Bergin knew I knew this. So what was it, then, that she didn't want me to know? What was she trying to protect me from?

THE FUTURE never used to scare me. Call it dumb sauciness. I just never thought there wasn't anything I couldn't do. It was August when Bergin and I first moved here. She was six and I was twenty-nine. The days were so hot, they were like standing over a pot of steamed clams. Mildew, the color of soot, crept up the sides of everything. I remember pouring whole bottles of bleach on it in the shower of the little house we rented. But I loved it, loved it as a sign of being back only 150 miles from where I grew up, and from my father. Of course I could have gone to law school in Tallahassee, moved right back into the house with my father where I grew up. But that would have felt too much like failure, too much like a retreat. I loved being, once again, in charge of my life, choosing its direction, moving around in the feel of my days as if they, too, were a new place to live.

We set up house in the little place near the law school. It was made of concrete block, painted green. An oak tree dripped moss across the roof, and the front yard was mostly sand. I began my long hours of studying and paid close attention to the budget we struggled to stay within. I borrowed money from the bank for tuition; I borrowed money from my dad for living expenses. (Doug was prompt and religious with Bergin's child support. That was never an issue.) So we did fine, Bergin and I. We ate simple meals, though I have to be forthright and admit they were most often anchored by frozen macaroni. We entertained ourselves with simple things: trips to the park, discount movies, Saturday morning bike rides. Every Thursday night at eight o'clock sharp we watched the *Cosby* show together, and every Wednesday when I had a break in my classes, I went to her school and ate lunch with her. It was 1987; Reagan was dealing with the Iran-Contra mess, Gorbachev was planning a visit to D.C., a new cereal called Just Right hit the shelves, and I started eating it and serving it to Bergin, as much on the hope of its name as the taste.

On October 1, Los Angeles had an earthquake that killed six people and injured one hundred, and I sat watching the victims on TV, feeling kin in a way, knowing, too, how the earth could shift and fall out from under your feet in more ways than one. I went out on a limb and bought a used IBM computer to write my briefs and papers on, hoping it would save me valuable time. Yet, half the time I seemed to spend on the phone to the IBM hot line, trying to figure out how to work the blasted thing. Every night, it seemed, Bergin went to bed with the old daisy-wheel printer slamming words onto the computer printouts that fed out onto the kitchen table like a paper worm. Late at night, I'd keep the radio on to help keep me awake. Tommy James and the Shondells would sing "I Think We're Alone Now," which easily could have been my and Bergin's signature song.

I was lonely. I have to admit it, and often bamboozled. I didn't know how to get the squirrels out of the attic, or how to get the toilet to stop running when I couldn't find the landlord. I was such a dummy when it came to mechanical things and using common sense. I missed companionship, real companionship, and intimacy, terribly. I started doubting what I had done: leaving Doug, pressing for a divorce, signing myself up for law school as if I'd be the next Sandra Day O'Connor; and, in general, retreating from all but my academic life. I had hightailed it into the solitary dedication of wanting nothing more than raising my child and graduating with honors. Joining all the law societies open to students, and then some, I booked myself up with every minute taken. My dad was so supportive, it made me wince. There was nothing I could ever do to make him withdraw his love. I guess I could have committed murder, and he still would have defended me. He died of a heart attack in 1989. Bergin was eight. That's when I hit bottom. That's when I nearly lost my footing for good. I could barely think or function for a solid year after that.

I remember Bergin answering the front door, or the phone. It would be a classmate, or a friend of my father's, or a neighbor trying to be neighborly. "I'm sorry; my mother's lying down now. She has a migraine." Or, "No. She can't come to the phone now; she's writing a paper."

Bergin even wanted to protect me from Jack.

I met him in the grocery store in the frozen-food section. It was on a Saturday when Bergin was over at the Bateses' house, playing with Simpson. I was shopping in a store where I didn't usually go. And I couldn't find Mama Caldone's Spaghetti for the life of me. I was opening the freezer doors all up and down the aisle, sticking my head in, rummaging around awhile, then closing the fogged-up door in a huff of exasperation. While I stuck my head into the section of pizza, someone began holding the door open behind me, and when I turned around, I saw this man with a package of Split Pea with Ham, asking me if I'd ever tried one of those frozen soups? (Frankly I hate split pea in any form. But anything frozen is high on my list.) "Worth trying," I said, and kept hunting for Mama Caldone.

As I was heading off, we got the front wheels of our grocery carts entangled, so I guess you can say we'd spent enough time together to be at least familiar with how we each looked. The next week, when we were at a medical ethics conference, we recognized each other. Attending the conference was part of an assignment for one of my courses. At the break, we struck up a conversation. The only personal information about ourselves that we exchanged were our names and our reasons for being there. But I inadvertently let loose the fact that I lived with my eight-year-old daughter only a few blocks from the law school. I was aware that now, and here, I was not a high school star coasting on my and my father's reputations. Here my looks were not overlooked. Here I really *was* what I was at first glance: a dishwater blonde plain jane with a child in tow.

I saw him outside the law school one day. He was leaning against his car. I didn't realize then that he'd been parked there for some time, looking for me. "Oh, hey," he said, as though seeing me were a surprise. I remember thinking he gave the overall impression of being short and fuzzy, coppery hair curling all over his arms and at the base of his neck before it disappeared under his opened collar. He had (and still has) the most disconcerting, but wonderful, way of keeping his eyes aimed at your face, going from lips to eyes, to cheeks, to chin (a roving constant eye) while you talk. Which, of course, I am good at, so he has a long while for roving.

He was unmarried, he let me know, and never had been. Turned out he was five years younger than I. (Don't ask me to explain strange; I just live with it.) He had graduated from the university and stayed on in the little city he had grown to love. He had gotten a graduate degree in hospital administration, and he wanted to see me, date me, if I was amenable. I liked that "amenable." Yes, I said, I was amenable. (Horny too, but I didn't throw that in.)

I met him for our first few dates. I didn't want him—or any man—coming to the house for me, where Bergin would feel that her world was changing. I kept everything the same for her, as much as I could. She was Doug's daughter and always would be. No one else would come into her life and move it around; I was adamant about that. But I didn't share my rules with Jack. I saw no reason for him to know all that. I just met him at various restaurants, or at various concerts.

When Bergin turned ten, I decided she was old enough to trust to stay alone in the house for a short while. I was going to meet Jack for a cup of coffee. Simpson Bates was there with her. It was Simpson's turn to spend the night over at our house. But I couldn't stop wanting to check on them. I was worried for no good reason (or maybe for a million good reasons, considering what crazy things the world could unleash at times), except that it was the first time I had done this, and even though Bergin was a mature ten (already like an old-lady ten), she was still just ten. (Oh, how hard it is for mothers to leave their children, maybe knowing deep in their bones there is no escape from the day the children will leave them.) I called twice: once from Jack's and once from the coffee shop. "What're you and Simpson doing?" I asked Bergin when she answered.

"Nothing, just reading."

"Are the doors locked?"

"Tighter'n a tick."

Tighter'n a tick. Funny how Bergin constantly seemed to pick up my idioms—or whatever you want to call them. Often we sounded like partial echoes. Sometimes we seemed like black and white prints of each other: a hint of my immortality, I guess. She was a flesh and blood warning, too, for me to think twice about what I might not want to hear again. "All three deadbolts?"

"All three."

"That'a girl. So what'ya reading?" I tried to sound light, so I wouldn't come off as intrusive or worried.

"Oh, just some old magazine."

"What magazine?"

"One of yours."

I knew then she and Simpson were probably playing around with reading things way over their heads.

"What's it about?

"Warts."

"Warts?"

"Yeah, *gentile* warts. But, Simpson and I were wondering . . . do Jews get 'em, too?"

I went back to the table and told Jack. It took him a minute, but he caught on to Bergin's misreading of the word *genital* for *gentile*, so that in a half-embarrassed yet amused way, we both laughed for the next five minutes without stopping. I guess he knew, before he even met Bergin, he would love her.

Then there was that day he turned up at the house.

"No. You can't see my mom, " Bergin said, holding closed the door and talking through the chain lock as I'd taught her. "She's fixing the gol'dern computer."

In the kitchen, I was dealing with a paper jam, letting loose a string of cuss words—or rather what I had come up with as substitutes for profanity in order to shield Bergin. "Gol'dern whatchamacallit, flip-stitching holy-mama stump sucker!"

"Ask her if she needs any help?" Jack said and patiently stood outside on the stoop.

"Man out here says he's your friend and wants to know if you need any help," Bergin called. Then she looked up at Jack. "You a computer nerd or something?"

"Nerd," Jack said.

"No," I yelled. "Tell whoever it is we don't need whatever he's selling, and tell him to walk away quiet because I'm going to turn loose my pit bull."

I didn't have a pit bull, but the fantasy that we did was Bergin's and my added-on security system. We had signs nailed up all around outside of the house with pictures of a bulldog dripping saliva from his teeth, saying *Go Ahead. Break In. Make My Day.*

"It's Jack," Jack called out. "Tell the dog my name is Jack."

"Oh, Lord," I said, running out to him, pushing my hair away from my face. I was glad to see him, but as soon as I let him know that, I bawled him out for coming unannounced.

TURNS OUT, that's apparently part of what Jack fell in love with: my ability to bawl him, or anyone, out. Not my aggressiveness or flair with words, but my honesty, he says. The way I will not put up with shams, whether it is in a marriage where I could no longer sweep destructive feelings under the rug, or a teacher of Bergin's who would shuffle her off alone into a corner with a workbook, because Bergin was too far ahead of everyone in her class to fool with. It gets me in trouble, this willingness to say it like it is. Or, if not the way it is, the way I see it. It makes things rough for everyone around me.

The only person I have ever learned to be quiet with is Doug. I've learned over the years, only too well, that if I don't swallow words in his presence, I will be called manipulative and mean. (And whatever words he chooses to apply to me in my presence can still hurt as clearly as slamming my finger in a door.) With him, the less said, the better. And if there are really important things to be communicated between us, I know it is always best to write him a letter.

But not Jack. Not with the one I grew to know and love, and to live with. He will listen to me go on and on about anything, and no matter where. I think of Jack as a bisection of the earth. Layers in him seem as differentiated as sand and loam, rock and liquid, and yet they are there, always, *always* steadying me. He has a buoyant outwardness, funny and high, ready to be "on" at any minute where being on is called for, and yet there's a deep quiet sadness in the center of him. At times he will sit beside me with a quietness that resembles a rock, or an old cavern. I attribute his calm to the spring when he was in college and his parents were killed on a slick road in a small nearby town called Dunnellon as they were driving to see him. Serenity is not born; it is learned, he has taught me. And if anything now, I am needing Jack to show me.

I WOULDN'T sleep with him for the longest dern time, and when I did, I refused to ever have him stay in my house. Even when Bergin was away visiting Doug, I would go stay with Jack at his apartment. The year after I graduated from law school, I clerked for a judge. Every day I had to wear power suits, keep my hair fixed and my hose on. Once I was due at Bergin's school at 9:00 for a gifted-child program, and at court with the judge at 10:30. I had spent the night with Jack because Bergin had been at Doug's. Doug had moved here by then, and he would drop her off at school for me and would stay to see her program, and so would I; and from there I would go straight to work. But as I was getting dressed at Jack's, I realized I had forgotten my pantyhose and didn't have any clean underwear, either. Panicked and short on time, I borrowed some Fruit of the Loom jockeys from Jack. They were a little loose at the waistband, but otherwise seemed fine.

I remember how I stood there at the punch bowl in the school library with Bergin beside me, Doug not far away, while talking to her principal, talking to her teacher, hearing all these wonderful things about my daughter. I kept nibbling on a donut and sipping the orange juice punch, but all the while, every second, feeling alarmed at how much ventilation the Fruit of the Looms were letting in. I was praying to high heaven they would stay where they were supposed to. (I knew, too, that the panty line in my power suit was bound to be a doozy.) But all I wanted to do was to keep Bergin's world right, to never let her down.

All those years before I married Jack, it was just Bergin and me. It was just us two going along, just us two peas in a pod, us two chicks on a raft. And as I drove the van with the twins in it that day when we were leaving the hospital, I had the most awful feeling that I had forgotten something.

I pulled up to the school to drop off Maggie and Kirk. I maneuvered into a parking space and walked them to the door of their classroom. I kissed them goodbye, and then walked back to the van, running my hands down my skirt, checking for bumps, for straightness, for flaws. The whole time I was driving to work, I kept messing with my suit, rearranging my skirt, and fluffing my hair, and wondering, wondering: how much over the years had Bergin and I had kept from each other? How many times had we hidden our mistakes, our failings, our private fears? *What had we forgotten about each other?*

SEVEN

Bergin

"Where do you want to be for Christmas?" Dr. Cone was looking at me. There was a bowl with red camellias floating in water on her desk. The room smelled like apples, because she was pouring herself a cup of apple-spiced tea. "Your mother's house or your father's house? Where would you like to be?"

"Here," I said.

She looked at me and offered to pour me a cup of tea, too. But I turned her down. Then, "Why?" she asked, not meaning the tea, but my choice on Christmas.

There was that frigging word again. If I heard *why* one more time I was going to rip my hair out. Or hers. "I like it here," I said. "I like the O.T. room, and the food, and I'm crazy in love with Nurse Dottie Stewart."

Dr. Cone laughed. "Okay. So you just can't bear to leave us. But remember the first time I saw you here, with Dylan, and you told me that next time you wouldn't fail? Is that why you want to stay here? Is this the only place you feel safe?"

"Yeah, safe," I said, and started laughing. There were bars even on her office window.

"Do you still feel that way?"

"What way?"

"About ending your life. Do you still have suicidal thoughts?"

"Sometimes. But it's so much trouble—swallowing the pills and all. And I didn't count on throwing up. It makes such a mess."

"Escaping, though, sometimes is nice to think about, isn't it?" Steam was coming up over her face and fogging her glasses as she took another sip of tea. She went on, "Ending it all, getting out of a family. It's hard being your age. Some days a lot of people feel they want to just drive away from where they are and not come back, at least for the rest of the afternoon. Is that the way you were feeling? Did you want to leave—just for a little while?"

"Forever might have been enough."

"That's a lot of Mondays." She got up and walked to the window and shut the blinds where the sun was coming in across my face. "What was hurting you so much that you wanted to be away that long?"

"I think I'll have some tea now."

She poured me a cup.

"Whom were you protecting? Why did you want to hurt yourself instead of them?"

I took the cup of tea from her and held it. I let the heat of it move up over my eyes. I shut them against the warmth. If I said the truth. If I let the words cross my tongue and leave my throat, we would all be shattered. I thought of a tree limb falling through glass, into pieces. It was words that we had to watch out for. They were what was waiting to steal the last little bit of me I was hanging onto. After all, I'd chosen to not live rather than to say what she wanted me to say now. I swallowed the tea and looked up.

"Okay," Dr. Cone said. "Let's talk about Christmas. Or better yet, let's talk about Luke. Tell me about him. Tell me about the beginning with him. I want to hear about the good times."

OKAY. THE Good Times. That's what she asked for. The Beginning. Sure, I could tell her about the beginning. I could tell her about even back in seventh grade, when how sex-crazed everybody started getting, how every Monday morning being asked, had I gotten laid over the weekend? Had I done it? Rumors started like faucets. And I didn't know what to say. I didn't know what to do. My power—oh how I loved it and hated it at the same time. The yellow hair. The breasts. Bigger and sooner than most. My skin. I was at the top of the heap. Everybody wanted to be near me. Touch me. Talk to me. And every day I felt more of myself leaving. I was who I was with them. And who I was with me.

And then in high school, the hall that every girl had to walk down to get to the gym for P.E. How boys would line up and watch you. And reach out to touch you. And call you *cunt*. And in my case The Frozen Beaver. Or The Ice Pussy. And I didn't want to be touched. And yet I did. I did. *I did.* Wanted what everybody seemed to want, too. I must. And yet didn't. Not yet. Not yet. And, too, to choose who and how far and when. And I didn't know how to stop it. Didn't know any words to throw back. Words that could keep them from touching me. To keep me to myself. And the whole idea of fighting back. Saying something that would sting. I didn't know how. *I didn't know how.* I didn't know how. And then out of all of this came one thing. Belong to one, just one, who would stamp me with ownership. I'd be marked goods. I'd be declared out of bounds. And it would be so easy for me. Just choose. That's all I had to do: choose.

Sure, some girls would die—no pun intended—to have *my* problem. But it's a whole different layer of craziness to feel every minute. All the time. All the time. *All the time.* That it is the packaging that matters. I might as well have been cellophane.

I chose Luke.

He claimed me in the first month of the tenth grade. He was on the football team. A follower in my father's footsteps.

"Oh, Luke."

As soon as I said it, my head dropped. It was the first time I cried in front of Dr. Cone. Because, in saying his name, I thought of the end first, and not the beginning. And damn it, not only do I look like hell when I cry, but my words jam in my throat. And damn it, too, if I didn't slobber in my tea.

"So okay, let's go back to the beginning," she said when she figured out I couldn't get out another word. "Tell me about when you first knew him."

That's the way Dr. Cone works—zigzags through your life like she is lacing a shoe.

"Damn Jack," I said. "He about ruined it right off."

I had to paint the whole picture then.

It was late September, still hot. Still shorts weather. And Luke and this friend of his, Mike, who was older, who had his own car and a driver's license. Who could be hot on me in a short ten minutes, too. Drove out to my mom and Jack's farm. The place where we moved when they married. The twins then were barely two. And my mom and Jack had clearly set the farm up as a place for happiness. The sweetness is like a syrup that can slip down your throat and make you choke. For Maggie and Kirk, I guess it's their Honey Hole. Their Laughing Place. But I was still waiting for the god-o-mighty happiness to happen.

Jack named it Blueberry Hill after that song by Fats Domino, "I Found My Thrill on Blueberry Hill." He plays the tape of the song all the time. On almost any time of day on any Saturday you can hear the song thumping out of the barn. That's where he has a machine shop set up to work on his tractor. And all the while, he's singing along like he's doing karaoke, too. He planted twenty blueberry bushes along the back fence. Watered and fertilized them until they drip over every year with berries. Then he makes us all pick them like we are the Waltons living in glory. We fill the freezer slap up to the gaskets with blue Tupperware bent out of shape with blueberries. He bakes off them all year long. Blueberry pancakes, muffins, cobblers, pies. Even blueberry ice cream. Like I said, Jack is an Aunt Jemima in a pinstripe suit.

Dr. Cone laughed. And that surprised me. I guess it egged me on.

The house is a cracker house, high off the ground on blocks. White clapboard. A tin roof. It was built in the thirties. My mom and Jack put in a new kitchen and added on what they call the Family Room. You know, with a fireplace and a table to eat off of and to play board games on. My mother is as addicted to board games as some people are to nicotine. She hates to lose, too. So yeah, right off, soon as you pull off the main road, you can tell the whole place is set up as paradise. A pig in the front yard. Two peacocks walking around dropping crap for the twins to step in, and feathers to play with. The feathers because they have the shape of eyes made right on them. And the twins sometimes stick them in jars like flowers. Or swordfight with them. And inside the house are circles on the rugs where one of the three dogs has thrown up. Or where one of the seven cats has passed a hairball. Pure-T heaven, for sure.

Again, Dr. Cone laughed. When she did, it scared me. In fact I jumped at the sound of it. It didn't seem like something a doctor should do. Or like what somebody sitting there in a white clinical coat looking groomed to high heaven should do. And then there's the sound of it. It's completely out of tune with the way she looks. To tell you the truth, Dr. Cone's laugh is something that ought to be in the *Guinness Book of World Records*. It's an eruption like the bass notes of an organ being played all at once. It's a man's laugh, a redneck with a beer belly's laugh. And the whole while she's letting it go, she looks at you, looks at you, looks at you, looks at you.

So when Mike and Luke came to see me, Mike parked in the front yard under the oak tree where we all park. He came up the pea-gravel walkway with Luke beside him. They stepped over a little peacock crap. Then stopped to look at Spam under the shade of an azalea, snoring. When he lies in his hole under there, his stomach protrudes like a bathtub flipped on its side. A pink bathtub with black hairs across it. And since he's the color of dirt, you hear his snore way before you see him. If he cares to wake up and lift his head to look at you, his snout is like a place to plug in a toaster. I could hear Luke and Mike laughing. Making a to-do over him. You know, squatting down to get a better look. Yeah, coming here is as good as driving over to the Ripley Museum of Believe It or Not.

I was in my front bedroom, reading. I could see them but they couldn't see me. And they walked up onto the porch and rang the doorbell. My Doberman, Stella, was lying on the bed with me. Her legs are long and thin as yardsticks. And she went nuts barking at the sound of the bell. Jack opened the front door with an apron on. My mother was at the grocery store. Which is a ten-mile drive away, getting Jack cornstarch and lemons, since he was in his blueberry pie phase. "Yo," Jack said, then caught Maggie as she toddled out the door after Kirk, throwing flour on him. Jack had flour all over his hands, too. They all wore butcher-like aprons with *Kiss The Cook* on the front.

"Bergin here?" Luke asked.

"I think she's inside," Jack said. "Y'all come on in. I'll hunt her up."

I could hear them in the hallway. Jack must have taken them into the kitchen, since I could hear Kirk and Maggie jabbering in their no-word talk. They could carry on a whole conversation in imitation English because they didn't yet know enough words to keep it going. But already, you could tell, they were crazy in love with the idea of conversation. Then Jack knocked on my door and stuck his head in. "Two fellas here to see you." He put on his cornpone accent, doing Little Abner or one of the Beverly Hillbillies, I couldn't tell which. Jack has about a dozen characters he can become on any given occasion. "Reckon they was just driving past and decided to come a callin'. Cause I don't see that they're sellin' nothin'."

I didn't laugh. And I didn't instruct him on what to say to them. I was moving fast, myself. I was after Luke. And I was combing my hair and making sure my shorts were clean enough. I had on a red T-shirt. I slipped on sandals and went into the kitchen. Stella followed me. Then headed out the dog door punched into the back screened-in porch and took out after one of the peacocks. It flew up to the roof of the screened porch, then fell through a hole there and started walking around the hot tub. "Stella!" Jack screamed, doing his Stanley-Kowalski-in-the-alley act. I decided to ignore him and the peacocks and pretend that my family was as normal as anybody's.

"Hey," I said to Luke and Mike. And, "Hey," they said back. It was funny how words had almost nothing to do with what we wanted to say. Body language was everything. The body was all we talked about.

Luke smiled. He didn't look at me directly, but glanced at me about every ten seconds. Long looks weren't in his vocabulary when he was around other people. He had on shorts, too, black Umbros that came to his knees. Mike had on long orange ones, as outrageous as he could get. Luke wasn't real big then. This was in the beginning of tenth grade, remember? He was thin and angular and on the edge of being where he'd end up. His feet were already the baseboards for somebody six-one. He had on Nikes, white high-tops with thick socks. He had what I call a mop-top then, hair that wasn't combed in any one direction but that just fell over his head from a fountain in the center. It is the color of wheat bread. His face is square with straight even features. He has a tan mole under his right ear, just at the edge of his sideburn. Later he would cut his hair in a buzz. And his face would thin out like a balloon losing air. He would pump iron until his shoulders were the size of midget melons, thick and firm. Sweet, too.

But now, Jack picked up on how hard it was for us to talk and took over. Which was not making me exactly thrilled. He handed Mike and Luke each a rolling pin and their own roll of dough. Pie crust from scratch is Jack's specialty. He was dripping ice on the dough. Then sprinkling flour all over the pastry boards that he had set out on the counters.

"Like this?" Luke asked.

"Yeah," Jack said.

"No," Maggie threw in, sitting on the edge of the counter by Luke. That was her favorite word back then. She was about the size of one of Mike's thighs.

"I think I'll just sit and have a Coke," Mike said, pulling up a stool beside me where I'd parked myself. We were laughing and making fun of Luke as he rolled out his dough, because it wouldn't let go of his rolling pin. Kirk was sitting on the floor playing with the dropped dough like it was silly putty.

My mother walked in then, carrying bags of groceries. "Oh, wow," she said. "A band of cooks. Good thing I got here with the rest of what you need." Jack left to help her unload the car. Mike went to help, too. And Luke kissed me in between their trips back and forth with bags.

So the only witnesses were Kirk and Maggie, who didn't yet know enough words to tell about what they'd seen. It wasn't my first kiss— Lord no—but it was the first that mattered. His lips were soft, much softer than I expected. And he forced mine apart with his tongue. And as he explored me that way, it seemed that I could no longer see myself. I was just skin and feeling. Pressure and touch. But what I liked most, surprised myself by liking so much that I began to think about it all the time, was the way he could roll his shoulders around me. And I could press into his chest, my breasts pushed wide and soft and oblong. And I would feel surrounded. Safe, warm and safe. The smell of his skin was the farm fields in fall. Sun-baked and seeding. Musky but rich.

I wasn't saying all of this out loud. But it was close. And the parts that I did say surprised me. Like I could even forget Dr. Cone was in the room. Or who she was.

"You were in this relationship for three years?" Her question was a meat slicer whizzing off the fat.

"Two and a half. We didn't make it through this year, remember? And if the damn pills had worked faster. And it hadn't rained. And Dylan hadn't come home, I wouldn't have to remember any of it."

"The beginning was quite wonderful, wasn't it?"

"Damn straight."

I sat up. It was so strange talking this way. I didn't tend to use cuss words with anybody who wasn't my age. And I sure wasn't used to talking about sex with anybody as old as her.

"It sounds as though you thought you really loved him. That you learned through this first relationship what love feels like, at least. Would you say that? Would you say that at least you learned a lot?"

"Yeah, heaps," I said. I thought she'd pull back and back off then. Because I'd said it real sarcastic, real mean. She only poured us another cup of tea, though. And I hadn't even asked for it.

"It must have been special to last two and a half years."

"I guess."

"Tell me one good time that you think you will always remember. Tell me about something funny or outrageous or amazing that happened between you."

"One thing?"

"For right now."

"Last year. The Junior-Senior Prom." I laughed. The sound of my laugh came back to me as disgusting. Tinny. Shallow. Young. I cleared my throat. I told her about how my mom is a miser. A cheapskate. How she cuts coupons and stuffs them in her purse until the leather of it is so swollen it looks like a tumor slung over her shoulder. And when she buys something, she says at the checkout, "I know I have a coupon for that." But she never can find it. And she bought me my prom dress on sale. Good reason it was on sale. The stays in the top were missing. Only she didn't notice. Neither of us noticed. Hell, I didn't even know stays were a necessary ingredient for dresses with no straps. Well, not totally strapless, it had these off the shoulder sleeves, ruffled and all. And the dress was red. Well, not red, really, but cranberry. But still it needed stays to stay where it was supposed to. So here I was on the dance floor of the prom. And on the first slow dance, as soon as I put my arms up to go around Luke's neck, my dress begins to come down. And Luke was so sweet. So different then. All night he danced holding my dress up with his arms wrapped around me.

I laughed again.

"What made him different? What made him change?"

"Did I finish telling you how Jack makes those pies?"

"No."

"Wanna know?"

"Yeah. Do you know the recipe by heart?"

"By heart," I said. "You see, he never misses a chance to teach the twins things he thinks will enrich them. That's what he calls it, enriching them. Like they are pies, too. And he was cooking out of the *Florida Cross Creek Cookbook* that day, so Maggie and Kirk would be aware of their local heritage. Independent Blueberry Pie. That's what it was called. Five cups of blueberries. Two-thirds cup of sugar. Three and a half tablespoons of cornstarch. Two tablespoons of lemon juice. One tablespoon of grated lemon rind. Cinnamon. Nutmeg. Allspice. And of course the crust."

"What was it like, making love to Luke?"

"How do you know I did?"

"I'm assuming."

"Are doctors supposed to assume?"

"Sometimes. So is that what happened? You began having sex?"

"My mother would say you were leading the witness."

"In my field, it's allowed. And remember, there's no judge here. So, did you like it?"

"Sometimes." I said it straight out, honest, but with a half smile, so she wouldn't know if I were teasing or not.

Dr. Cone smiled back. "Often?" she asked.

"Often this year."

"Do you want to tell me?"

"Do you think I should?"

"If you want to."

"Will it make me less crazy?"

"You aren't crazy."

"What am I, then?"

"Wonderful."

I laughed. And I surprised myself. The sound had an oh-yeah hook to it. It was a wise-ass laugh, loud, and sort of outrageous. "I'm wonderful? I'm in a crazy house, and I'm wonderful?"

"Wonderful and very much alive."

We sat in a moment of silence then.

"So you don't think it's so terrible that I slept with Luke and then stopped. Stopped dead cold. So now he hates me."

"I doubt he hates you. He was probably ready to stop, too."

"I don't think any guy's ever ready to stop."

She laughed then. "You're so clever, I have to run extra steps just to keep up. Did you like it?"

"What?"

"The sex."

"Oh, yeah, sure."

"That's strange."

"Why?" I couldn't believe this woman. She could say such wild things.

"Well." She drank a little more tea then. "Often when young women first start going to bed with their lovers, they say they don't get much out of it at all. Some of them say it seems so . . . well, elemental, foreign, crude."

"Like he's going to the bathroom inside of you?"

We both laughed then. It was like she was my age and we were at a party or on the phone. This was beginning to feel a whole lot like I wasn't the only one nuts. Or if nuts was what I was, then maybe it wasn't all that bad, and I wasn't going to be all alone.

"It changes," she said. "Just like everything in life, it changes."

"What do you mean?"

"You're seventeen. It gets better. A lot better, in fact. But how else did it make you feel?"

"Used. It got to be all Luke was interested in. There was nothing else about me he seemed to want."

"So you asked him to change?"

114

"Well, I let him know I didn't want to just go to bed with him all the time, every time. I started to feel bad. I mean really bad."

"Caught?"

"Yeah, between what he wanted, and the way I wanted him to make me feel, and the bad way I was feeling about what I was doing."

"What did you use for birth control?"

"Condoms. Every time a condom. And spermicidal inserts." I said that with every syllable I could get out of it. Then I explained, "I drove to a far-off drug store and bought it myself."

"Well, that was responsible."

"What do you expect? I have a 4.7 GPA. That's weighted, you know. I might have been fucking around, but I wasn't going to get fucked up."

I thought she would break when I said that. I thought she'd pull back in disgust. The walls would shake. And it'd be over. I'd go back to my locked ward. And go to O.T. And work on the leather stitch-by-stitch billfolds I was making for everybody for Christmas. But she laughed instead. She laughed and looked at me, looked at me, *looked at me*. And the way she looked made me feel like I was somebody crazy funny. Or clever-dirty. Like I was Eddie Murphy in drag.

"So where did this all lead?"

The truth then slipped out of my mouth as if she had greased the exit. Which I guess she had. "I told him I wanted to slow down. And he said we were through, it was all over. He dumped me. And then he called me a lesbian."

She didn't wait a beat. "That was a terrible thing for you to hear. That was a hard retaliation. He was hurt and threw this at you. But that isn't why you took the pills."

"No."

"You wanted to die because of something else that happened after this, didn't you?"

"You want to see something? You want to see something disgusting?" I was grabbing the bottom of my T-shirt. My fingers were making fists around the hem. I was scared of her now. I knew how she could lead me to places. And I'd find myself there before I even knew where I'd been headed. So I knew I had to give her something that could keep her occupied. A detour. I pulled the T-shirt up over my breasts. "See this! See what I've done here!"

She leaned toward me and bowed her head toward the breasts that every boy and every man everywhere all the time in the whole world seemed to be so damn crazy about. Small white scars dotted the tops of them like flesh stars. They were all that was left now of the circles I had burned into my skin with the end of incense sticks, which I could burn in my room at home. And no one would wonder why or what I was doing. So over the last two months, soon after Luke left me, and three months after I moved out of the farm of paradise—the Blueberry Hill of Thrills and Pies—and into the house of my father, I had made them. I would lock myself in my room and lie on the bed. And let the white-hot pain seep into me. Bringing calm and release and a sense of feeling *me*. Just me. Just me. Just me. Without anyone inside of me. Or touching me and wanting me. And I wouldn't have to think, either. About the worse pain of what I was about to lose. Lose. No. I wasn't going to lose. I wasn't going to lose *that*.

Dr. Cone didn't touch them, but she was close. "I've known they were there," she said. "They were written down on your chart as a possible rash. But I suspected more. It was easier to hurt yourself than to hurt them, wasn't it?"

She was standing in front of me now. She put her hand on the hem of my T-shirt, and together we pulled it down. She was leaning close and looking into my face while I felt tears coming into the backs of my eyes. "It's okay. I'm not going to tell anyone," she was saying. And I could hear her voice. Just barely hear her voice. Like it was something someone was pouring over me. Seeping in. Going in. All over me. "And I promise you, together we're going to do this. Trust me. We're going to give you back to yourself."

I wasn't looking at her. I wasn't looking at anything. I was just holding on to the arms of the chair like it might move. Or dump me out. And my head was down. But I could tell she was leaning on the edge of her desk but bending toward me. And then I could hear, clear as anything, one of the cups of tea rattle off its saucer.

EIGHT

Leslie

O n Christmas Eve I woke up at 4 A.M. The digital clock on the bedside table was looking back at me like animal eyes in the dark. Jack and I had gone to bed only two hours before. For, at ten, as soon as we were sure both of the twins (especially Maggie) were deeply asleep, we'd started putting together a swing set by flashlight in the backyard; and between Jack and me together, I don't think I'd ever heard so many cuss words uttered in one place at one time, in my whole life—or laughter. It was stolen laughter, though, fly-by-night mirth, for I couldn't forget where Bergin was, and I couldn't get out of my mind how all of our lives had been turned around. But laughter, at the time, in the burst of the moment, we accepted. In fact, I sounded a bit hysterical—tension, pent up and shoved down for weeks, leaking through.

During the whole Rise-and-Take-Shape Production of the swing set, Jack recited suggestive pronouncements, like handing me a long-bodied screw and quoting Lady Macbeth's speech about screwing my courage to the sticking-place, and we'd not fail; and then, "There's nothing like a good screw at 2 A.M. for the dark of the soul." He cited his own self on that one. Or, when I whacked my thumb with the hammer, instead of the dowel I was trying to force into a hole, he cried, "Wondrous hole! Magical hole! Noble and effulgent hole! From this hole everything follows—the baby, the placenta, then for years and years and years, a way of life. Cynthia Ozick, *The Hole-Birth Catalog*, 1972." Oh, how Jack could make me laugh! How much he reminded me of my father! He was like a retrieval device. That thought made me stop in the dark of that Christmas Eve to realize that love hooked to love could be pulled through a life, like hands linked in a tunnel. It made me wonder, too, if the love I had passed to Bergin was now going to be enough.

How could I have ever made us ready for this? I had never imagined a time such as this. Car wrecks, cancer, broken legs, acne—all of them, at one time or another, had crossed my mind. With dread and held breath and my fingers crossed, I had thought of all sorts of likely disasters, as though *if* I thought them, they wouldn't happen. That was my own personal way of inoculating us against them. But this. Not this. Not what Bergin had done. How could I have ever imagined *this?*

And worse, other than the sheer horror of the act alone, it was connected to me somehow. It had to be. For I felt as if she were taking the life I had given her and was throwing it back at me, smacking me with it across my face, a gift she did not like and would not accept. This, of course, sent my mind threading back into Christmases past, of all the things I had stayed up late at night wrapping, putting together: Barbie apartments, Cabbage Patch Dolls, chemistry sets, pink boom-boxes, pearls—all of which she liked, loved, played with, kept.

Out there in the backyard it was cold, the moon full and the stars like rice spilled on dark cloth. There were inches of leaves under our feet that we scraped around in, and Jack sometimes would scratch his head the way a squirrel in the daylight would scratch in leaves for nuts, as though irritated at the top layer. I wrapped a red velvet bow around the seesaw, and Jack quoted Hamlet and popped a beer against the swing set as a way of christening it, saying now the deed was done and sweet angels would sing us to our rest—and also hopefully the twins until at least 7 A.M.

But there was no rest, and no angels, only sore muscles and a swelling thumb, and a soul so bruised I could sleep only two hours and then wake and think, again, of Bergin. I remembered her and Simpson swinging on the rusted swing set in the tiny backyard of the block house where we had lived, single, just she and I. And now, she would be home in four hours. At eight I would drive to the hospital to get her. Dr. Cone had said she should be with all of us for part of the day. None of us could understand why she didn't want to leave the hospital. The twenty-one days that our insurance covered were up, but Jack and I both said that whatever was best for Bergin, we wanted. Doug agreed, too, though you could tell he was nonplused by all of this. A suicide attempt was a bit hysterical in his book. It was probably an act of cowardice, in his opinion.

The day before, I had gone in to see Dr. Cone, alone. "We have signed a suicide contract, Bergin and I," she had said. "She can call me at any time; she can come back to the hospital at any time during the day. She'll be given her medicine here. She will have nothing but her own personal belongings with her. I want her to stay out at least until dark—the beginning of the day with you, the last of it with her father. I've talked with him, too. There are to be no guns in the house, no prescription medicines. I want you to go over your house carefully. Baby-proof it, in a sense."

God, how awful that sounded.

"Do you yet have any idea?" I asked, and then added as a lawyer might, "of motivation?"

"Everything between Bergin and me is totally confidential."

"Of course."

"But I can tell you, I don't know much more than I did last week." Then she added, as a good doctor should, "She'll let us know in her own time, in her own way. We'll get this sorted out. Just be patient."

But there in the dark at 4 A.M., lying awake beside Jack, patient was not anything I could be much longer. He must have felt that I was not asleep. My lying stiffly there, breathing shallowly, woke him; and his hand began rubbing my back, moving down to my thighs, and then, between them there. And I wanted to, wanted to believe, as his joke said, that in the middle of the night, there is nothing better for the darkness of the soul than to make a little love—good love. But I couldn't. I couldn't respond. And sensing it, he stopped. He pulled away and let his hand rest across me, heavy and quiet. Clearly, my dumb sauciness about the future was over.

At six sharp, the twins were up. They burst into our room, yelling that Santa had come, and to come see what he had left. "Oh, boy!" I added, then asked (jolly only half to the core), had they yet looked out of the window?

Maggie stood on our bed for a clear view. Her reaction was a squeal equal to one of Spam's when Stella, Bergin's Doberman, gets after him. Oh! beautiful swing set—it had done its job. On this Christmas morning, the twins' delight was running over. They banged out of the back door and scrambled over Jack's and my engineering marvel in their bunny-feet pajamas. The dogs were barking, and the peacocks were strutting and then flying up in terror and falling through the screen roof of the porch onto the top of the hot tub, as usual. The two horses out in the field snorted and took off, their tails high in the early morning fog. One of the cats bolted into the tool shed.

"Touchdown," Jack said, putting his arm around me as we stood in the backyard, watching the twins. He meant he was relieved, too.

We'd generated our own merriment, and so far so good; our Christmas Day was off and running. While I went to get dressed to drive to get Bergin, Jack got on the seesaw with the twins opposite him. He was holding himself up with his toes rooted in the leaves as though Kirk and Maggie had him suspended in air. Pretending to be at their mercy, he pleaded, "Let me down! Let me down!" He was in *his* pajamas, too: sweat pants and a *Gators* shirt the color of an exploding orange.

Underneath the water running, I could hear Maggie outside the shower door. "Hurry, hurry; we want to open the presents under the tree." Earlier we'd agreed to wait for Bergin to do this part of our Christmas ritual. "I will, I will," I promised, rinsing shampoo out of my hair. Not since the twins were born could I ever remember taking a shower without one of them being somewhere in the bathroom.

I heard Maggie run out and then something walk in—one of the dogs. It was one of the dogs in the bathroom with me now. I wrapped a towel around me and stepped out into the room where the mirrors were whited-out with steam. I saw then that the dog had chewed off one of the straps of my brassiere. I had to really rush now, scramble, and at the same time, try to contain my excitement, along with my apprehension. The two emotions were braided together now, whenever I thought of bringing Bergin home.

I wanted to look okay. I didn't want to look as though I were struggling. I didn't want Bergin worrying about me. I wanted her worrying about *her*. All eyes on Bergin now. But I had to take time to fix my hair, put on make-up, do all the things that would outwardly make me look as if I were, as usual, on top of everything. Flustered though, I used by mistake the lip-liner pencil on my eyebrows. Then I couldn't wipe the dark mauve completely off. So as I turned around to look at myself before walking out of the door, I gave off the appearance of being somewhat diseased—more ready for Halloween than Christmas.

The last glance in the mirror turned my thoughts back to when Bergin was ten, and I had taken her to the circus. She had gotten this obsession with the sideshow, the tent where the man with alligator skin stood out front on a platform, up above us, chest-high on me, half a foot overhead on Bergin. Beside him was a woman with a baby sticking head-first out of her side, and beside her, a lady fat enough to make Spam look slim. All around them were barkers promising more outrageous freaks inside. Bergin was more interested in going into that tent than the main one, and she was after me: "Why not?" she had asked.

"Because it's a waste of money," I had said.

"After the show, then."

I had tried to appease her with, "We'll see."

But she'd kept after me. "So what if it costs too much? I want to! I really want to."

Why? Why had she been so fascinated with all that fake deviance? I could so clearly see what a sham it was: the alligator skin, plastic; the baby and the so-called pregnant woman's skin, rubber—the whole hideous thing had probably been slipped on like a monkey suit. The fat lady was the only one who was real, poor thing. But Bergin didn't see that, and I couldn't make her understand. I wouldn't take her, wouldn't buy the overpriced ticket when we came out of the main tent three hours later, either. I bought her off by buying her a monkey on a stick, instead.

Getting in the van on Christmas morning, I was ashamed of denying her that sideshow. I should have indulged her. I shouldn't have been so serious, so much of a tightwad. I shouldn't have been so focused on honesty. I should have just let her be ten, just ten, when reality is never just reality. I shouldn't have bought her that discount prom dress that threatened to make her topless in front of the whole school, either.

WHEN I PULLED up to the hospital, I reached in the back of the van and took out a basket I had packed for Hoot. He was out of the hospital now, but he had gotten a job on the cleaning staff there. Jack had helped to arrange that. It was keeping Hoot busy and focused, and close to the help he needed. I knew I could get the admitting officer to page him, and he would come down into the lobby. I called for Bergin on the phone, too. The fifth-floor head nurse on duty answered, and I said back. "Yes, I'm Bergin's mother. Yes, Merry Christmas to you, too." Then, "I'm here, down here in the lobby. Thanks."

One elevator door opened and Hoot walked out. A second later, another opened; and Bergin, with a nurse escorting her, stepped out. "Merry Christmas, Hoot," I said, handing him the basket while he thanked me. Then I reached to hug Bergin as she walked up. "Hey," I said. "You look great."

She smiled. Over the last week, I'd brought her a whole suitcase of clothes, and for today, a new red sweater. It was red with snowflakes on it, which in snow-free Florida was ridiculous, but still right, because Christmas was Christmas anywhere. Its rituals and stories and fantasies we could surely turn over and find comfort in, in any place. I wasn't sure when I bought the sweater if she would wear it, though. But she had it on. It, and a pair of stone-washed jeans. She was carrying a paper bag in what, I supposed, were presents. The name of the hospital gift shop was on the side.

"Have a good time," the nurse said, stepping away. "We'll see you tonight."

"How's it working out here?" I asked Hoot while I was still holding Bergin's hand, still holding on in a remnant of the hug we had exchanged. Side by side we stood watching Hoot, listening to him telling us about how much he liked working there, how much he liked having someplace to be on holidays and Saturdays. "And the uniform," he said, looking down at the blue jumpsuit with his name *Richard Murphy* embroidered on the pocket. "This is great."

He rooted around in the Christmas basket. Bergin leaned forward, looking in, too. We made a big to-do about the jars of blueberry jelly that were in it, jelly Jack had put up. I had thrown in wrapped hard candy in red cellophane, so the jars were nested in a festive clutter, along with oranges and pecans in their striped shells.

"Bye," Bergin said to Hoot as we walked out. And "Merry Christmas," I said, too, as we headed out the big double doors to the parking lot. We dropped hands as we opened the door. I tried to talk to Bergin as if we were not where we were, as though what had happened had not happened. I was counting on Christmas being my script. It was to be the usual American-family-all-out holiday, in particular our Southern one with its cheese-grits breakfast and cornbread-dressing dinner and warm afternoon. It was a Christmas Day warm enough that a swing set or a bike was not just a sitting frustration.

"You should see the twins," I said. In a verbal flourish that I milked for a good ten minutes, I painted the picture of how I'd left them and Jack on the seesaw. Bergin laughed. She sounded so *all right,* so appropriate. She didn't look or seem damaged, deranged, *oh! but where was she? Where was my daughter?* My mind skated over the old parts, the pasted hearts in construction paper, the handprint in plaster of Paris, the notes, *I luv yu.* Or when I disciplined her, *I hat yu.* And then an hour later. *I sory.* How I grieved for the time when our relationship was simple and uncomplicated. When we could say anything, and it would not be chewed over and harbored, to become, often, too often, secret sores.

As soon as we drove up, the twins and Jack came barreling out, along with Stella, whom Jack had put a red turtleneck sweater on, as well as reindeer horns tied over her ears. The twins and Jack were cheering as though we were stars on a team. *Merry Christmas, Bergin.*

Merry, merry Christmas. Stella jumped up on her, licking, licking. And "Come see," Maggie said, pulling on her hand, running her to the backyard to view the swing set, then into the house to open the presents under the tree. "Hurry, hurry!" The tree touched the ceiling in the family room, ornaments on it glued by the twins and the ones Bergin herself had made all through grade school. Oh, how I'd agonized over what to give Bergin! The present I had ordered and picked up weeks before, I had decided against. It was a whole set of flowered tapestry luggage that I had hidden in the hayloft of the barn. It was to have been her going-away-to-college present, an endorsement of her future. But I couldn't give her that now—not now. Instead a blue cashmere sweater was in a box under the tree.

The rest of that day, I see now, was manic. I was even tempted to brew one of those herbal teas: *Mood Mender* or *Tension Tamer.* But all through the morning, we kept playing the day in a high pitch, beginning with the presents we opened under the tree, with Maggie acting as gift distributor. She could read all of our names on the name tags and was so proud of it! I sorted through the ribbons and torn paper, eager to save what I could for next year. Bergin had bought us small things and trinkets at the hospital gift shop: Jack, a wallet; me, a silver bookmark; Kirk and Maggie, modeling clay and paint sets. Jack cooked breakfast in an apron that said *I thought about being naughty to save Santa the trip, but . . .* And then on the back, *my wife wouldn't let me.* Throughout our holiday breakfast, Maggie told knock-knock jokes, and Jack did his version of imitations of Santa's reindeer on the morning after Christmas: Donner, with a split hoof from landing on our neighbors', the Taylors', roof; Blitzen, with a sprung knee getting over the Millers' oak across the road, and Rudolph, having a sneezing attack from all the peacock feathers on our roof. I have to give him credit—Jack is good in any pinch.

At midmorning when we were winding down out of sheer exhaustion, Bergin went into her room with Stella. I swear, Stella knew more about Bergin than any of us. For Bergin had, no doubt, told the dog any number of secrets, had counted on the dog ever since the eighth grade, when Bergin had found her abandoned on a road near our back woods, to greet her, every day, with gusto. That's what Bergin had called it—gusto—the jumping up chest-high, nearly knocking Bergin down, the licking of her face, her hands, and the dog's rooting of her nose under Bergin's fingers for constant attention. Stella had no manners and no hope of any. But Bergin liked her that way, liked her exuberance and rudeness, she said. She had even insisted on moving Stella to her father's house when Bergin left us to go live with him. It hadn't worked out. Stella was too much of a handful for a shiny, spick-and-span glass house—or so I assumed. I hadn't really known what exactly had happened, only that one day, Stella was back home. Bergin had driven her home and left a note. *Stella needs to stay here. She's not happy over there.*

Not happy over there. What exactly had happened there? Bergin wouldn't talk about it. She hadn't wanted to explain. *She* hadn't been happy over there, either, but she had offered no explanations, no details. *It's just not working out.* That was all.

Now at noon the twins were lying down in front of the TV watching a video of *The Lion King.* Kirk, poor thing, was half asleep. Maggie always drove him hard and wore him out. I walked into Bergin's room. She was lying on her bed. Stella was curled up on a pillow on the floor, having a dream. She was running after something, chasing whatever it was and yelping in her sleep. I looked at the dog, still in her reindeer hat, and then at Bergin, and both of us laughed. It was so easy, so easy to look outward and pretend that nothing else was going on. Yet I knew we were both dying inside. The circus monkey on a stick—seven years old now—was hanging from one of her bedposts. "I'll drive you over whenever you're ready," I said.

"I guess I am." She stood up. It was 12:30, and she was expected at Doug's house at 1:00.

"IT WAS a pretty good day, wasn't it?" I threw out on the ride over.

"Yeah, it really was."

"And you think the sweater is okay? It fits okay?"

"It's great."

"You like the color, too?"

"Yeah. It's perfect."

I restrained myself from talking about how many times it would be cold enough here in Florida to wear it, and how it might be just right for going to college in the East. And I'd stopped myself from asking, too, if she had wanted to drive. Dr. Cone and I had not discussed that. On her medication, would she even be allowed to drive?

Better to keep my mouth shut and aimed on safe things rather than getting into water over my head, where I had no guidance.

I turned on the street that would lead to Doug's house. Some people had their outdoor Christmas lights on already, and decorated trees were visible in windows. Kids were riding bikes and skating in the road. The day was warm now and dried pine needles, blown onto the shoulder of the road, covered the grass in a color of rust.

Teaching Bergin to drive had been one of the hardest things, I think, I have ever done. Turning over to her all that power—1,000 horsepower, or whatever the hell it was, along with power brakes, power steering. It was frightening. For the longest time, it seemed she could never judge distance, pulling out in front of other cars with only a breath's space so that horns honked and other drivers gave us crazy looks. And sometimes Bergin was teary-eyed as though she'd never get the hang of this. "Go now," I'd coach on turning left onto the high-way.

"Now?"

"Yes, now. No! You've waited too late."

It's a miracle we hadn't killed each other, if not in a car wreck, then by murder. When I'd drive up to Doug's house on those weekends when it was time for her visit with him, he'd come out into the drive-way to meet us and tell us what we were doing and not doing and how we should improve.

"You've got her putting on the brakes around a curve," he told me one day. "That's all wrong."

"I'm doing my best," I said.

"Well, I'm trying to get her to understand the importance of trac-tion. The wheels have to be turning to safely go around a curve."

"So why don't you take her more? Why don't you drive with her a couple of afternoons?"

"I don't have time right now. I'm in the middle of something; besides, driving a car isn't all that hard. You just have to learn it right."

By then Bergin would be out of the car and walking into the house, leaving us two still going at it. (Should have brewed up then that tea called *Tension Tamer*. I wanted to serve him right there and then in his own driveway my own brew of *Shove It*.) "Well, I'm going to be driving with her this afternoon some," he said, looking at me, leaning on the car window, "and I'm going to teach her on my straight-stick, and I'm going to concentrate on getting those wheels turning on curves. And I'd appreciate it if next week, you'd follow up."

I drove off then. If I'd stayed with him, all my life I would have been following up.

Then when Bergin came home that day, she was rattled, I could tell. As soon as she jumped in the car with me and I asked her if she wanted to drive, she had said no, she'd had enough for one day. Then in almost full-blown tears—"And next weekend he wants me to parallel park! He gave me his Jaguar to drive, and if I dent it, he'll kill me. And why the hell anyway does somebody need to parallel park? Nobody does that anymore. There's almost no place you have to do it, anymore."

That week I pulled two garbage cans out onto our road and let her practice maneuvering my van back between them. She knocked both of them down twice and one of them four times, but she pulled off three perfect parallel parks. Then, "Next to this van," I told her, "that little ol' Jaguar's going to feel like a bar of soap."

Now sitting beside me in the van on the way to her father's house on this Christmas Day, she was looking out through the front windshield, self-contained in silence and her own secrets. I had to remind myself that this was my daughter, the person I knew so well and loved beyond measure. "See ya," she said, opening the door after I pulled into the driveway and stopped. "And thanks for the sweater; it's perfect." We reached to hug each other, a long stretch; and for a second I squeezed her arms, trying to say all that I could not find the words for, but that love, love was at the center of it. And my hope for hope. My hope for her to come back.

I sat there a minute while she knocked on the front door with its huge green wreath, and it opened and Vicky was there, stepping out on the steps and waving at me. Then Doug appeared, holding the door open and waving at me, too. They would have turkey and dressing. They would open gifts and play at being merry. Then at dark they would drive her back to the hospital where for some reason, in her own way, Bergin was choosing to hide.

At home, Jack was trying to thicken the gravy. I pulled on an apron to help him. Gravy is Jack's only nemesis. He just can't get the hang of using what I resort to—McCormick's Instant. Whisk in one cup of cold water and *voilà*.

131

While the twins were still lying in front of the VCR-doing-its-thing, both of them just about in La-la Land and fully asleep, Jack pulled me into the pantry and closed the door. He kissed me there, passionately there, pressing me against him as though he feared I, too, might disappear. Then he pulled a small box out of his pocket and handed it to me. "Merry Christmas, Leslie," he said. Inside was a bracelet, a wide silver bracelet. "Turn it over," he told me. So I read what he had had engraved there, and the sound of my own laughter startled me. I laughed until I realized how hysterical I sounded. For it wasn't the tender sweet-nothings I had expected to read there. It was instead something he'd borrowed from a greeting card, a funny prayer: *Give me Patience, Lord. But hurry.* I thanked him, and kissed him, only I initiated it this time. As I did, I felt myself accepting and forgiving and hoping, all at the same time. Sure, it was borrowed and canned words that, all day, we'd been using. But as yet, they were the only ones we could trust.

NINE

Bergin

Dr. Cone said I wasn't crazy. But if I wasn't crazy. Tell me what this was. Stepping into my father's and Miss VickyLaTour-Talbot-Now's house at one o'clock on that Christmas Day. I had no more of an idea than a fly at sunrise where I was planning to settle down for good on any other day. At any other time. Because I wasn't intending to stay there. And I wasn't intending to stay with Jack and my mother. And I wasn't intending to stay in the crazy ward where Dr. Cone was turning out to be maybe the best friend I had ever had. No. And I wasn't even thinking about why I wasn't thinking about it. It was more like I was just planning to be air. And so nothing, not one little thing, or *iota* of a thing—as Miss Vicky likes to say—needed to be paid attention to.

Seems to me that's proof I was nuttier than the fruitcake Miss Vicky set down at that Christmas dinner on the glass table that was turning lemon yellow from candlelight. "That's the perfect pair of earrings for my new suit," Miss Vicky said, looking at me. "Black and silver and gold, it's just got a little bit of everything." She was talking about the fact that as soon as I'd walked in the door, we'd opened our presents. I'd decided against giving everybody the stitched leather wal-

133

lets I had made in the crazy ward. Instead I had bought honest-to-god gifts in the gift shop. Earbobs for Miss Vicky. A key ring for my Dad. And a Puff Daddy CD for Dylan, who wasn't there right then. He was spending the day over in Palm Key with *his* father. "So how in the world did you know it would be perfect for my new suit?" Miss Vicky had talked through the turkey. And now she was talking through the fruitcake. And throughout it all she had been jumping up and sitting down, serving this, serving that. And talking all the while, all the while. While my dad and I sat cattycornered with candles in front of us. "It was just a lucky guess," I said.

I'd received from the two of them the same cashmere sweater my mother and Jack had given me, only in peach. Same sweater, different colors. And I was living where I'd get maybe a handful of days cold enough to wear it. But it was a nice sweater. Pretty. And expensive, for sure. After all, what little room did I leave them? It's hard to choose gifts for someone set on becoming air. "Looks like your high school's team is going to end up number one," my dad said, stirring sugar into his decaf. He had on a gray sweater and khaki pants; and when he looked at me, his eyes, or at least what he was seeing, were hurting him, you could tell. "Which team?" I asked, to be devilish.

"The Sharks," he said, confused. Like maybe now I had a memory disease, too.

Football is what he meant.

He didn't even know I was messing with him. After all, there were swimming teams. And volleyball teams. And debate teams. But I knew which teams he followed and which he did not. "Yeah," I said. "The offense is really strong this year."

I was praying he would not mention Luke. For Luke was one of the reasons the team was doing so well. And Luke was, no doubt, being scouted for any number of college scholarships. Like a good father, my father didn't say the name Luke. And then when he looked at me, you could tell he was afraid to. Afraid to mention anything that had anything to do with my past. Afraid, too, of anything to do with my future. Which left us a pitiful little amount of subjects to mess around with. You could tell, too, when we looked at each other, that I would never again look the same in his eyes. And he had, even before now, changed in mine.

It had been in August. Mildewy and hot-as-Hades August. When my mother and I had had that knock-down-of-a-doozy fight. I'd been volunteering at the clinic, doing filing. And old Dr. Wilkins was letting me do blood pressures. And I would come in hot and tired and worn out. And planning to go out with Luke. I was on to my future like Spam after table scraps. I was going to be a physician. Marry Luke. Live in a terrific house somewhere terrific. Where it snowed. And have half a dozen kids who wouldn't have Christmases and Thanksgivings and weekends split down the middle like oranges ready to squeeze.

On that August day of the Great Fight, my mother was following me into my bathroom. Into my own shower, for Christ's sake. "Eleven-thirty," she was saying, "I don't see why in the world you can't agree to come home here and have Luke here. Park the car at eleven-thirty and be where at least I'll know where you are."

I had twenty minutes before Luke would be there. "I don't know anyone my age who has a curfew, Mom. In six months I'll be old enough to vote. Nobody that age has to go home and be with their mother by midnight. I'm not going to turn into a pumpkin."

"But you could at least get off the roads. There are drunks on the roads after midnight. Be where I know where you are. I only want you safe."

"I *am* safe. I'm safe with Luke. I'm safe with myself. Stop turning me into a tragedy-about-to-happen."

"I'm not turning you into a tragedy. And it didn't turn me into a creep, either. Or whatever it is you say these days—dweeb, loser."

"Tool."

"Tool? So okay, whatever, and I came home every night when my father asked. And it didn't turn me into a tool, or ruin my life. It didn't make me one less bit popular at school or anywhere. I only did what I was asked."

"And *I'm* asking that you leave me alone. Give me some breathing room. I'm not living the life you lived thirty years ago."

"Twenty."

"All right, twenty," And then I reminded her straight out. "It's different now. I'm different from you. I never want to be like you."

She turned away and sat on the bed. But she didn't leave. I could hear her in there in my room while I finished my shower. The twins were coming in, too, bouncing on my bed. Turning on my radio. "The twins and I wanted you to go with us to see *Pocahontas*. Jack's going to meet us. He's coming straight from work."

"I don't want to see *Pocahontas*. Luke and I are going out to get pizza."

"You've been out with him every night this week."

"So?"

"And then?"

"Then? What does it matter what then—we're not going far. We're going to be hanging around. We'll probably go over to Mike's."

She followed me out to the barn. She and the twins stayed after me all the way out there to feed the horses. Feed the dogs. The peacocks, Spam, and the cats were her job. "I don't like what's happening to us," she said behind me while I had my hands in oats. Maggie and Kirk were chattering and moving all around us while she said, "You only come home to eat and sleep, and I don't know what's going on with you. This is the last year you're going to be home, Bergin. You'll be going off to college. I want the twins to have a lot of memories of us together. I want . . ."

"Well, *I* don't want to spend tonight with you and them and Jack."

"Bergin!"

I was climbing up the ladder to the loft, more to get away from her than to go after hay. It was August, the pastures were still lush. But it was at least some place I thought she couldn't go. And then Maggie started yelling up after me, "Mama doesn't like your tony voice." That's what my mother always said to Maggie when Maggie gave her grief, *I don't like your tone of voice.* And now my mother was climbing up the ladder after me. One hand after the other. One foot after the other. And fast, coming fast. She reached across the hay bale I moved in front of her.

Before either of us could see it or stop it, she raised her right hand and slapped me in front of my ear. Right there across part of my mouth. The sound and feel of it was so foreign. It was like hot liquid had been poured over both of us. Freezing us. Turning us into statues that, for a second, were speechless. I put my hand across my cheek where hers had left. Then she put hers, her right hand. The perpetrator, as she might be inclined to call it. Across her own mouth, and said, "Oh, I'm so sorry." There was a moment of hard silence. A silence which, after a moment more, gave way to a laugh. Both of us. Both of us letting go. Short, soft, astonished laughs kin to a giggle. It was a reliever of shock and tension. And embarrassment, I think. And then I said, "I didn't think you could get up here that fast."

She sat down on the hay bale then. "I only want you to be part of us, Bergin. Part of this family Jack and I have made."

"Well, it's not the family I want." And for once in my life it seemed that I was speaking what I really thought. Warmed up now, I went on, "I wanted the one I had when I was five."

She looked at me and with cold hard realism she said, "Well, I'm sorry but I just couldn't make that one work, Bergin. I just couldn't . . ."

"Well, that's the one I wanted. That's the one where Dad was always home, where it was always fun, and . . ."

"No, he wasn't. It wasn't that way at all."

I stood up. "Why is it always the way you say? Always the way you say!"

She stood up, too, and started down the ladder. "Well, maybe it's time for you to figure this out on your own. I don't seem to be able to help with any of the answers."

"Yes, maybe it is. Maybe it's time I left here. Maybe it's time I went to live with *him*."

She looked back up at me, halfway down now. And with her mouth drawn in that way she has to show when she has really had enough. When her temper is cold-hard-steel and mean-to-the-bone. She said, real calm, "Let me know when I can help you pack your bags."

That night I called him. Right after she had driven off with the twins, mad as a wet hen and with her mouth still a tight line. I dialed his number. Miss Vicky answered. "Vicky, is my father there?"

"Just a minute. I'll go take the phone to him. " Then she chatted on the portable all the way, carrying it to him where he was parked in front of the TV.

"Hey," I started. "What ya doing?"

"Watching *Wall Street Week*. "

Then simple, straight, and with all the fat sliced off, I said, "Can I come live with you?"

NOW I LOOKED at him at the head of the glass table, his fruitcake gone and his decaff about all swallowed. His answer that day had sounded surprised but pleased. Calm and matter of fact. "Sure. Why not? That'll be fine. When?"

"Tonight. I'm going to pack up and head over there tonight. Luke will bring me. And then tomorrow I'll come back for my car and the rest of my things."

"You and your mother have a fight?"

"Yeah, a fight."

"Did you ask her about this?"

"Yeah, she agrees. She thinks it's time for me to come live with you, too."

"I'll tell Vicky, " he said before we hung up.

Miss Vicky. She was clearing the table now. I got up to help. Picked up my plate and my dad's as he pushed back from the table and got ready to get up, too. "Oh, no," Miss Vicky said, taking the plates from my hand. "I don't want you doing one iota of a thing. You two just go sit down in there and enjoy each other. I'll get these."

Enjoy each other.

He got into his leather chair and picked up the remote. I got on the couch and he popped on CNN. And we got the Christmas Day news. The fat-sucker cat, old Liposuction, jumped into my lap. And I stroked him, stroked him, stroked him. Gray fur so soft I could not think of words so soft. And I studied the way his black fur ran right up to, and yet did not cross over into, the gray one-by-one-drawing-a-straight-line of hairs. Then I started counting the windows. For Dr. Cone had given me what she called homework. While you are there, she said, I want you to count all of the doors and windows in every room you spend time in. I want you to look around and count the pencils or pens that are lying around, if any. I want you to take down notes about where paper and things to write with are kept. I want you

139

to put it all down in this ledger. She had handed me then a little black book with *Accounts* written across the front in gold. She wouldn't tell me why. And she wouldn't say any more. And I was beginning to seriously wonder which one of us was the one needing to be labeled nuts.

Miss Vicky was talking over the bar that separated the family room from the kitchen. She was clanking dishes and clunking pots. Good old Vicky was the one whose tongue had been greased in some prebirth machine shop. She was telling us to get the *TV Guide*, to look up what specials were on. She was asking if we wanted hot apple cider or popcorn. Or what was the weather supposed to be tomorrow? Check the Weather Channel. Check the sports. See if the Dolphins had won. Check on the Disney Channel for a parade. Or a movie. Or, if my dad and I really wanted to get wild—and she giggled—turn on MTV. Let him see what videos are like. Let him see first hand what Dylan and I were really crazy about.

Crazy. The word. The sound of it hung like a bad smell. There we all were—paying attention to it. And yet at the same time, turning our faces away from it.

But thank God for Miss Vicky. Because otherwise I would have drowned in my father's silence. It was all I could do to just sit there and sit on the memories of the past five months. And not let them sweep me off like one of those typhoons that come up onto India. Or somewhere so far away I can never picture anything about it but the horror. And be drowned. And all the while. All the while. All the while. The TV people were talking up a storm, blowing out whatever came into their minds. Or speaking whatever they were reading on a script. And doing it so fine. All fine. So easy.

What I hadn't told Dr. Cone about me and Luke breaking up was the way I had made myself be okay about it. How I had been able to go back to school and be pretty all right, really. Stand the rumors and ugly words that I heard whispered. Or said straight out, sometimes, to my face. That I was gay and queer. And a bitch on top of all of that. I could be okay with resigning my cheerleader thing and move on over to the soccer team. Even though I knew doing that made me really look like what was being said I was. But I was feeling okay. In most ways, I was knowing I was going to come out all right. I could wait it out and move on. That was my plan, at least. Even though I knew that part of what I had hoped for about me and Luke. That people could love each other. And do fine with each other. And it would last. Was now like a round dead piece of flesh I had to try to keep from touching. *Don't touch. Don't look at. Don't get close to that. That* was what I could not bear to lose.

So my dad and Vicky didn't even know we had split. Except when she, at first. Then him, asked why they hadn't seen Luke around? And I had been lying on my bed in there in the room Miss Vicky had fixed up for me. Victorian stuff just about everywhere. And pink ruffly curtains long enough to kiss the pale blue rug. And the dressing table with a mirror big enough to reflect only me, and what is called a skirt around it in blue and pink flowers that Miss Vicky had sewn herself. She had just had a ball decorating that room, she had said. And she was just happy. So happy. Happy as a June bug, in her words. Happy as a fly in shit, in my unspoken ones. To have me living with them. Oh, yeah. And I was lying in there with Stella on the rug beside me. Which didn't please anybody because she had fleas and tracked in dirt and chased Liposuction and tore around on the tile floors. Slipping and crashing into things and breaking glass. Always the fear of breaking glass. And my father had come into my room, outlined by the door. His hand on one side of the doorframe. And looked at me. "Haven't seen Luke lately. What's been happening with him?"

"Oh, we parted ways. He went his. I went mine."

"Oh?"

"Yeah."

"Well, those things happen. But I sort of miss him, though. He was a nice kid."

"Yeah. Well. We're still friends."

I could lie so good. I impressed even myself. Luke and I were enemies, if anything. But I could stand it, stand it, stand it. Because the whole while the loss of Luke was slicing me, I was looking at my father there. Or thinking of him, there. This time leaning into the doorframe asking me things about my life. About me. Wanting me there. Living there. It was what all along. All my life. Since that day I was six and got on the plane with my mother. And rolled the line out from my mind to him. To him. I had wanted. He had wanted, too, always. Always had, I was sure. The two of us together just every day. Living in the same house. Just like it was supposed to be, and to happen. Hell! I was rubbing my mind across the Daddy Juju every minute of every day like it was the sun. Or God. Or the secret of Mother Earth. It was the Daddy Juju saving me.

That's what I didn't tell Dr. Cone. That's what I couldn't tell anyone. I couldn't speak the idea out loud, because it was too hard. And silly. And stupid-sounding to explain. I think I knew, too. Feared all along, too. I might do something to make it disappear.

Disappear. *Oh God don't let it disappear.*

Now on Christmas night, he clicked the TV off with his remote. Might as well. Miss Vicky's mouth wouldn't let any other sound get through. "Wanna play some chess?" he asked.

"Sure."

By then I knew there were eight floor-to-ceiling windows in the room and three doors.

"You want the black pieces or the white?" He was emptying out the chess set now.

"Black," I said, while wondering if you would be treated any differently if everyone in the room knew you were dying of cancer.

Because learning I was going to live sure seemed to have the exact same effect.

We set up the chess men and went at it. We both thought so long between moves, it was like we were living in slow motion. And when neither of us could checkmate the other. And dark was coming through all the floor-to-ceiling windows. We called it even. And I went to pack up. The peach sweater in a big bag with the blue one. CD's and stocking-stuffers. And a whole lot of other stuff. Then, damn, if nature didn't call. All that apple cider and tea and the little sip of champagne at dinner that Miss Vicky insisted I have. But not too much because it might mix all wrong with the medicine I was on, which made my dad ask, "Are you sure it's okay?" And Miss Vicky's answer, "A little sip can't hurt, just a little sip." And me, taking a little sip and saying nothing, nothing. Feeling crazy to the bone. And feeling how they, too, were thinking I was crazy to the bone. And taking medicine made for people who are crazy to the bone. So I had to go down the back hall to the bathroom. And pass by the room where I had died. Then the room where Dylan lived, but wasn't in at the time. His posters of motorcycles and football players on the walls. CD's stacked to the ceiling. A computer eye blinking in the dark, licking up his e-mail. He would be home in a little while.

"We just loved having you, Bergin, honey," Miss Vicky said after I came back from the bathroom and was on my way out to my dad's car.

He drove me back to the nut ward with the radio on. Christmas tunes. "You're too good a chess player for me," he said, smiling, teasing in his way.

"Yeah, you taught me too good," I said.

He parked the car and walked me into the lobby. We got in the elevator and he escorted me up to the fifth floor. When the elevator doors opened, we stepped out. He rang the bell at the locked doors and then reached over and hugged me. Hugged me in his way, hands on my shoulders, just lying there a second. A second. Then the locked doors swung open. And I walked in.

"SO WHAT did you find out?" Dr. Cone was sitting on the edge of her desk the next day. I was sitting in front of her with a wrapped present in my lap, along with the account book. I opened the book to page one and read out loud, "The Family Room, Jack and My Mother's House—four doors, six windows, those little golf-score-like pencils on the game table. But no paper."

"Okay, so what about your father's house?"

"That's easy," I said. "The whole place is practically glass."

"And how much of it can open?"

I turned the page. "The Living Room—two doors, five windows, paper and pens on the antique desk. The Family Room—three doors, eight floor-to-ceiling windows, and two of them slide open."

"That adds up to a lot of ways to get out." She stood up and shut the blinds where the sun was coming in across my eyes. "You are never really trapped there, in either place, are you? And with a little scrambling around, you can always write down what you want to say. If not to them, to yourself, right?"

I closed the account book. "Guess so."

"See, you have a lot of things in each place to help you out. So overall, how was your Christmas?"

"Fair to middlin'."

She laughed.

I explained, "That's what the patients say in the clinic where I used to volunteer with Dr. Wilkins. I'd ask them how they are and that's what they'd say, *Fair to middlin'.*"

"Well, that's not so bad."

"No."

I handed her the wrapped present. "I got you this."

She opened it. And as soon as the edge of the wrapping paper gave way, she started to laugh. There it was—that sound that was all hers, so explosive it was contagious. And she held up my gift. Then opened it and offered me one. Then reached in to eat one herself. It was a can of mixed nuts.

She asked me to tell her all about my visits over the past day. And after I gave her the menu, with all the family conversation mixed in, we moved on to the beginning of my senior year. We talked about Luke a little. And how he handled the hurt of my breaking up with him by saying those things about me. Then she said, "There were other disappointments during that time, weren't there?"

"Yes."

"So tell me. Tell me about one."

So I told her about how I'd applied to be one of the three students who would go to the state capital and spend the day with the governor. Like student legislators, in a sense. It was a special program just my school had set up. And it was to be a great honor for the whole community and school. And sometimes these kids got chosen to go to Washington and be a page in the Senate or House. And it made sense for me to be part of this. Because I'd done so much school-wise anyway. As president of this and president of that. And everybody thought I'd be a shoo-in. A done-deal. A natural. That choosing me would be a no-brainer. Because along with what all I'd done, we had to write an essay about why we wanted to go. And that's how the teachers who were on the committee to choose the three to go, were going to choose. By this essay. And I'd worked hard on mine, really hard. I'd written about what I'd learned volunteering at the rural clinic. And how I was interested in learning all about government programs for health care. And the choices about it and the changes.

I'd stayed up nights writing it and researching it. And it was good, really, really good. My mother proofread it. And Jack talked over some points of it with me. Because he knows all the latest stuff on how hospitals are run. And my dad even read it and said it was wonderful. Really, really wonderful. As good as any essay he could have written even when he was in college, he had said. And that was wonderful. And that was so nice. And I was feeling really good about it. Everyone was expecting me to win. Then Mr. Whitstruck, my biology teacher, sent me into the teacher's lounge to get him a bag with aspirin in it that he kept there. Because he had a headache. And a sore throat. And was in the middle of a class that I knew everything about anyway. So I stepped into the part of the teacher's lounge where the sort-of-like lockers are kept. I was reaching into Mr. Whitstruck's for the paper sack with his aspirin in it, when on the other side of the locker, where I could not see them, were some teachers. And they were talking. They were talking about the essay thing. They were on the committee to choose. And they were talking about . . . well, it took me a minute to realize it. But they were talking about me. *Me.* And it was not anything I ever thought a teacher. Or someone should ever say. And . . .

"Say it," Dr. Cone said. "I want to hear you say exactly the words they used."

I cleared my throat and looked straight at her. I put on a voice like Jack would. Like I was some big farty-assed teacher I was imitating. And I said, "That girl has too much already. She's got money, looks, an important family, a car. She thinks she can just do anything. And I think it's time we took her down a peg."

Dr. Cone looked at me and handed me a Brazil nut. "It's hard to realize," she said, "but sometimes the people we think are the grownups aren't always the grownups. They fool us into believing they are. And then we find out something like this, something that shows in how many ways they are still children. In a sense even younger than you. Emotionally younger, anyway. Still a child in that sense."

"But maybe some of what she said was true? That's what I kept thinking and wondering. And yet it was so mean, so mean. That wasn't the worst, though."

"What was?" She sat on the edge of her desk holding the can of nuts. "And oh, by the way, I don't think what she said had any truth in it. Sounds to me she was a bit jealous and was just acting like a ten-year-old. And jealous of you, if you can believe it. But anyway, tell me. Tell me what was the worst?"

She leaned a little toward me then. She was still sitting on the desk, half on, half off. One leg on the floor, the other swung over the desk with the can of nuts resting on her lap. Her white clinical coat was spread open over a brown tweed skirt. "Well," I said, going on. Ready to tell her just about anything right then, I guess. "When I was walking out, she was coming out the other way. She didn't know I had heard her. She hadn't even known I'd been in there. I hadn't embarrassed her by catching her. But she stopped me in the hall and told me I had written one of the most beautiful essays she'd ever read. *Exquisite*, she called it. That's the word she used. She two-faced me. And said all that. And she was grinning all the while." I looked down at my lap. "You know," I said, "sometimes you get to see what you shouldn't."

"Yes."

"And sometimes you wish you hadn't," I added, too.

"Because you can't stop yourself from seeing and hearing it over and over again. Is that the way it was?"

"Yes. And you know, sometimes the meanness of people just sinks deep inside of you, and makes you sick."

She sat down behind her desk and put her arms up on it and crossed them. When I looked up, I saw her sitting like that. The can of nuts was still in her hand. But she was looking out the window. And then she looked back at me. Looked at me. Really, *really* looked at me. We stayed that way for a good long minute. And then, "Yes, it does," she said. "Yes, it does."

TEN

Leslie

I didn't sleep all of Christmas night. The day kept playing over and over in my mind, and even when I went to work the next day, I kept seeing it, the way we had all been, and how small and lost Bergin had looked as she stood on the steps of Doug's house, ringing the bell. For a while I could do nothing else but sit there in the drive, looking out of the front windshield of my car and seeing the light from the rooms of Doug's house coming from inside and wondering what was happening there. In fact, what *had* happened there?

All of this, and us, were connected somehow. I was wondering myself, what was I afraid to look at? What was I not remembering? What could I not know, not realize, feel, about my own daughter?

But that's the thing about having a child that, in the end, crushes mothers: giving them life and then once again having to give it to them to live as they choose. And in their choosing, they rip it from you, go off in their secrets and hold you at arm's length with their looks and words and ways. Talk about labor! At this point, I probably knew more about the personal lives of the people in my office than I did about Bergin's.

By 10:00, I was sitting at my desk reading the files of a case that I was taking on, a robbery of a Handy-Mart. I was being forced to focus on that. As I did, I thought about the confidentiality rule that I practiced with my own clients, then the one between Bergin and Dr. Cone, and realized that that one was starting to rankle me now. If I put aside all of our mother-daughter-in-adolescence angst, I should be able to know what Dr. Cone was learning before Bergin even told it. And furthermore, she probably ought to tell me first.

William Tiner, one of the law interns, stuck his head in the door, "Wanna go to lunch and discuss this?" He was holding up another file for a case he'd been researching for me.

"Sure," I said, picking up my purse. It was hard to sit still anyway.

We walked down the street and then crossed over to an Italian place that specialized in about a hundred different spaghetties. We both ordered wine, which I rarely, if ever, did at lunch. But I was starting to feel that maybe a little alcohol could slow me down. Lord knows, I might have swapped one of the twins for a nap, *if* I could have been offered a deep-sleep guarantee. And *if* anyone would have swapped for the twins, especially Maggie. Often I thought the two of them were like the little boy in Mark Twain's "The Ransom of Red Chief"—that if anyone kidnapped Kirk and Maggie, *I'd* be offered money to take them back. Anyway, that's how I liked to joke about their all-out, all-over-everywhere personalities. I remembered how more than once, and with inside-out affection, Bergin had declared Maggie a certified Motor Mouth. "She's going to beat Miss Vicky in the Talk Olympics," she once said. "Proof that she's got my genes," I added.

Today Jack and I were swapping off. Always in the past, over the Christmas holidays, we'd have Bergin stay with the twins. But now . . . well, even Lydia, our housekeeper, was off. So Jack would keep the twins while I went in to work for a while, and I would keep them tomorrow. Later today he was going to stop at his office at the hospital to check on things, taking along the twins. Then all four of us were going to meet there and have dinner with Bergin during her visiting hours. She had phone privileges now. She could go off the ward if she wanted to, down to the cafeteria, the gift shop, to the gardens outside. Dr. Cone said it was all up to her now.

William Tiner and I took a corner table. He was probably all of twenty-five, tall, bespectacled, a sharp dresser. He was so eager to please, he reminded me of me.

"I don't think this is going to see the light of day," he said.

"Why?"

"I think the State Attorney's evidence will unravel before it even gets on the trial docket."

"What about a plea bargain?"

"Yeah, it could go that way, too. Which means that, what—we spend fifty hours on this instead of two hundred?"

I looked across my bowl of minestrone, through the round clear glass of his glasses and into the round clear eagerness and intelligence of his eyes. *He* had gotten through those young-adult years, had made it, and now was doing what he was doing quite well. He'd even taken on the appropriate whine of an overburdened professional—dumping the stress to his colleagues where it was safe—while pretending to hate what he loved. At one time, Bergin was heading into becoming like this.

At some time in the near future, this young, intelligent, and compassionate man would marry someone like Bergin. He would have a good and fine life—somewhat predictable, and surely full of a lot of whine and the normal amount of hurt and hard times—but he would be okay. Thinking this made me suddenly feel sick. I pushed my soup away and drank only water. It scared me to realize that I was on the edge of giving up on Bergin. On the edge of grieving for what I feared she could never be.

"How's your daughter?" William looked at me. His eyes were steady, really concerned, and he was asking what anyone who worked with me would.

"Coming along," I lied.

"Any more results on the tests?"

"No. Not yet." In my whole life, I'd never been so tight-lipped and such a master of the white lie. I'd had to take days off from work. And to take days off from work you have to tell why; at least close to why, because it is expected—not required, but expected—at least if you're normal. *My daughter's in the hospital. We're not sure. The possibility of hepatitis, more than mono, that's for sure. We thought it was just a relapse of mono—but no—it could be more serious, more complicated, we're just not sure.* Oh, how shame drove me! It echoed from my childhood from all the times I white-lied about my mother—the migraine, the out-of-town trip, the school notice that got blown off by the wind. I surely knew how to dance around embarrassment. The patterns for shame were set, and I hated that. But I pulled them out, ironed them out, and put them on.

"That's rough, I know." William picked up the check. We stood up, and the chairs scraped on the tile floor the way my teeth felt as I clinched them. More than hating my own lying, I hated condolences. "Don't worry about this case," William added. "I'll do all the leg work. In fact, what else can I do to help?"

On the walk back to our offices, we talked about the case all the way. One of the streets we crossed was brick, and I tripped, and William grabbed my elbow. "I'm fine. I'm fine," I said, shaking him off. His hand on me made me feel infirm. It was as if tragedy were taking me in its teeth and shaking me until I was old and bedraggled. I felt a hundred already. Outwardly my body was going on without me. Inside, I was racing. By now I could have reached the moon.

I remembered the moon and the book and the way I would read it to Bergin when she was not even a year old. *Good night, stars. Good night, moon.* Oh! the sweet accompaniment of those words to help the letting go into the darkness, accepting sleep. In her crib the light fuzziness of her hair was like duck down on the pillow, her forehead so wide and broad it echoed the babyhood of all things: forest deer, colts, calves, puppies. Is it possible to *not* trade off your own life for that one, that one there—if it were ever in the need of doing so? I would have done anything—still would—to protect her. It was impossible to not love her with total abandon, too. The rhythmical instinctive suck of her mouth on my breast. The mouth like a pump—on and on toward nourishment. Whatever it took, whatever it needed, it would have and fight for. Such evidence of a life force was rarely on display. And so often we forgot it: the thrust for survival, the kicking and screaming insistence to be here alive and awake.

She never wanted to sleep. Slipping into the bed in the middle of the night, she would get between me and Doug. Those were the long two-year-old nights when dreams split her sleep—old cave-dweller dreams, I felt sure, because I saw so clearly her fear of strangers, her fear of the dark, the fear of what her instincts and imagination told her to fear, even dangers way beyond her experience—rape fears, bodily harm fears, abandonment fears.

WILLIAM LEFT me at the door, and I walked into my office and sat down. I called Jack.

"What ya doing?" I needed the sound of his voice, and the sound of the twins', as desperately as I needed sleep.

"We're making cookies."

"Oh? What kind?"

"Stained Glass Window—you know—where you put a Life Saver in the middle and it melts."

Maggie must have pulled the receiver out of his hand. "And mine are going to be red," she said. "I'm going to make all the red ones."

"That's wonderful," I assured her. "What about Kirk? Let me speak to him."

"Here, Kirkie," I heard Maggie sing, then whisper, "Don't talk long or your cookies are gonna burn."

"How's it going?" I asked Kirk. He hadn't yet said anything, but I knew he was on the phone, because I could hear him breathing.

Then, "OK," he said.

"So what color are your cookies going to be?"

"Green."

"Oh, that's going to be nice."

"Yeah."

And then here came Maggie again, "We got to go, Mom. The buzzer's going off."

"Let me talk once more to Jack then."

I could hear the oven timer in the background like the buzz of a trapped fly. "I'll see you later, okay?" he said.

"Yeah. I'll meet you in the waiting room outside the ward."

"Fine." And then the oven timer stopped, and Jack hung up; and as soon as he did, I wanted to call him right back.

I couldn't think about cases or trials. I couldn't stand the silence in my office, and yet I couldn't bear to join any conversation going on around me. The only conversation I could pay any attention to was the one going on inside my head. I reached down on the floor beside my desk and picked up the books I had gotten Jack to check out of the medical library for me. I closed the door to my office and began reading, once again, looking over what I'd already read over the last three weeks, trying to understand, searching for something that made sense. Teen suicide took up a sizable section. But it mostly had to do with treatment and medications and types of therapies that were found to have success. I looked at that word for a very long while. *Success.* Success in treatment. The unsuccessful attempt. Thank god, Bergin's attempt had failed. For once, she'd been unsuccessful. I almost had to laugh at that, thinking how well she did almost everything, but thank God, not this, not this. *Most often the child feels trapped as the result of being placed in a double bind. The only solution he or she can see is to be totally removed from the situation, and thereby chooses death.*

I spun my chair around. It is one of those chairs that sits on a pedestal and casters so that it can change angles in the room or toward the desk. It sits on a big plastic oval that protects the carpet from the rollers and also makes the chair move with the ease of sliding. I opened my eyes onto the solid vanilla wall where the pictures of my family are stuck in haphazard fashion on a bulletin board. The window was closed. Coming from an old box in the corner was the smell of pizza. We'd had it here, William Tiner and I, one night before Christmas, and apparently the custodian hadn't yet emptied the trash baskets. *What kind of pizza does a dog like?* I could hear Maggie's voice asking over the last few weeks. For a million times, it seemed, she'd set me up for her favorite—and latest—joke. I had heard it from the back seat of the van, in the kitchen, in the bathroom, from across a table in a restaurant. And sooner or later Kirk would answer, just as if he and Maggie were a stand-up comedy team, a four-year-old George and Gracie Allen. *Pupparoni!* Kirk would shriek after he gave you two seconds to try to come up with it on your own.

The next to last Saturday in November, we had been with Bergin and had gone to the Pizza Palace. Jack had a late meeting at the hospital, so it was just me and Maggie and Kirk who drove to Doug's house and picked up Bergin there to take her out for dinner with us.

Since she'd moved in with Doug, that's the way we did things. I would see her on weekends the way Doug used to, or, if she wanted to, she would come out to the farm and stay the night with us. Usually, though, she had some place else to go. There were so many things she was involved in at school. Packing up and spending the night with us didn't happen often. So I went every weekend, either Friday or Saturday, to be with her. It was our time, just our time.

The next to last Saturday in November, a week before the *attempt*, the thank-god-unsuccessful attempt, she and I and the twins were sitting in a booth at the Pizza Palace ordering a large pepperoni pizza and a Caesar salad and Cokes, and Maggie was talking nonstop. Kirk was making hills on the table out of salt and pepper. Then the waitress brought the Cokes, and Kirk and Maggie began shooting each other with the paper over their straws, because Jack had recently shown them how to tear the paper and put it back on the straw and then blow it off. Bergin was getting several in her face, and I was getting my share of them in mine, and though I was on the verge of putting a stop to all of this, it was their exuberance I didn't quite have the heart to squelch right off. Then, "Two more blows apiece, and that's it," I said.

"I want to move back," Bergin said.

Kirk hit her with the straw paper right on her forehead. She grabbed him and playfully rubbed her knuckles in his hair. I wadded up the straw paper, then reached for Maggie's. I don't think I had totally heard what Bergin said the first time she said it. Then when I looked at her, she said again, "I want to move back."

"You want to come home?" I guess it was not just repeating her, but more of a paraphrase in the way I preferred to hear it, that I said back.

"Yes."

"Anything wrong?"

"No. It's just not working out. And I'll be closer to school and all."

"Okay. That's fine. In fact, I'm glad." I put my hand on top of hers. *Make as little of this as you can,* something in my mother-to-a-teenager's brain said. For let a teenager know what makes you happy, and they are as likely to spin their wheels and blast off opposite as to go through with it. I was just glad, glad, happy as a clam at high tide, or Spam under his azalea—as someone happy as I was might be likely to say. My daughter had chosen to come home and, for the moment, that was the only thought I was letting swell inside of me. Our pizza came, and the waitress cut it in its pan there in front of us. Maggie got up on her knees and sat in the booth that way.

"When?" I said.

"Now. Next weekend, I guess."

I smiled. "I'm glad you're coming home, Bergin. I've missed you. We all have."

"Yeah," Maggie added. "And Stella's been sleeping in your bed."

"Will you tell him?" Bergin looked at me. She had her elbows on the table, and her pizza was on a plate in front of her. She wasn't yet eating, and I should have picked up on the fact that this change was carrying more weight with her than it was with me. Because by now Maggie, Kirk, and I were digging into the pizza, winding the hot cheese around on our forks. I knew instantly who *tell him* meant. Doug. She wanted me to explain all this to Doug, to let him know that she wanted to come back home with us. But I couldn't talk to Doug. If I told him that Bergin wanted to come back to live with me, he wouldn't have believed it. He'd have assumed I was being manipulative, or that I was reading into it things that weren't there. I would more than likely be accused of talking her into it. He would have insisted that Bergin tell him, anyhow. Hear it from her own lips, that's what I knew he would insist on.

And now I realized something else, too. For that next weekend, she had not come home. *I just couldn't get it all together,* she had told me on the phone. *It'll be next weekend. I'll get all packed up this week. It'll be next weekend for sure.*

In my office, going over all of this, I suddenly saw, saw so clearly, saw so painfully, horrifyingly, in fact, exactly what I had done. I could hear how what I had said next was wrong, so very, very wrong, for she had asked me, me, asked me. *Will you tell him?* I could again hear how softly, how earnestly, how so without any seventeen-year-old tone, or attitude, I guess you'd call it, in her voice. She had simply asked me, *Will you tell him?*

Would I tell him? *Could* I tell him? I had no choice but to answer Bergin as I had. Not with Doug's and my history. Not with the way things were with us. Now I whirled my chair around and picked up the phone. "Jack," I said, when he answered. "I want to see Bergin tonight by myself. Okay? All right? You understand? Yes, I'll be home by nine, or I'll call. Kiss the twins for me. I have to hurry."

I waved to William Tiner as I sprinted out. I got into my car in the parking garage. I drove like I was on fire, which I was. My urgency was like someone who is sick, terribly, like the alarm of someone desperate. I pulled into the visitors' lot at the hospital and walked into the lobby and tapped my feet waiting for the elevator.

On the fifth floor, I walked to the locked doors. My heels sounded like hammers on the tile floor. I had to stand there and call in by an intercom. When the head nurse answered, I told her who I was and that I had come to see my daughter. "It's not visiting hours," she said.

"I know, but my daughter can leave the ward now. Tell her I want to take her down to the cafeteria for a Coke, or a cup of coffee, whatever."

"Just a minute, please."

I stood tapping my heels in the hall and looking from one wall to the other and through the wired window in the locked doors. Finally the doors opened. The nurse stood there with the keys. Bergin was behind her.

"Hey, Sweets," I said.

"Hey."

She had on jeans and a blue sweatshirt. Her hair had been recently washed and was still damp, you could tell. But she looked beautiful, so naturally beautiful it squeezed my heart. *And she had done what she had done to save me.* To save me and Doug, but mostly me, because I couldn't tell him, either. She didn't want to hurt me with the truth of this, take my life away as I had known it, with the truth of what I had done. Or had refused to do. I took her by the hand as if she were still seven or eight, so she would have no choice, no choice at all. I walked her into the elevator. It was empty. I said thank God to that, because I needed privacy and silence, and there seemed no better place than this—that black moving box with only the two of us inside of it. I punched the button to the top floor. As we moved up toward nowhere that we wanted to go, I stepped in front of her to stand close and, with my two hands on each of her shoulders, I practically yelled, "I know why you did this. I know now. I told you to tell him, didn't I? And you couldn't. And you asked me to, but I said I couldn't . . . And you . . ."

She leaned back against the side wall of the elevator. We were still speeding toward the roof. I kept pressing with my hands, holding her in place, waiting, waiting, and then the tears that began to come out of her eyes were wet with all of the sorrow and pain, and the answer of *yes* in them, that I could ever hope to see.

ELEVEN

Bergin

I was standing at the window of my room. My hospital room. Watching for my mother's van to pull up into the parking lot below. She was coming to pick me up. She was taking me home. Home to her and Jack's house. The farm. A fog like the beginnings of someone's backyard barbecue hung over the parking lot asphalt. Because the days had been warm. And the nights cool. And the pavement held the heat that then rose up in what I remembered from probably fifth-grade science—*ghostly layers of tiny globules of water, liquid in a gaseous medium.* The physical world has always made such easy sense to me. And damn it. But bless it at the same time. My mind—which my mother says is inherited from my grandfather—never seems to let go of anything.

It was only 7:45. Behind me, lying on one of the beds, was Dee Dee Hamilton. A week before she had been moved into my room as my roommate. She was overweight. And had a bad case of acne. And an alcohol problem. And was holding up a make-up kit that I'd put together for her.

"Thanks for this. I really mean it," she said.

Blush and foundation and a lipstick pencil were in the little tapestry bag with Scottie dogs on it that I'd bought at the gift shop. I'd picked out everything for her. I'd fixed her a French braid that went across the top of her head. It showed that her ears stuck out. But oh, well. And I'd made her up and shown her how to use everything in the bag. And now she was pretending to feel like a million bucks. Now she was half in love with me. And half hating me. Because I didn't have acne. And I had a waist. And I didn't have a runaway desire to drown myself in alcohol. In fact, "What're you in here for?" she'd asked on the first day they'd moved her in.

"I killed myself," I said, and she'd laughed.

"You mean you tried."

"No. I mean I did."

She'd laughed again. "Well, at least you lived to tell it."

And tell it is exactly what I'd had to do after my mother cornered me in the elevator and made me say out loud what she had guessed. So Dr. Cone had called a right-away, next-day, family session. A pared-down get-to-the-meat-of-this meeting with just me and my mother and my father and her.

"Yes," I said. "I couldn't say it. I couldn't tell him. And I knew my mother couldn't, either. I should have done it. But I couldn't."

"Why?"

Dr. Cone was looking at me. But it wasn't her voice asking me this time. It was my father's. He was looking at me, too, sitting right beside me, wearing another gray sweater and with his face scraped from shaving and his hair looking a little wet. And asking me, why, *why?*

So I told the part that I could say out loud. "I was afraid of hurting your feelings." You could tell when I said it that he didn't have any more of an idea than Spam of what I was really talking about. He was clueless about what it was like to disappear while still here. To check out before the real adios takes place. So that then, leaving is more like an afterthought, like just a matter of paperwork. And then I thought, *Damn!* Because this was making me out to be Saint Bergin and them to be the ones who would suffer for all time with the meat-headed truth. We were wedged between it and no way to undo it now. Old Rock-Hard Truth.

"This sometimes happens," Dr. Cone went on saying, looking from one of them to the other. Doing her head-doctor thing. "When divorced parents know they can't speak freely with each other. And the child feels caught between. But that only means the future doesn't have to be this way. It doesn't mean that you, solely, were responsible for Bergin's act. After all, she's the one who interpreted that the situation couldn't be solved." Now she was looking from him to her to me, her eyes like things with wings with *where to light?* on their minds.

That whole session ended with me answering questions that let me say what I could not say straight out. Like, yes, I wanted to move home with my mother. And yes, I might as well go now. "You can leave here tomorrow, then." Dr. Cone had said. "Twice-a-week visits with me here, in the office, and probably in a few weeks we'll stop the Zoloft. Then I can see all of you together weekly or biweekly. Whatever turns out to be necessary."

SO I'D PACKED up and was standing by the window looking out through the fog for the blue van. Dee Dee Hamilton on the bed behind me. Watching me. And saying she was feeling more lonely already. And I hadn't yet gone anywhere.

But that morning session with Dr. Cone, where I'd told it like I'd told it, wasn't how she let it lie. She called me in that afternoon. She called me in from my room, where I was giving Dee Dee that makeover. And while I had my fingers deep in that braid. So when I walked back into her office, I had hairdos and Revlon and *how in the hell to get poor ol' Dee Dee to look better* on my mind.

"What was it like—living with your dad?" I have to hand it to her. Dr. Cone can shoot straight, once she decides where to.

"Okay. Just not exactly what I expected."

"And what were you expecting?"

"Oh, I don't know. Just that maybe he'd let me drive his Jaguar any time I wanted. And he'd take me to Las Vegas. And we'd gamble away about a half million dollars just for the hell of it. And every day we'd have cotton candy for breakfast."

She laughed. "I know you well enough to know that everything you've named is not anything you care about. So, if none of those things happened, why was it so awful?"

How could I tell her? How could I put into *any* words the stupid-sounding bone-headed idea of the Daddy Juju? That it was as necessary to me as air? As much me as my name, my skin? How could I tell and still sound like *me?* How off and on, and just all the time, for over ten years and always, right there, right there at the center of everything that happened to me, was this god-o-mighty radiating power ball that I'd rubbed my life against. The sticky ball in the center. That for as long as I could remember made everything make sense. This bone-headed six-year-old-sounding thing? Rubbed like all get-out through the whole Luke thing and the farty-teacher-essay thing and fight-with-my-mother thing. And the *I'm not so crazy about Jack but I guess he's what I've got to live with* thing?

And then, my father didn't see me. He really didn't see me. I was in the house, his house, and he looked at me, let his eyes sit down on me. But he didn't see me, never did see me, never tried to really, really see me. Always before it was him and me on weekends or at school things where he had come to see me, me, just me. And I'd be getting awards or doing special things, and he would watch me. Be proud of me, see me, *be* with me. Putt-Putt on weekends, seeing *Annie* in the dark with only a bag of popcorn between us, learning chess with him, just him, one whole day or half day with just him.

And now in his house, there was Dylan and Miss Vicky. And he would go to Dylan's soccer games and throw around the old football with Dylan in the backyard under the trees, where moss dripped like Christmas tinsel out of season. And he was thinking of Dylan playing that, playing what he loved, getting big enough to do what he loved. And I'd go out there with them, too. But he wasn't interested. Didn't really give a rat's ass, you could tell. And he'd have Dylan drink milk-shakes with eggs in them, *making Dylan big*, is what it was all about, making him big enough to play what my father loved. And he would come to my soccer games and get up and leave in the middle when it was clear as a pimple on poor ol' Dee Dee Hamilton's fat-swollen face that we were going to lose. No, I couldn't tell this. None of this.

It was dumb. And would sound dumb. And would make me out like I was only two or three or four, like I was someone who just could not share. And then I couldn't see myself *there* anymore. I was in his house but disappearing. I was alive but leaving. He didn't take my phone messages. He'd use my hairbrush and not put it back. He'd leave the toilet seat up, for Christ's sake. And Miss Vicky would say only, *Doug dear*. But I saw *You Are Not Here* in a damn stupid left-up toilet seat. Everything he did and said told me that my life didn't count. Didn't count. *Didn't count*.

And yet inside of me my mind was saying *I want, I want, I want*. The holes in my ears started to hurt. The pierced holes. The tiny lit-tle holes. So I got so I couldn't stand to touch them, put an earring in. And yet I did, shoved them in and swallowed screams. Words to songs wouldn't shut off. First one, then the other, singing between my ears all day, all night. I would be at school and go through the day, split in two. There was the one world on the outside where I could touch

165

things and move around. And there was this other one where I sat back and watched myself move around and touch things. And more than not, when I went to him to ask for a minute, to do something, a calculus problem. He's good at that. Or something about my car, a knocking under the hood. Or a door handle that was feeling jammed. He would make that *humph* sound, a sound kin to a sigh, that said my interrupting whatever he was doing was just that, an interruption. An irritation. I was an irritation. Something added on to his life. A sales tax. The label on a new pillow that you tear off once you get it home.

And then I got so I couldn't look into anyone's eyes. I couldn't give anyone any more power over me because I knew if I was hurt one more time, I couldn't survive. I held onto the last of myself by never letting my eyes light on any one thing. Not any one thing long enough to let it take me away. And then I started in on that incense. Burning all that incense in my room. It blocked out the smell of Stella. It blocked out the smell of me. And Miss Vicky would walk by my closed door, and I could hear her outside as she would be putting her nose up and taking a whiff and say, "Oh, that's so nice. So nice."

Stella chased Dylan's cat. She made a mess in my father's house. No one liked her. No one liked my dog, and they were only tolerating me. I was a third wheel, the shithead that no one really wanted there. And so, *no*, I could not say to him what I wanted to do. Not after Luke. Not after knowing how mean the world can be. And end. How things can end. Never last. I could not make the words come out of me that I wanted to leave from there. I couldn't let the last little bit of all I was hanging on to disappear. Or let my whole life up until then become nothing that was true or that I should not remember. If I told him the words, said them out loud so that even I could hear them, the last little bit of the power ball, the Daddy Juju, would go. Die. Be dead forever. For good. It was just simply a matter of words, of this, of all of me coming down to living in four little words. Say *I want to leave* and nothing after that could go on. And I didn't want to be here, any-where, go on anywhere, without the god-o-mighty power ball, my Daddy Juju, my center. Easier to take it with me. Better to pull out than to stay here and be without it. That's the way I decided to go.

I looked up from where I was smoothing the cloth of my jeans over my thigh. For a while I kept rubbing back and forth across my knee. Dr. Cone was watching me, looking at me, saying nothing. But waiting. Waiting. The silence was like water that moved. And that I could see my own reflection in. But that I could not bear to go near or to touch. No, I would not tell her. No, I would not say any of this out loud. I would not let her hear how stupid and silly and mean and ridiculous I was. *Really* was. Or see how crazy I could think. And yet how, to me, it made perfect sense. And then the whole while I was telling myself this, my mouth was opening up and starting to.

"So you see," I ended about a century later. "It was stupid. All the time I was hung up on this stupid thing. And it was only something that I had made up when I was little. And I was still believing in it. Holding on to it."

"And where is it now?" She smiled.

"A little of it's left," I said.

"And?" She looked at me, steady and hard. The lines like paren-theses beside her mouth were curved like smooth arcs, sitting still and waiting.

"It's here with me," I finally said.

I laughed out loud then. We were like two little kids playing make-believe. Just knocking around in a made-up, just-ours, secret language.

She stood up, then walked across the room. She picked up a pitcher of water and started pouring it onto one of those awful-look-ing burned-leaved plants. Greenish brown and ugly, they were. Two steps from dead, if you want my cold-hearted opinion. "Sometimes what we see isn't always there," she said, still pouring. She was still looking at that ugly-as-hell plant. "In other words, what you thought your father was doing, and saying by doing, might not have been totally, really, what was there. He might not have meant a bit of it. Not a bit. But if you felt it, it made it true. And all of us, all the time, have to struggle with the fear of losing something. Something that is crucial to us. Something that with all of our hearts we believe in."

She put the watering pitcher down. Then she handed me a wrapped piece of candy from the bowl she kept on her desk.

"Or better yet," she said, opening the bottom drawer next to her feet. "Let's have these." It was a can of mixed nuts. "I've really gotten hooked on these. Those that you gave me at Christmas were a really good idea."

We both laughed, again, at that.

For what felt like a million years, we sat there. Just sat there, eating nuts. And I told her more and more about all the times I had pulled out the Daddy Juju and rubbed my life across it. And as I did, I could see in her eyes and hear in her voice, that somewhere along the way she, too, had lost something. Or had something that she loved change to where she could no longer reach it. And I might have been making it up. I might be still as crazy as everybody thought I was. But I swear, to me, it looked like, in the liquid way that beneath the ice-lenses of her glasses, her eyes filmed over. And in the way that, as I learned in biology, her lachrymal gland seemed right on the edge of just cutting loose while looking at me and listening to me. Really, really listening to me. She knew all about loss. And the fear of it.

I STOOD THERE at the window, Dee Dee still behind me, and watched my mother's van bounce up over a speed bump in front of the automatic gate. She punched the button on it and took hold of the ticket that the gate-thing spit out. The automatic arm lifted then, and let her in. She pulled into a space in the last row. It was only 8 A.M., and people were walking everywhere. Coming into the hospital. Coming to work. Or to get some god-awful body test done. She'd probably been battling traffic since seven. I watched her get out and walk on the black fog-wet pavement. Dark blue slacks and a white tight sweater. A long silver chain at her neck that was swinging like a pendulum as she headed fast toward the door. She looked so small. Like someone I could reach down and move around with my fingers. As she got closer, I could see she had blue flats on her feet. And from looking down onto the top of her, you could tell, too, her hair was puffed up on top like she'd back-combed it. This was a bad-hair day for her; that was clear. And she'd been rushing since sunrise. That was a given. I just hoped she'd stop and check her shoes for peacock mess before she stepped into the lobby.

"How often will you be coming back?" Dee Dee asked me again, as though I hadn't told her earlier.

"Twice a week for a while. Less later," I said, and turned away from the window. For my mother had disappeared into the building now.

"I don't guess you'd have time to stop in and do this again," she said, patting her French braid that went from ear to ear.

"Yeah, maybe. I guess we'll just have to see."

"Because you've got exams and all, right?"

"Yeah."

"I'm so far behind, I don't have a rat's chance of passing anything," she said, half angry-sounding, half pitiful. Poor ol' Dee Dee was in the tenth grade for the second time. It was hard for me to even imagine *her* private hell.

"Tell Dr. Cone," I said. "She could get you a tutor."

"It couldn't be you, by any chance, could it?"

"I doubt it. I'm pretty loaded down right now, Dee Dee. But I'll stop in to see you. I'll make time. Now here." I handed her a CD, one of my favorites. And she knew it, too. And then there was a knock on the door. And my mother stepped in.

"All set?" she asked.

Sure enough, her hair was backcombed up on top like two rats had spent a passionate night there. And there was a telltale green stain on the edge of one of her flats. I picked up my suitcase, the heavy little black one that had been my mother's for about a hundred million years. And that she had packed things in and brought to me the day after I ended up in the emergency room. "Yeah," I said.

She was acting false-cheerful. Because we didn't yet know how to handle me coming back from the dead and now being taken home in a blue Aerostar van.

"See ya, Dee Dee," I said, going out.

"Yeah, see ya," she called back.

My mother reached down to take the handle of the suitcase away from me. And then she stopped. For a second both of our hands touched each other's on the suitcase handle. Then she let go. Her carrying it for me. Me carrying it alone. God! There was so much to decide on. Everything seemed to say so many things. And all of them different.

I got in the front seat beside her in the van. She started the engine. "Have you had breakfast?" She glanced at me as she put the gear in R and backed out.

"Just juice," I said.

"Let's stop then," she offered. "Let's just pull over some place and have us a man-handler breakfast, whatta ya say?"

Whatta ya say? Now she was going into cowboy talk. God-o-mighty! I'd gotten us *all* crazy. "I'm really not hungry," I said.

"Something quick, then." She pulled into a drive-thru line-up at Hardee's. We were waiting behind lawn-care trucks. And electrician trucks. And plumbers' vans. Everyone was tanking up on the way to some job. She turned on the radio. "You choose," she said, pointing to the knob that would let me scan the stations.

I rolled it over to some hard-ass rock that she'd never let me listen to ordinarily. And that I didn't much like myself. But I figured I might as well test the benefits from just being checked out of a nut ward. She didn't say a thing, only asked me what I wanted to eat. Then she ordered me anyway a cheese-and-egg biscuit and a large orange juice.

We drove out through town and headed toward the farm. The fog was burning off now. We went under the canopy of about a dozen oaks reaching their limbs across the highway. They were probably older than all the years of everyone in my whole family added up together. Older than I would get, now that it looked like I was going to be staying alive and would finish out a normal life span. Whatever that was. And whatever that meant.

"We could go to a movie this afternoon, if you want, " she said. She took turns glancing at me and at the road. "Or out to the mall. The after-Christmas sales are still on. And I have the whole day off."

"I'll think about it," I said. I didn't want to just flat-out refuse, just yet. And then it hit me that her taking the day off meant she and Jack had been discussing what to do with me. *What to do with Bergin*, I could hear it now. They were going to take turns babysitting me just like I was one of the twins.

We turned onto the single-lane dirt road. Then pulled into the long drive of Blueberry Hill Farm. *Oh, for Christ's sake*, I thought, and wanted to say out loud but didn't. As I saw a banner strung across the front of the barn with my name on it. And then I saw Jack and the twins standing outside. Waiting for me. Waving at me. No doubt Fats

Domino would be hitting his high notes out through the barn windows, too. At least as soon as we got to where we could hear it.

The fog was only on top of the sinkhole in the front pasture now. Just a film of white. Just a remnant of what had probably thickly and totally covered it an hour before.

My mother pulled the van up to the hitching post that was its usual parking space. We opened the van doors without even thinking. We slid them back so quickly we wouldn't have time to let anything else enter our minds. Or at least I did. Because if I sat there and looked out at them. At the twins and at Jack and at Stella running to meet me. And at the peacocks pecking around. And at Spam stuck up there snoring under his azalea. I might have gotten a little shaky. For I hadn't expected to ever see any of this again. Hadn't planned to ever even *be* here again. And now, damn! Here everybody was giving me to what amounted to a birthday party. And I was only certifiably alive.

Part II

TWELVE

Bergin

A nd so I had stood there in the drive and looked at the party set up for me, to be given for me. It was a combination birthday party and coming-home-alive party, I guess you could say. I ate cake and played horseshoes with Kirk and Maggie and Jack while my mother put hamburgers on the grill. For a while I rolled Stella over and over in the dead winter grass until she had short little hay-colored streaks of stuff stuck all over her. Somewhere in the afternoon, too, I finally sang the piano-thumping chorus about finding a thrill on Blueberry Hill along with Jack and Fats Domino, while feeding most of my hamburger to Spam. But I wasn't there. Never, never, really there. Not there.

And now I have been home for two weeks. Night before last it turned cold. Down below freezing. Streaks of moisture like the ruined colors of a painting ran down all of the house windows. I went to sleep listening to the faucet in the bathroom next to my room drip into the sink. And into the tub. Outside, the faucet under my window ran a thin stream into the clay-hard ground. For no pipes anywhere on Blueberry Hill are freeze-proof. They are wrapped in black foam. But still, we keep them dripping all the time, every bit of the day until it warms up, and through the night. Tonight we will drip them again. Out in the pasture where the water trough has run over, ice puddles lie in the mud like giant coins.

Yesterday I took the Biology AP exam. Sat in Mr. Whitstruck's room wearing that blue Christmas sweater, as if I were the god-o-mighty school queen. Which, once upon a time, I guess I was. Luke was there sitting in the back corner, wearing shorts like he was shooting a finger at the cold. That's the thing about living here. When a little bit of winter comes, some people hop on it and pull out maybe a total of two wool things. While the others go around refusing to believe it. Shorts and a sweatshirt. Probably that's all Luke will ever take to.

It was funny how I got to use that Krebs cycle ATP stuff, after all. Got to draw the little hexagon of adenine. And the pentagon of ribose. But what was really going through my mind was that nothing that had happened to me was like I thought would happen to me. Because I had this idea. Or at least, I'd been led to think that what happens to people—from watching movies and all—is that once you tell the secret. Once you let out the dirty. Retch up the goods. Or whatever you want to call it—to a shrink or somebody, you are set free. Made well. It's supposed to be easy. You see it over and over. In books. In films. And everything moves along after that. Fine. Really fine. And you can get to go around saying how you grew from it. Were changed by it. But I am here. And ain't nothing happening.

It's like I am breathing and eating behind a wall of *Where I've Been* that won't let me move out to where everybody else is. A fence. A coop with sides that I can see over but cannot go through. My ticket stub is on display. But I don't have a flea-sized idea how in the hell to get back.

Every day I pull into the parking lot and park where the seniors have places set aside. I walk down the halls and eat my sack lunch sitting on the brick wall that rims the inside patio. I stay open and look friendly, but I know what's in everyone's mind. I can hear their voices saying what they would be saying if they were speaking out loud. And I can hear them thinking: *There goes Bergin Talbot, Queen of this, Captain of that, President of whatchamacallit, Honor Society, god-o-mighty honors galore, once. And now . . .* Yes, I am the All American Girl blown up. I've exploded. No one can say why. I am walking proof that having what everyone is led to believe they should want is not worth having. *What did she ever have to complain about? What could have been so wrong with her life that she did this?* This. So now my fall is a comfort. I am sour grapes in Birkenstocks. All of my exams I could have been excused from, too. The principal had asked me. And then the guidance counselor had asked me, as if they were going to practice doing head-stuff, too: "Would you care to wait, Bergin? You don't have to do any of this right now, if you don't want to." Their voices had been so sugary sweet, it was like swallowing molasses straight.

But no. No. I have said *no* to anything that has waiting in it. Because standing still, being still, is the worst thing I can do, Dr. Cone says. And besides, I have one of those minds, she also says, that dips into learning, that takes on new things as a way of keeping calm. I didn't lose my concentration for new things. It was the old that did me in. And so, "Keep moving. Stay involved. Don't pull back," is what she told me last week. "Make a list of things you have seen that have moved. A chair, a book. Things that are gone that once were there. A kid in your class. A wastebasket. A stain. Anything." I've been to see her four times, so far—which is twice a week. And I know better than to ask what in the hell she is aiming at. Because she won't tell me until she is ready. And says I am ready. So I do my homework for her just as I do it for Mr. Whitstruck and for everybody else.

There were only eight kids taking the AP Biology exam. It isn't what you'd call a gotta-have course, seeing as how most kids in this county school are in no hurry. Most will stay home next year and commute to the community college. Which, when you really think about it, sounds pretty good. More than likely they will live and work near here their whole lives. While I don't have a rat's ass clue where I'll be. Or what I'll be doing one year down the road. Much less in ten. Can't think about it. Don't want to think about it. Sure as hell *not* going to think about it.

Carbon. Hydrogen. Nitrogen. I filled in the blanks. *Cyclic degradation and regeneration within the cell. Polysaccharides, proteins, lipids, deoxyribonucleic acid and ribonucleic acid.* Then I moved on to the reproductive system of the starfish.

During that first week, Carol Ann let me practice with the soccer team pretty much like I was someone with a bone disease. She said I could sit out whenever I wanted to. She had replaced me as goalie with Diane Taylor. Diane is a freshman and isn't real sure of the rules, either. But Carol Ann is hot on Diane. It was only when Diane got her period last Tuesday. Which she called having a visit from her aunt, for Christ's sake. That Carol Ann looked at me on the bench and asked, "Do you feel up to it?"

"I don't have any aunts," I said, and got up and put on the shin pads and goalie gloves with sticky on them.

I saved two goals and had pizza with the team. Now I am reinstated as the goalie with the mostest. Or hot shit on cleats. Because I don't seem to give a rock-hard damn about anything but winning. I have to win. I want to win. I want to feel what it feels like to win. *Most starfish have separate sexes. They spawn both sperm and eggs into the water. Sometimes the mother retains the eggs on the bottom and protects them.* I was tempted to glance back at Luke.

I made a mental note instead to write down on the ledger page in Dr. Cone's account book under the title Things That Have Been Moved: *Luke. Jason Murphy's case of acne has jumped to him.* It is clear he is about to explode with backed-up testosterone.

Most starfish have great powers of regeneration of body parts. And in some, this becomes a regular means of asexual reproduction, producing whole new animals from each fragment. Which means, I guess, that if I were a starfish, I could cut off my thumb and start all over.

I handed in my paper. While everybody else was walking out, Mr. Whitstruck leaned over the desk and looked at me. He held my paper and glanced down at it. Then back at me. He has these brown circle-frame glasses. And brown-blond hair that he keeps cut with long bangs that he lets flop loose. I don't think he's much older than thirty. A dark tie and a striped shirt, and he wears tennis shoes with Gap khakis, trying to look like one of us, I guess. And cool. "How's it going?" he asked while adjusting his glasses. Then real quietly and softly, he touched my arm. Let his fingers rest on the blue of my sweater. And what was going through my mind was that no other man in this whole school would be allowed to do this. Because it would come off as sexual. And because it might come off as harassment. The whole world is screwed up. But Mr. Whitstruck is gay. Everybody knows that. It's not something he can really hide. And then last year some kids saw him marching in a parade downtown. And there was a good bit of stink made about it by some parents. And I guess by somebody on the school board.

My mother even got involved. Said she'd defend him if he wanted to bring a suit. He has a right to be hired, to work here, she says. But so far he's just being watched. Watched all the time. Eyes on him like on me, too. Lose a pound, and somebody will say he has AIDS and is dying. And he's probably more faithful to whoever he's in love with than half the husbands in America. "Pretty good," I said back, and realized how good it felt to be asked. I thought, then, of a joke. The whole thing moving through my mind just as I'd heard it on the radio. *Why is it so hard to find a sensitive, caring man? Because they already have boyfriends.* I looked straight at him and laughed. Out in the hall,

I laughed louder. People looked at me. Mr. Whitstruck can touch me and be nice to me. Because I am a girl. He cannot be suspected to be after me. And I can laugh when nobody else does, or knows why. Mr. Whitstruck and I are alike now. When you get right down to it, this *is* a kind of freedom.

At soccer practice, I left early. This is one of the days I go to see Dr. Cone, and Carol Ann doesn't ask. She knows I have other things to do. Important things. Getting-my-head-worked-on things. So she lifts her hand and tip-waves me off the field when I signal that it is time for me to go. We have made this plan, though. Next week in our game, it is me who will set a trap. An off-sides trap. I understand the whole game now, all the rules.

I got into my car out in the parking lot, took off my cleats and pulled on a sweat suit and running shoes. I rewound my hair up under my wool headband and looked over at the kids in a group beside me. It was Claire Foster and Denny Rook. The year before they'd asked me to a party. It had been one weekend when Luke and I had nowhere to go. And I had talked him into going to it. Because I thought we ought to be nice. Nice for no other reason than to be nice. And now Claire and Denny were waving to me. They yelled *Hey* to me. I got into my car while waving back.

But going through my mind was that party. And how I had realized, in-cold-surprise realized, that they had not wanted me. They had wanted only to *see* me. See what I would do. For everyone there had been doing whippits. Sucking nitrous oxide out of capsules that someone had gotten a whole case of. And they were getting dizzy drunk. And talking in crazy-made voices. And pretending to be opera singers, for Christ's sake. And Claire had six tablets of Ecstasy. And was telling everyone to choose a number between one and twenty, and whichever six got closest to the number she was thinking of, they would get the Ecstasy. And dance till sunrise and the rest of their whole god-o-mighty lives, for all anyone knew. So it was a trap. A joke to see how I would take it. What Luke and I would do. And now Denny was coming close to the car, sticking his face on it to make his flesh smear and his nose go flat. "Come on. Come go with us." I waved him off and pretended to be in a rush somewhere. Which I was. I backed out with my head turned around to look behind me. Dizzy would feel good. Dizzy could make sense. But I was living out what has turned out to be my own joke now.

Driving to see Dr. Cone, my mind was on the night before and how, when we'd heard on the TV news that it was going to freeze, I had gone out to the barn to get the peacocks and Spam inside it. The horses, too. I'd had to dangle one of Jack's oatmeal cookies in front of Spam to get him in there. Then I'd locked them in. And turned on the naked-light-bulb lights, and let the closed doors and their body heat warm up the place. The peacocks had headed straight for the tack room to peck up sweet feed that had fallen on the floor. I climbed up the ladder to the loft for hay. It was stacked to the ceiling. Jack had just recently bought hay. Had gotten it from a farmer from down the road. Ordinarily I can sit still or stand and smell hay for about half a century. But it was like my nose was stopped up. I didn't smell anything. I slipped each of my hands under the thin hairy ropes of one of the bales and lifted it. Then rolled it to the edge of the ladder in the dim light to throw it over. To let it fall onto the concrete floor below. And as I was pushing it, then lifting it, then about to roll it over, I saw to one side, in like what was a little tunnel of hay, this suitcase. And beside it, two other small ones. All matching, tapestry and flowered.

It was so strange. It made no sense. It was like seeing a little kid's picture puzzle where you pick out things that do not belong. I let go of the hay. And it crashed down. And the peacocks flew up. And Spam squealed. But I went back to look at what did not make sense at being there. I opened the suitcase. It was empty. It smelled so new it was like the insides of an unbought car. All vinyl and clean. Then I knew. My mother had often hidden Christmas presents for the twins up in the loft with the hay. And this one had been meant for me. It was so new and unused. Who else could it have been meant for? But my mother had forgotten it. She had just not remembered. She had often done that. Found weeks later a gift she had hidden and forgotten about. And then I understood. Realized in cold surprise, too, that it was not that my mother had *not* thought of it. It was instead that she had thought *too much* about it and chosen to change her mind. This was not something that could be given to someone who might never be able to go anywhere. This was not right for anyone like me, now.

I PULLED INTO the hospital parking lot and punched the chrome button on the gate to pop out a ticket for me. I put it on the dash and drove to an empty spot. Then I walked into the hospital while studying the sidewalk. All the while. The whole while, seeing again the hay and the suitcase hidden in it. It was strange when I felt something stop me, stand in front of me, to get my attention. When I looked up, I saw Hoot there on the sidewalk with one of those gas blowers. I hadn't even heard the sound of it as he had been blowing leaves off the walk in front of me. And now he was standing there. The motor cut off to silence.

He was asking me how I was doing. He grinned. The yellow-onion squares of his teeth were like a broken bracelet. His eyes were steady, too, looking at me, waiting.

"Okay, " I told him back. "How about you?"

"Hanging in there," he said, then asked if I had any gum. He had nervous twitches that broke out one minute in his shoulder. Then a second later in his wrist. He nodded his head while I dug down into my purse. Then he told me, "I found it's best to keep every part of myself busy. 'Specially my mouth." He laughed and thanked me as I pulled out an old piece of Dentyne. "I reckon without this, I'd be smokin' and drinkin' and doing who knows what else."

"Sounds like maybe you should make a gum commercial," I said, handing him the piece. We both laughed then. And he sang, "*Yeah, oh yeah.*" When I turned and left him on the sidewalk, I heard the motor of the blower starting up like a small jet plane. I glanced back. The leaves were flying up off the walk in front of him and rolling in a pile that was adding up, adding up. I made a note, too, that on my way out, I really ought to stop by and check on Dee Dee.

"It's too strange," I said to Dr. Cone, when I got to her office.

"What?"

"Being alive."

"Because?"

"I hadn't meant to."

"So what's so strange about it?"

"I don't know how to act."

"Feels a bit like parachuting down into a foreign country?"

"Yeah, in a blindfold."

She nodded and got up. She sat in the chair beside me.

We are not looking at each other now. We are just here, side by side. We are looking at the vanilla wall in front of us. And at the gray tweed rug. And at the coffee-brown side of her desk. I can hear her breathing because every once in a while she lets out a long sigh. I cross one of my knees over the other and play with the sole of my tennis shoe. "Let me see your ledger," she asks now.

I lay it open. She turns the pages slowly while I keep it balanced on my knee. She is leaning toward me, looking carefully, carefully at each of the pages. At every word. She studies everything I wrote down today under the title Things That Have Moved and puts a finger under each line.

She reads out loud, "Jason Murphy's acne has jumped to Luke." She looks at me and laughs. Then, "Mr. Whitstruck's pencil sharpener is now in the back of the room." And, "Jack has finally gotten a decent haircut." She looks up at me after that one. "How did that happen?"

"My mother sent him to her hairdresser," I say.

She smiles and looks down to read again. "Spam smells better, but I don't know why." She laughs louder, then looks down at the last thing I wrote today. *A limb on the tree in the front pasture is cracked and lying on the ground. The ice from last night has broken it off. Yesterday nobody noticed that it was half-dead. Now Jack will cut it up and move it into the house as firewood.*

"See," she says finally, looking up and looking at me. "You have a whole long list, and it keeps growing. Things move. And the way you feel now won't be here forever, either."

Our eyes lie on each other's like they need to be here and to be still. And what she has said *does* make sense. Her words move inside of me, and they seem to bring with them a certain warmth, as if I am, too, a log or a circle of ice, so that one day even I will not be as I am now. But at the same time that she has made me feel better, I want to hear, to have her tell me, to feel that she knows. *Yes, but can't anything last?*

I'm too afraid of the answer, though. I'd rather not ask. Than to know.

THIRTEEN

Leslie

I will not let this be. We cannot go anymore like this, walking through the days like the past is an oil drum, turned over and dripping through our lives. I want us back—all of us back, as we used to be, better than we used to be. Last Saturday I had to go to Tallahassee for an oral argument at the District Court of Appeals. It was all about getting a piece of evidence in a robbery trial to be admissible, and I didn't want to go alone. I didn't want the family to be split up for the whole day, either; for it is like I am cradling Bergin once again, trying to hold her in my sight and in the protection of our small nest, the nest of me and Jack and the twins. Over the last three weeks I have been watching her sit at the dinner table, walk through the back hall to her bathroom before school, head out to her car, drive in, drive out; and I keep track of everything she does. Of course this makes me feel ridiculous and crazed, like she is the child who has swallowed the loose change at the bottom of my purse; and I need to see what damage has been done, and if, indeed, it will be passed. Her thoughts are all hidden.

But what is out in the open is the way I accidentally, incidentally, in a manner of speaking, committed manslaughter of my daughter's soul. Did it with my big mouth, and went about jeopardizing her life with no more thought to it than the way I drape the dishrag over the faucet every night after supper—neat, rinsed out, with me on automatic pilot. My dishrag ritual is something I demand—a cleanliness to it, a finality, permission to end the day. Yes, I insist on it, as I insisted that Bergin keep everything clean and honest in her life—and to speak for herself—because what has gone before has been so ragged and indirect.

Sort out what you are responsible for from whom you are responsible for, Dr. Cone told me the last time I went to see her. I go to see her sometimes alone. I need to be with somebody who knows what I have done, who has seen the hole I—or at least Doug and I—have ripped into my family, and understands that I have to fix it, to stitch it back, or, at the least, stuff it full with something good.

The business at the Court of Appeals would last only an hour at the most. I would have the remainder of the day free, so I suggested to Jack that he and the twins go with me, and that we would include Bergin, and I would find something interesting for them to do while I was at court. Listed in the newspaper was the schedule of a Native American Powwow to be held at a campground outside of Tallahassee, and I decided *that* would be perfect. I would drop them off there, go do my court stuff, and then join them. Jack was all for it. There's a teaspoon of Seminole mixed into his family way back somewhere, and he was eager for Kirk and Maggie to learn of that, as well as of their country's heritage. I invited Simpson Bates to go along. Bergin hadn't hung around with her in years and she doesn't even go to the same school now, but I am taking over. *I am going to get us back.*

Simpson pulled up in front of our house at 7 A.M. sharp, which on a Saturday is like asking a teenager to donate a kidney. It gave me a funny charge seeing her driving. For I still think of Simpson as that little girl in mismatched short sets, arms and legs like a spider's, who spent almost every waking moment with Bergin when they were eight, nine, and ten. And now here she was dressed head to toe in black and driving a gold jeep. She was all smiles and nearly six feet in tight knit pants and a knit top and tall black boots, as if she intended to do chimney sweeping on the side. She held out her arms and balanced through the peacocks and Spam, and dodged the dogs that sprung at her like they were mounted on pogo sticks. Bergin stood at the door calling out, *Hey.* Bergin was dressed in jeans, a sweatshirt and headband—all in black, too. I swear, this is a black-fabric generation. And I myself was packing snacks and drinks in the back of the van in one of my navy blue power suits with mid-sized heels. Jack was shutting up the barn.

Jack drove, which gave me plenty of time to play car games with the twins, as well as to watch Bergin and Simpson who, after a little polite conversation that included me as we pulled out old memories (the summer they dressed up the cat, the year they cut each other's hair, the spring of the dance recital in which Bergin kicked off a tap shoe and Simpson fell down), each plugged in earphones to pocket-sized CD players. Then over the next one hundred miles they swapped CD's. I kept glancing back at the twins, still so innocent and connected to me. And oh, how I wanted to let that sweetness reign while it could: Kirk's sticky fingers as he touched my cheek, wanting to turn my face to see what evil Maggie was doing to him, and Maggie, patting my hand and saying *But see, I didn't mean to.* She'd sat on his new box of crayons and neatly bisected a whole handful. In court I might be a red hot mama, but here, with the twins, I was . . . well, there's no sense saying it like it is. I peeled back the paper on the broken crayons so they were now usable, then for the rest of the trip I swapped riddles with the both of them.

As we pulled into the campground I was just finishing *What's worse than a giraffe with a sore throat?* with *A centipede with sore feet,* while Jack stopped beside a line of trailers. The tops of two teepees were visible through the trees. I kissed the twins good-bye and told them I'd be back as soon as I could. I slid over into the driver's seat and watched them all walk off—the twins holding each of Jack's hands, Bergin and Simpson a step behind and off to one side, with their backpack purses banging between their shoulder blades.

COURT IS where I am comfortable. Court is where I follow the script that I have been trained to follow, where my anxieties fade, and I can fight like a man. I forget to worry about what I lack, whatever it is that my mother could not teach me. Here, I am my father's child, as long as I keep my suit coat buttoned and stay in dark colors. Here, I am hell on wheels, or rather, high heels.

In what amounted to only ten minutes, I stood up there in front of the judges and laid out a polished argument that gave me what I asked for. Then I hurried to the parking lot and got in the van. I should have, but I didn't, change clothes. I didn't even think of it—so used to rushing, I guess. So here I was heading back to the camp-ground in power suit and heels to hunt for my family. *Getting her life back is Bergin's job now,* Dr. Cone told me three weeks ago, and now she says it every time I go, over and over. *Get it back. Get it back. It is her job now.*

I stood at the edge of a large circle where Native Americans danced in tribal clothes. I saw Jack and the twins on the other side, sitting on a bench, Kirk in Jack's lap, Maggie in her purple jeans and an orange top beside him, transfixed by the event in front of her. I rarely saw her so quiet. I scanned the crowd for Bergin. I looked for the height of Simpson to stick out.

Four or five men were under a hut, beating drums; one was stand-ing up with a microphone beginning to speak. *Each dance is different,* he said. I looked at every face around the circle. No Simpson, no Bergin. I looked back at Jack. How could he be so calm, not knowing where my daughter was? *You have to sort out what you are responsible for from whom you are responsible for.* What did Dr. Cone's words mean here? Sometimes I thought she was like going to a priest to be taught about sex. What did she know about losing a child! Or nearly losing a child? And still not having her back? There were no pictures of family members anywhere in Dr. Cone's office, which was probably part of her professionalism—not letting anything of her personal life get in the way of treating Bergin, and us. She was older than I; she should even by now have grandchildren. If she did, had she forgotten? Could she really know what being a mother can do to you? *The Drum is like the heartbeat of the nation.* The old man in beads and what looked like a deerskin vest was going on: *And one thing you will never hear is our drum being hit in that one-two-three beat. No. Oh, no. That's what Hollywood came up with. That has nothing to do with us.* My head and eyes were moving and looking, one step from frantic.

Staying calm and not thinking the worst has nothing to do with us now, I was thinking. We have seen the worst, been too close to the worst, to ever be quite the same again. I twisted my Christmas bracelet on my wrist. I began weaving in and out of the people standing in the circle. I wedged myself between bodies and looked up at each face. I touched shoulders and arms when I needed to make a space for me to pass. "Excuse me, excuse me," I was whispering with every step. But faintly I was aware I was all the way into being rude.

Hands grabbed my shoulders from behind, strong, forceful hands. I stopped and turned around. A tall thin man, his face wrinkled and his hair white, leaned toward me and whispered, "You cannot move through here like this once our ceremony has begun. You can't turn your back on our sacred circle, either."

"But you don't understand," I rasped back, my voice louder than a whisper. "I've lost my daughter."

His face relaxed somewhat. "We have a place for that. See that trailer over there? That's where lost children are taken. How old is she?"

"Seventeen," I blurted, pulling away from him, and walked on. His last look at me made me see how crazy I seemed. What would he do? Call out the security tribe? *Track down this nut in the midst of us—* that's what he would tell them. But what did he know? What could he understand? The old man in the center of the circle with the microphone was following me with his eyes, and he was still talking about that drum. *Many Native Nations refer to the Drum as the Horse, because it carries their spirit into other realms and other times. Ride the Horse is a saying which means to free your mind and allow your body to feel the power of the Drum, which can let Mother Earth resonate through your feet and into your heart.*

My feet were pushing toward Jack, and when I reached him I leaned over him where he was sitting. "Where is Bergin? Where is she?"

"Around here somewhere." He glanced back over his shoulder. I was touching him like he was a fencepost, as if he were wood that I could lean on. "You mean, you don't know exactly?"

"Did you see the alligator feet?" Maggie asked, tilting her head to look straight up at me. "And the buffalo teeth?" She meant the tables under some nearby tents where crafts—genuine dried alligator feet, and buffalo teeth, and who knew what else—were for sale.

From my angle, Maggie's face looked like a heart upside down, her chin the meeting point of lines. I saw then, too, on her cheek that an eagle's head had been painted. Kirk sat quiet, mesmerized by the drums.

"How could you lose her?" I persisted with Jack. Anger and frustration seeped into my voice. He swiveled around now and whispered loudly at my rudeness, if not at me, "Calm down. She's not a little child. She's here somewhere."

"She's with the alligator feet," Maggie said. She swirled around, too, and pointed. "She went in there to see that stuff." Her finger led my eye to a trailer with a huge buffalo head mounted on one side. A canopy was attached to that side of the trailer and, below the curtain that acted as a door, I could see feet, not alligator feet, but human feet. Four feet in black, two Birkenstocks and two boots. I stepped back into the circle of people who were behind Jack, and I stood quietly, alternately looking over at the feet at the trailer and out into the hut at the drummers. Then as I glanced back, I saw Bergin holding up the flap of the tent and looking at me. The sound of the drums now I could feel inside of my own body, coming up and mixing with the chant of the dancers. No doubt, over all the years of whatever was our future, I would lose sight of, or be ignorant of, where exactly Bergin was; and would I each time, every single time, feel this panic, this rising sickness that would make me think all over again that I had lost her?

WE DROVE out of the campground belching buffalo chili and carrying our secrets and our loot: two dollars and fifty cents' worth of alligator feet, twenty-five cents of muskrat jaws, dollar fifty of buffalo side teeth, a sack of passion flower for tea, and five face paintings: Kirk's goose, Maggie's eagle, Simpson's dog, Bergin's snake, Jack's cow—and me, empty of everything but a sad heart wrapped in a power suit.

Before we'd left home, I had put in the back of the van two pots of dormant lilies to put on my father's headstone. I wanted to drive by my childhood house, too. A young family lived there now. I had done this with Jack many times before, so he knew the way as he drove. We stopped on the street outside the house and looked at it for a moment. A swing was in the front yard, and an ugly dog was locked behind a back fence, barking at us. Memories oozed out of all of it like something squeezed and liquid, and I turned to look back at Bergin. "Do you remember when we hung you up a swing there, too?"

"No."

"You remember that little swimming pool we blew up for you in the backyard?"

"No."

"Aw, come on, Bergin, of course you do. And how my father would ride you on his shoulders down to the creek in the woods behind here?"

"Yeah, well, if you say so."

"I remember," Simpson volunteered. "I came that one weekend, remember?"

"Where was I?" Maggie piped up.

"You weren't here yet," I told her.

"You were a twinkle in my eye," Jack said, putting the gear in drive. I couldn't decide if Bergin had been snippy so as to sound cool in front of Simpson, or if she really did not remember. I also suspected she had witnessed my ruckus at the powwow circle when I'd lost her, and she was now pissed off at me for that. *Ridiculous* was becoming my new name, in her opinion; I could see it in her eyes.

Meanwhile Jack was trying to explain to Maggie what a twinkle was, or more precisely, what his particular twinkle had meant.

"Let's head out to the cemetery then, if you don't mind," I said to Jack. I hated the thought of the word *cemetery*. I hated even the thought of Bergin and anything to do with the end of life in the same breathing zone. But what was I going to call it: graveyard, burial ground, potter's field? What right did she have to encroach on my time and memories with my father? What right did she have to rearrange all of our lives like this, inhibit us like this?

I got out of the van and stepped in mud without so much as a notice. I went to get the lilies from the back of the van, where they'd been riding under Bergin's and Simpson's feet. I pulled the lily pots out from around their shoes and boots with an, "Excuse me, you getting out now?" and walked off before they could answer. I was going to take my own life back if she wasn't going to reach for hers. I could feel them behind me—all of them: Jack and the twins, Simpson and Bergin traipsing up the hill to where my father's grave is. Later, or maybe even then, I knew they would be whispering something about my being on the warpath.

Bergin. The headstone with engraved words stuck out as we climbed up to where it is under two oaks. I knelt down in front of the granite stone and dug a hole with a trowel I'd brought along. My mother was here in the same plot, the two of them, side by side. As I began lifting the earth, I began calling on the strength that my father always gave to me, wanting it to travel up through my knees to spread out throughout me, filling me with his resilience. I began to apologize silently to him, and to me at the same time, that I had not fully remembered and realized the longing for father-love that I should have known would pervade all of Bergin's life, too. Then I whispered inside my mind an apology to my mother. For I regretted now more than ever that we had never really known each other, or tried, and that I had so few thoughts and memories of her. This job of mothering, I told her, is too fraught with danger. There is too much perfection expected from it. You have to forgive yourself from the moment you begin.

I patted the soil. The lilies would spread and bloom over both, and I weeded around the daisies that were already there, and dormant, then tapped the lilies out of their pots and put them in. Maggie helped me, patting the dirt down around them. Usually when we stopped here, we all spent a few minutes in prayer or silence, much like we do at the dinner table before we eat. And sometimes we held hands. Bergin had done this with us in the past. But she and Simpson had walked a little way down the road that cut through the hill.

Maggie grabbed my hand and then Kirk's and pulled us into an arc in front of the headstone. "I'll go first," she said. Then Maggie lowered her head and looked at the planted lilies. "We just came here from a powwow." Her voice was steady and even, and she didn't even seem to have to linger to think. "Indians there said the earth is like a mother, and so I guess that means you're lying in her lap. Well, I hope you have a good time. Everybody says you were quite a fella. I'm just sorry you didn't get to know me. Amen." It was a mixture of prayer and a one-way conversation. Jack and I glanced at each other and smiled. I turned around, hoping Bergin would come join us. She was sitting on a tombstone, though. Simpson was standing in front of her. They were eating something like peanuts out of a bag. The way she was, her irreverence and nonchalance, shocked me. Or was this what happened when you have been where she has?

WE ENDED that weekend without much of any significance being said between us. What *could* we say? "It's not going to happen all at once," Jack told me that night. "Some miracle isn't going to come along and push us all through to somewhere else. And somewhere good."

"Why not?"

I looked at him while rubbing Pond's for Dry Skin on my face and wearing a pink nightgown with ruffles at the shoulders that is way too youthful-looking for me. But Jack gave it to me, so what can I do?

"It doesn't work that way." He patted the bed beside him.

"Well, I want it to. I want everything to be different now."

"Shhh," he said, rubbing my shoulders under the ridiculous lace.

I wish I could say we made love like prisoners on a conjugal visit, or like sailors on shore leave, or like the rabbits down in our back pasture who hop through the tall grass at night like they are paid to make tunnels and a whole new generation. But we didn't; my mind was too stuck. Instead I got up and brewed us a pot of passion flower tea.

NOW IT is Monday. I am sitting in court waiting for the start of my second case on the docket. I am super-prepared, and I have told the State Attorney I don't want to drag this out. Cut to the chase, I told him earlier, because I want to get out of here by four to be at Bergin's soccer match at least by the half. Jack has already picked the twins up and is at the soccer field. The judge is coming in and we are all rising, and now William Tiner is coming down the aisle toward me with a piece of paper in his hand. He places it on the table in front of me.

Call the County Hospital E.R., it says. My breath sucks in, and I pick up the paper and walk with it as though I do not know where I am going, but then I head straight to the judge. I ask for a postponement, I think. I think I say everything I am supposed to. "An emergency," I add, holding up the paper and flapping it as though I need evidence. He looks toward the State Attorney. But I do not wait to hear what comes next. I know this procedure—and the judge—too well. "Take my things back to the office," I say to William Tiner as I half run, half lope—but am all the way terrified—up the aisle to the door.

FOURTEEN

Bergin

You should have seen my mother's face. Because from where I was, propped up on one of those crank-up tables in the emergency room, the angle sure said this was a woman on the high end of freaking out. None of it was pretty, either. For she ran in, pulled back the curtain from around where I was. Her eyes big. Her hair frizzed. And her suit coat off so the deodorant rings on her silk blouse were on for-the-whole-of-mankind god-o-mighty display. That caught me with a tickle in my throat—if I could have laughed, seeing as how a towel was over my mouth and blood was still coming out of me like a water balloon had just been dropped. Because only about twenty minutes before, a soccer ball had been kicked from close. I mean up-close-and-personal range. And straight. With no detours whatsoever. Into the center of my face. My nose was broken. And my front teeth had gone through my upper lip. Everything was swelling about as fast as a balloon could be blown up, too. A nurse was holding towels over my nose. And I was holding one over my mouth. And Jack was holding one of those little kidney-shaped basins under my chin to keep me spitting the blood out, so I wouldn't swallow it.

It was him who'd run onto the soccer field as soon it happened and bent over me. He'd picked me up. I mean embarrassingly picked me up. Like I was a little kid. Or someone out cold or dead. While saying all the while that everything was going to be fine, fine. Because my teeth were still in. In fact, he said *Smile* and he could count them. You see, the blood was just scaring the ever-lovin' bejesus out of everyone. There was so much of it! My hands were covered with it. And the whole front of my soccer outfit was turning stiff with it. In fact, I think the only part that wasn't touched was my eyebrows. And so that's why I couldn't laugh at how my mother looked. I was too busy bleeding. But it was crazy funny, since she prides herself on being someone who never loses it. I mean, her voice never shakes and she can crack a book open anywhere at any time and figure out how to impress a judge. Or solve a quadratic equation. Everything except cook a half-decent meal or fix a toilet. And here I was lying on that table, cranked up and bleeding like Spam stuck with a pitchfork. And it was this. This that had undone her.

But then I learned there was more to it. And what was really at the root of it, as well as maybe begin to know what I'd really done back in December. And what it had really done to her. And wouldn't you just know it? There as part of it was my dad and his sparkling communication skills. All over again.

For practically everybody in the whole ever-loving family had come to see me do my thing in the soccer game. My dad. Jack. The twins. And Dylan. My mother planned to be there before the whole shebang was over. I had set my offsides trap in the first quarter, yelled out to my team to *Move up! Move up!* so as to come close to me, so the other team would follow them and be caught offsides. And we did, and caught them once. But then the next time, their forward cocked her foot sideways and blasted a shot that caught me with my mouth open yelling, and my mind on the trap and not on the whole reason for being there. Which, of course, is to guard the holy god-o-mighty goal. The hit knocked me back. And I just lay there. Not knowing anything. Not feeling anything until I felt Jack lifting me up. Then Carol Ann put a towel over my face. But Jack wouldn't let go of me. Wouldn't let anyone else touch me. Yelled to Carol Ann that he'd take care of this, then half carried me to his car and left the twins to—get this!—my father and Dylan. He told my dad to call my mother to tell her what had happened. Then with all that done, there was nothing left but to drive me like a bat out of hell to the E.R.

Now while I was in there bleeding. And my mother learned it was not me dying again but only my nose blasted to kingdom come, she went out onto the other side of the curtains and blasted my father to the same place, if you know what I mean. It seems Jack was such a big-wig with the hospital, the whole lot of us were pretty much getting the run of the E.R. So Lord help us, I could hear her clear into the treatment room. *Why didn't he tell her it was just a soccer ball accident? Why did he just send word to her to come to the E.R. as soon as possible? Hell. Damn. And Holy Mama. Didn't he have any consideration for her? Didn't an ant-sized streak of compassion for her pass through his brain? What was she to think receiving a message like that? Being told to just call the County Hospital E.R., and nothing else? Not one iota of any other word. Didn't he remember how fertile her imagination could be?* At least that was the gist of it. And then I could hear the twins running up and down out there and doing God knows what. They were telling her that my father had tried to color with them, read them books out in the lobby, and that Dylan didn't know even one riddle, only two pretty stupid knock-knock jokes. And no, they couldn't sit still. They'd just never seen so much blood as was coming out of me.

To them, I guess I *was* like a freak movie. Like something on cable they weren't supposed to see.

I lay back and just let myself become on the high end of fascinated with what all a broken nose was bringing out. A young doctor,
maybe an intern or someone like that, leaned over me to say he was
going to put my nose to sleep to set it. Which a plastic surgeon was
on his way to do—at the request of Jack. Nothing less than Dr. Miller,
the bona fide plastic surgeon on call, would do for Jack. That's the first
thing he asked for when everybody got a good look at how my nose
was aimed off to the left. And the intern said they were also going to
give me something for the pain. Which to tell the truth, I really was
starting to feel.

As a nurse was getting ready to shoot something into my left arm,
the intern said just sort of commentary-like that he'd never known a
soccer ball could do this much damage. I wanted to say it was probably because I had my mouth open yelling at the time. But I had a
towel in my mouth. And then Jack, who was sitting on the side of the
treatment table holding his little basin, looked straight at the intern
and asked, "Are you questioning the fact of what happened?"

"No. Oh, no," the intern said, while the nurse pulled the needle
out.

"Well, I should hope not," Jack said, still sounding so touchy I
couldn't believe it. "And where is Dr. Miller? Did you page him?"

"Yeah. Oh, yeah. He's on his way."

"Well, I don't want anybody else touching her nose until he gets
here."

I laughed. But no sound came out, I was so drugged up. I remember Dr. Miller coming in, though. And that intern sticking a needle in
my cheek to put it to sleep. And then Dr. Miller putting a metal thing
up my nose that looked like something you'd use to turn over meat on
a barbecue. Which he then pulled on hard to the right. For a long
while after that, I just sort of floated around. Off and on hearing and
seeing everyone coming in and going out.

It was about another hour that I just lay there, ice packs all over my face. And Jack sitting on the left of me. My mom on the right. My dad popping in and out with the twins. And Dylan who finally came up with a good, if not acceptable, joke for the them. Which is the first thing I remember waking up enough to really hear. *What does the H in Jesus H. Christ mean?* And then Dylan's funny little voice like a radio halfway between two stations, answering himself: *Howard, from that part, you know, Howard Be Thy Name.* Dylan was proud, but my mother was nonplused, you could tell. She kept telling the twins this was not a riddle they should add to their collection, that it could offend people. But by the time they understood *that,* practically everybody in the E.R. had been asked about Jesus's middle name.

And then a nurse came in and said we could go.

But before we were checked out, I tried to ask all of them something. The words wouldn't come clearly out of my mouth, though. My face was still numb, and my lip was so swollen. It was like I was trying to get sound through a pillow. I said it three times and got everybody there so flustered and guessing, it was like we were playing charades. Finally, and with a hitch in his shoulder and a smile that said it all, Jack handed me a little pad of paper and a short yellow pencil. And I wrote down on it, *Did the goal count?*

When I handed it to him, he held it for a minute. It seemed he read it twice. Then he laughed. In fact, his laugh exploded about like Dr. Cone's. And then he passed the note around the whole room. Pretty soon everybody was heehawing and going just pretty much wild, if you know what I mean. Which struck me that they were doing probably out of relief. Or maybe it really was because of the outcome. For Jack said, "No, Starlight with a Crown. You stopped the shot with your face. And it bounced back to almost midfield. Score still zero to zip at the half. But I don't know who finally won."

My father added, "I think it was the greatest goal stop in history."

And then my mother threw in, "I'm just sorry I missed it."

By the time it was okay for me to check out and go home, I was walking on my own. No blood in sight anywhere. My face was bandaged like someone after a car wreck in a cartoon. This metal contraption was taped onto my nose. And my mom had gone down to the gift shop to buy me a T-shirt so I wouldn't have to walk out all covered in dried blood. So I was wearing kelly green down to just about my knees, that covered up pretty much every bit of my soccer shorts underneath. So anybody who looked at me was sure going to look twice. My mother said she thought I'd get a kick out of that particular T-shirt. And when she said it, she laughed like a woman who's been sniffing household cleaners. Then she said it again, "*Kick*," *get it?* Yeah, I was still a good bit fuzzy in the head, but I got it. Because on the front of the shirt was a cartoon of two horse heads talking to each other over a fence. And one of them was saying *What's your name? Mine's Whoa Dammit.* So I got my mother's pun, and I got the gist of how we were playing cheerful to the hilt. So I was clumping along on the pavement in my soccer cleats. All of us walking together out into the parking lot where there were three separate cars.

For a while there, I felt like a dog in one of those old western movies where different people who love him call him at the same time to see where he'll go. I got into Jack's car with him. We'd started out this whole thing together, so I figured I might as well end it this way. I sat in the front seat in his little black Toyota.

He slipped a homemade tape of him singing "Starlight with a Crown"—and *a cappella* for Christ's sake—into the little tape-deck slot. And we listened to it all the way home with neither of us needing or, I guess, feeling we had to say a thing. The sound of the tape was so awful it was funny, and it pretty much wiped out anything else in my mind. In fact, we couldn't help but laugh a little the whole way, listening to that stupid song.

It was strange, though. And it was crazy funny, too. Because when we first pulled out of the hospital parking lot, I looked back up at the fifth-floor window and remembered how Dee Dee and I had looked out it and down onto this exact same spot. And the week before, when I'd gone up there to see Dr. Cone, I'd stopped in to see Dee Dee just like I'd promised myself—and her—that I would. But she wasn't there. She'd been discharged and sent to another place, and she was evidence again of just what Dr. Cone had promised me that I would see—that things move. Even people. But what was crazy-funniest about the whole broken nose thing and driving off from the hospital while I looked back at it, was that the whole while I was in there and getting worked on, and my nose getting pulled back into being lined up even with my chin, I was aware of being fascinated. I was thinking everything about it was saying something to me. The biology, the good, the bad, the successes. What you could do. And could not do. Even the failures. I was thinking I might want to spend more time there. And not just being in it either, crazy. Or smashed.

I looked down at my fingers lying there in my lap. I could see a remnant of blood in one of the creases at the base of my thumb. Purplish red and thin, as if a pin tip had left it. When I put my tongue to my lip it felt like it came to a huge point. Like the mouth of a turtle. That's what I was thinking about. About a turtle and his mouth and the way it is shaped. But as we drove away, it was strange and funny and fascinating, too. Because I found I was starting to worry about how my new nose was going to turn out.

IT WAS the weekend after that that my mother got this harebrained scheme. Maybe she got it because I was not fit to appear with in public, seeing as how the metal thing on my nose made me look a good bit like Hannibal Lecter in *Silence of the Lambs*. You know, when they

203

put that contraption on his face to keep him from biting everybody. And maybe my mother got the seed planted in her brain by that T-shirt she bought me down in the gift shop. Because she came up with this idea that she and I should take a mother-daughter horseback ride, out through the back pasture and down the road to the trails in the state park. Yeah, yeah, yeah. And like I said, my mother thinks she can get a book and, out of it, learn how to do anything. Mutton and Chops, our two senior citizen geldings, hadn't been ridden in over a year. Not ridden much at all in fact, since I got into high school and got so busy school-wise. They were even one second from semi-wild, if you know what I mean. Too happy to be retired and not prone to take to any piece of strapped-on leather. So my mother checked out of the library that book on horse whispering. Apparently she was hell-bent on cussing or shouting Mutton and Chops into giving us a heavenly mother-daughter ride.

We started out early in the morning, first luring the geldings into the barn with an extra dose of sweetfeed. "I think Chops has worms," my mother said, looking over the gelding's belly.

"No, I wormed him last month," I said. "He's just old—his rib cage is sprung. "

When she set the saddle on him, Chops dropped his dong and peed all over my mother's foot. "Oh, for crying out loud!" she said and went out to hose off her boot. Chops stayed spread-out like that, all four feet splayed like an old table, until my mother and I both pulled him out to the round pen. My mother started swinging on a dead tree limb, trying to break it off. "The book says to chase him until his head drops and he begins to chew, and then he'll turn to you and join up," she was telling me, about like she was passing an exam I was giving. I hadn't asked her one thing about horse whispering. I was just ready to hop on Mutton and be done with it, but my mother was out in the round pen now, chasing Chops with the tree limb.

When I walked up to watch her, and help if she screamed for it, Chops took one look at me and bolted across the round pen. He side-swiped my mother's shoulder and knocked her down. "Stump-knockin' tig-o-friggin' crazy horse!" she muttered, getting up. "He charged me."

"No, he didn't," I said. "Something spooked him. He actually tried to miss you."

She turned around and looked at me closely. Then she started this really ridiculous laugh. You know, that holding-back-but-letting-go laugh. One guffaw right after the other. And she wouldn't stop. "What? What?" I said, which got her to finally be quiet and look at me. She said she really wasn't making fun of me, but the sun really was glinting off that metal thing on my nose, and it was indeed a very credible possibility—that's what she called it, *credible possibility*—that Chops had been taken aback because of my new look.

"New look?" I said.

"Well, new-for-the-next-two-weeks look," she said.

"Yeah, well," I said, ready to let it go, because I could tell she really was pretty nervous about doing this whole horse thing.

And the way she was acting was bringing back one of the things I learned when I first got into wanting to do the horse thing and was hanging out with horse people a good bit. It was back when I was thirteen. It seemed to me that I, and everybody I was hanging out with, wanted more from a horse than he could give. Love and to take care of us and to let us ride him to just god-o-mighty anywhere. In fact, do all sorts of things, one step down from handing in our homework and dropping us off at the mall, until we were just reading all sorts of things into him. Thinking he was thinking one thing, then another, and almost always something about us. And then pretty soon I figured out that it was food, and the fear of shiny things, and an empty belly, and the longing for a herd—that was all. And I mean *all*. That ever went through a horse's head. But out in the round pen now, my mother had set her jaw. The book was open on the ground. She was totally determined that Chops would join up with her and let her become his alpha mare, then go on all the way and give her human love. Or at least do whatever she said, so she could think it was human love. And she was reading out loud, "It says here to spread open your hand and let your fingers look like a bear claw, and the horse will run even faster."

She spread both hands across her chest while Chops just stood on the other side of the round pen and ate grass.

"I think he's given up worrying about bears," I said. Then, "Why don't you ride Mutton. And I'll take Chops."

I handed her the reins. She said something like *Yeah, well maybe*. Then she pulled Mutton up to the mounting block we have out there near the round pen and got ready to swing up. As soon as she had one foot in the stirrup, Mutton moved his rear end one step to the right, which left my mother hanging in a pretty tight bluejean splits, if you know what I mean. He did it three times. Finally she said out loud and to the whole heavens that the damn horse ought to be thrown to the ground like they did in that horse whispering movie. Then, "Slip him this lump of sugar," I said, and handed her one. When Mutton started sucking on it, she swung up.

The weather had changed into something that told us this was probably going to be the last cold spell we would have. In the pasture under the tall bahia grass, there were green shoots like fistfuls of clipped ribbon. When I looked out over the length of it, it had a color like the skins of old limes—part yellow, part green, and with splotches of brown. Trees in our woods were bare, though, gray-brown bare with moss hanging in a few of them. Balls of mistletoe like giant squirrel nests were high up in some. My mother and I had on jackets that we could unzip. Before the day was over I knew we'd strip off about two layers. The sun was coming through the trees in thick shafts. Straight and yellow-white, hitting the dew and splashing it with silver. By the afternoon it was supposed to be near seventy degrees. I had a canteen over my shoulder with Gatorade in it.

Chops walked like he was part camel, the front part doing a waltz, the back part trying out a cha cha. My mother's red jacket weaved on ahead. At this point she was too scared to be talking, because I was certain the only dream Mutton ever had was to be a stallion at the front of a herd. He was walking and half trotting, and toying around with galloping all out. Which was keeping my mother one second from screaming and jumping off. But she wasn't going to let that out into public, or at least the public of me. Oh, no. Not come hell or high water, as she herself liked to say. She was playing cowgirl on a Saturday, as if later an Acting committee was going to hand out awards.

At the back pasture gate, she was busy getting Mutton to line up next to it, so as to let her open it without getting off. Or cussing too many times. She was aiming him up sideways to the latch, telling him he was going to do this come hell or high water. I stopped and just sat on Chops. Then I looked back and saw Stella, and then the other two dogs, and Spam, and the peacocks, and two of the cats, following. All of them were splitting paths through the tall yellow bahia.

We went through the woods. Then came out on the other side. We were ready to open the back gate to the road and head to the park trails. But my mother held Mutton back with a fistful of reins. She was waiting for me to catch up. By now she, too, knew there were more of us than just me on Chops and her on Mutton to head down the road. Spam and the dogs could squeeze under the fence, and the peacocks could fly over. That would be a mess, not to mention somewhat of an embarrassing display, going down the shoulder of a public highway with our whole menagerie following. "You know, I think it'd be nice to just ride around through the woods, don't you?" she said.

"Oh, yeah," I answered. Then uncorked the Gatorade.

My mother unzipped her jacket. Underneath she had on a long-sleeved T-shirt and a leather belt. There was a bracelet on her wrist that she'd had on almost every day since Christmas. But what really caught my attention was that her shirt was on backwards. And her belt missed every one of her jean loops but one, so they looked hiked up and crooked. I didn't say anything. It worried me, though. In fact, it scared me, to tell the truth.

We headed back through the woods. We circled and looped through them about half a dozen times. I think Mutton was excited about the herd he really was leading, seeing as how the dogs and Spam and one of the cats were still following. The peacocks had taken to the pasture fence and from there were watching us pass as we made each of our circles. Two of the cats were lying down in piles of leaves. Mutton never settled down. He jigged and jogged and rattled my mother's teeth until she said she understood fully why cars were invented. We stopped for a rest at our neighbor's fence, where his back acreage was planted in pine trees for lumber.

I handed my mother the canteen. She put it straight up and drank from it. Some of the orange liquid ran down her chin. Chops licked it off my mother's thigh as it dripped onto her jeans. Mutton stood still, for once. That was the nicest thing about him. He didn't mind Chops getting close or licking things off his rider's thigh, as long as he had some leather somewhere over his head strapped on to remind him to behave. "Oh, look," my mother said, suddenly pointing up. The angle of the tipped canteen had let her see it before me. At first I thought it was a buzzard. Thought, too, how fitting that'd be—a buzzard flying over us. Making circles. Turning back. Looping over us.

"Oh, but don't you see?" my mother said. "The white head? The feet? It is. It is!"

Her excitement made me look again. And when I did, I, too, realized that it was an eagle. I had seen only one other one in my whole life. I mean, one time when it was out free. And wild. But recently Mr. Whitstruck in Biology had told us how the population of them was coming back. There were supposed to be about two thousand of them somewhere now, living in our part of the state.

"What a wonderful gift," my mother said, "to be here today and to see this."

I kept my eyes pointed up, but the eagle wasn't all that I was seeing. That's not what really stayed with me. For I kept seeing the flapping label of my mother's shirt. And her hiked-up jeans. When we got back to the barn, after I got off of Chops and was ready to lead him in, I looked up, though. And that eagle was still there. Still flying around. Seemingly going nowhere. Not to somewhere like I would have thought. Not like how the egrets were out over the pasture. Or the crows. Or sparrows. Or finches. Going somewhere, then coming back, some obvious errand on their minds. All business. No. Not the eagle. Not him. Instead he was seemingly on no business. He had stayed up the whole time we rode back to the house. And now as I glanced up, he was still swooping and diving. Circling and gliding. Out of nothing. Not anything. I'd never seen anything like that. The word that came into my mind was *joy*. He was doing it out of nothing but joy. I never thought I could think like that.

"YOU DIDN'T?" Dr. Cone is in a yellow blazer. Black pants, too. The clinical coat looks recently starched. Earlier, she had given a lecture to some students, her secretary had told me. Because she'd been a little late to see me, and I'd had to wait. And so that is when she gets a double-dip of starch in the coat, I guess. And the dark of her pants brings out what there is of the same color in her hair. So that it seems she is framed at the top and at the bottom with a darkness like tilled earth.

"No," I replied.

"It takes time," she says. "And the feeling, too, will come and go. You just have to wait until it circles back again."

"I guess," I say.

Through all the parts of what I have just told her, she has laughed like I myself am sitting behind a desk running a late-night talk show. Her laughter is like water, warm water, going up and down and all over on me. I hunt for it now. Go after it like I am in woods and camouflage gear.

"So what did you write in your notebook this week?"

"Not a whole lot. But I did make a short list of all I did wrong."

"Intentionally wrong, I hope," she says. For she has given me the job of messing up on at least three things, then writing down what happens after I do them. I hand her my notebook. She moves to sit beside me so when she turns the pages, we can both see what she reads. *Turned down the wrong street on the way to school and had to turn around.* She flips over to the next page to see what I have written down under the title she gave me: *Repercussions. Was two minutes late and had to go to the office and get a tardy slip for Christ's sake.*

"Okay," she says, flipping the page back. "That one cost something. But not a whole lot, really."

Wore my watch upside down for two days, she reads next. Then, *Fed the cats dog food and the dogs cat food. Wore a Reebok on my right foot and a Nike on my left and went all day like that. Then made out applications for college and mailed them. But left off the stamps.*

She looks up. "What are you going to do when they come back?"

"I don't know. Maybe they won't."

"Oh, but they always do. The post office is the biggest stickler in the universe. They'll get you for the lack of a penny or an ounce over the limit."

"I guess I'll decide at that point," I say.

She turns and faces me. "What did you think of this homework? Did it start to make you feel you could make mistakes and everything would still be okay?"

"Yeah. I guess. Yeah, maybe. But I wonder?"

"What?"

On my mind is that day my mother and I had gone on that horseback ride, and my mother's backward shirt and belt that had missed its belt loops, so I ask, "Did you give this same homework to my mother?"

Dr. Cone smiles. She gets up and goes to her desk and opens the top drawer. "I can't answer that. You know I'm sworn to secrecy." Then she hands me a book of stamps.

FIFTEEN

Leslie

I wanted to apologize to Doug. I *needed* to, for the way I had blasted him in the E.R. over the note he'd sent me while I was in court, which had certainly done nothing to endear me to him, to say the least. In fact, it had pretty much amounted to throwing a whole new bucket of ice water on what was not exactly a warm and fuzzy relationship in the first place. And the hysterics he'd pushed me to by letting my imagination run away with me over his note made me feel like Stella when she forgets how to be housebroken. I was working on *calm*. I had ordered *calm*. I'd put it on my Visa card a hundred million times. Besides, Dr. Cone was saying over and over (like Chinese water torture, drip, drip, drip, on our foreheads) that we have to communicate, Doug and I. So here I go, ready to take the risk, to learn how to talk to each other, no matter what. I called him from my office near the end of the day.

"Doug?"

"Yes?" Blindfolded, and with only one word, I could have picked him out of any police lineup—that baritone close to a low G.

"I'd like to talk to you."

"Fine."

"So can I come over?"

"Sure."

"When?"

"How about a little before five?"

"Good. I'll be right there."

It was no more than a ten minute drive.

Doug's office is the top floor of an old frame house downtown near the post office. Below him is a lawyer who likes Victorian. So Doug has gotten to show his stuff by renovating and redesigning the second floor to look like the inside of a spaceship, which, if you ask me, seems to be his hidden desire of where he really wants to live. His waiting area is black tile with a red and black rug on it, black leather couches and chrome tables. One whole wall has been knocked out so that a round window of slick glass looks down onto people pulling into the post office. Mindy Sparks, his new secretary, was behind a white desk with headphones for a telephone. Everything he designs is supermodern—at least for himself, and if he is given free rein—metal and tile and marble and glass just about everywhere. The framed photographs of buildings hanging on the wall behind Mindy testify to this.

"Can you please tell Doug I am here?" I said.

"Sure, but can I use a name?"

It was hard to realize she didn't know who I was. Recently Vicky had told me that Doug had a new secretary, a pregnant mother of three who on Saturdays sings country at a club downtown called The Potted Geranium. I guess I'd been to Doug's office so rarely (and no photographs here with me in them—only Dylan, Bergin, and Vicky) that to Mindy I was an unrelated stranger. And that alone made me feel strange, to be so wiped out of Doug's life. "I'm Leslie," I said.

"So?"

"Leslie—Bergin's mother."

"Oh."

I stood there in my navy blue power suit, watching her hit the buzz button on her telephone. "Mr. Talbot, your ex is here." And then she looked at me. "He says he'll be just a minute. He's just finishing up a phone call."

I walked over and sat down on the black couch. Mindy started humming "Sleeping Single in a Double Bed," while clearing off things on her desk and clearly getting ready to leave.

Doug appeared in the door—black pants, loafers, a white shirt, a red tie. Every bit of him seemed groomed to high heaven and worthy of a magazine ad. He ushered me into his office, his hands doing all the talking, pointing the way, then pulling up a swing-like black leather chair that, when I sat down in, took the gabardine of my skirt and made it slide. "I came here to apologize," I said.

He sat down behind his desk. "For what?"

"Blasting you in the E.R. over that note."

"Oh. *That* was a good bit out of control."

"But you do understand, don't you?"

"What? That I can count on you to lose it like that in any stressful situation?"

"I'm not here to fight."

"What else do you do?"

"I'm here to apologize."

"Go ahead then."

"I'm sorry."

He looked straight at me. For a moment neither of us said anything else, and then he looked off to the side, at the wall where there were more framed photographs of buildings. "This has been so hard," he said.

I thought he was talking about our conversation, about me being there and the ultimatum it seemed we were under from Dr. Cone. It seemed he couldn't go on, either. Clearly he was struggling for words, or at least struggling more than usual.

"I shouldn't have jumped to so many conclusions," I added.

He looked at me. And then, "You were right, though. I didn't think out my note very carefully. I just wish you hadn't let me know about it in front of so many people."

"That's what I'm apologizing about."

He looked again at me very slowly, very steadily. "How are you doing?"

"Oh, fair, I guess."

"I don't see any end to this."

"Oh, let's just call it even." I stood up. I knew Lydia would be starting supper, and I'd promised Kirk I'd bring home a kit for a glider airplane that I could pick up in a Jiffy store.

"No. I mean an end to what has happened."

I looked back at him. He put his head in his hands and leaned toward his desk.

I'd never seen Doug do anything like this. I'd never seen him wear any emotion this clearly.

"I think she's better," I said. "I think things are much better, in fact."

He looked up at me. "I've never had anything take me over like this. Our daughter. That child I once held. Bergin. Who is she?"

I sat back down.

He looked at me and asked, "Can we go out to dinner and talk about this? It doesn't have to be anything elaborate, or for very long— pizza or a burger. Something like that."

I nodded. How could I say no?

He grabbed his suit coat and again ushered me with his hands. I'd rarely seen him move this fast. He told Mindy to please lock up, that he'd see her tomorrow. And then he led me through the waiting room and out to the parking lot to his car.

AS WE GOT in and he drove, I pulled out of my purse the cellular phone I'd gotten in the last week. I couldn't take the chance of being given another note in court or anywhere that could make the bottom of my life drop out, not again, not any more. I'd learned my limits. And even though I knew I couldn't take the phone into court with me, it still made me feel a little more in charge. But I sure hated like the devil to think how much it was going to cost me, as well as to make my life more hectic. I dialed home now, and Maggie answered.

"What's Lydia planning for supper?"

"Something stinky. Where are you?"

"On my way to do a little more business. Is Bergin home?"

"Yeah. Daddy too."

"What's Bergin doing?"

"In her room on the computer."

"Well, tell everybody I won't be there for supper. But I'll be there in time to put you to bed."

She yelled off to the side then, "Take Mama's name out of the pot." And then I could hear Kirk's voice in the distance, and then Maggie said to me, "Kirk says not to forget to get him the airplane."

"I won't," I said, after which Maggie told me that Jack and Lydia were making meat loaf and broccoli and mashed potatoes, and that the broccoli was making the house smell like horse gas, and that Daddy was going back to work for only an hour and would probably beat me home. "Fine," I said, and hung up, or rather turned the power off and put the phone back in my purse. By then, without my being aware of it, Doug had pulled into the parking lot of the Pizza Palace and was now parking in a spot two rows from the door. I didn't say anything; pizza was fine with me. But the memory of being there with Bergin the night she told me she wanted to move out of Doug's house and back home with me—and that I had said yes, sure, wonderful, but *she* had to tell him, not me—were whispers stored in the brick and wood, none of which could I block from my hearing. "This okay?" Doug opened his car door.

"Sure. Fine." I hauled out my purse, which seemed to be getting bigger every day.

Doug ordered a pepperoni pizza with extra cheese. I ordered a salad and promised him that, yes, I'd share part of his pizza with him. Then he looked at me and spoke first, which startled me. "I still don't understand. What did we do that made Bergin so desperate?"

I looked at him, then down at my fingers. I was trying to think of exactly what I could say, and how. But then he took over my silence and said, "I know what Dr. Cone has said, that she felt trapped, and that you had told her she had to tell me she wanted to move out, and that she said she couldn't tell me because it would hurt my feelings, but, what does that mean? What does all that exactly mean?"

His eyes were steadily aimed on my face. He had folded his arms in front of him on the table. He had gray hair on his temples now like someone had made small white paint strokes. And his eyes have deep creases beside them. He loosened his tie. He seemed so desperate to understand, or to feel peace, to be freed from all that had happened, that I felt intimidated. I can't say, either, that what moved through my mind was logical or sensible, or how it moved as quickly as it did, seeing as how the feelings were so complicated and layered with what felt like a fast-forwarded series of dreams, dream-memories of all the years we had known each other. But yes, I felt grateful to him and grief at the same time, grateful that he had known me when I was growing up, grateful that he had known my father, grief that he was the only one in my life now who did. In fact, there was so much history between us that I felt exploded by it, stripped by it, hungry for it to exist between Jack and me and not Doug and me. But it was Doug who owned my youth and the joy of Bergin's birth and what the actual presence of my father had been like. I was known to him in a way that I could never be known by anyone else. That alone would connect us forever. Nothing could ever change or diminish that.

To this place, too, I was joined, and always would be: this place where we were sitting where I had made such a drastic mistake without knowing that I was making a drastic mistake. I was also having move through my mind the awareness of all the times I had sat with someone I was legally defending while they searched to understand what they had done wrong—or at the least, what they had done to get caught—as well as how to undo things. I thought even of Hoot and the times I had dug him out of trouble, the cars he had wrecked, the injuries of one magnitude or another, that he had caused over all the years of his drinking.

And if there is one thing I know certainly from having seen it over and over, in the human mind there is a space, a place where by necessity thoughts will not go, or if at all, not go deeply, but will instead skip over when trying to comprehend pain for which one is responsible. As if, *if* that mind did go there, it could no longer exist. Going on would no longer be an option. As if, *if* the pain comes in, it will do so only in seconds long stretched out one from the other, flying in, but not really touching down, no not down, never really down, but only heading off again, so as to allow the mind to go on at all.

And so I wanted to avoid telling Doug about what part the place we were in had played, for both of our sakes. And what exactly I had said and he had said that had brought us to this place in our lives. I could have been reluctant to answer Doug, too, because I was so conditioned in knowing that if I spoke what I thought to be the truth, he could deny that it was, and not just that it was the mind defending itself, but that (of course) was our pattern. But it was also more even than that. For the despair I could sense so close to spreading and taking over the whole of him scared me off.

For a moment I considered trying to turn things light, to say something to the effect that Bergin was at *that age*, you know, of raging hormones and all of that, and how sensitive that can make a woman—by God, take me as an example. And I knew he would smile at that, and I knew, too, that after I said it, I would feel like a traitor to my own sex. And so all I did, all I could think of doing, was to reach over and touch his hand and say, "I think you're more important to Bergin than you realize."

He looked at me and said back, "I don't know. I don't understand any of it. I don't know that I ever will."

On the tip of my tongue—for it was habit—was *Damn right on that*. For I knew no way to tell Doug how he left me and Bergin emotionally thirsty, time and time again. And maybe it was not him as much as us. But he was the keeper of my youth, and our history, and I felt protective. So instead I gave him something safe. "Time. Time will make all of this better."

He looked off and signaled to our waiter. "I'm just glad I never had any more." For a minute, I thought he was talking about the pizza. For that's how I think of Doug, speaking so elliptically that it can feel as if at times you are playing charades. But then he added, "Dylan is Vicky's and that leaves me pretty much out of it. Besides, Carl is his real father, and that's where the real responsibility lies."

I added, "You're talking about *children*, aren't you? "

"Yes. And thank God I don't intend to ever have any more. Thank God, too, you and I never had another one."

"But thank goodness we had this one." I slid out of the booth.

"This one was enough." He paid for the meal, and I thanked him.

"And she's turning out just fine," I added, saying it for the good of both of us, knowing, too, that he was enjoying the darkness of his mood so much that he was probably going to hold onto it for a good long while.

Doug drove me back to my car where I had parked it in his office's parking lot. By the time we got there, it *did* seem that a lot of stiffness had been eased between us. We vowed to talk more and to stay good friends, that we would practice whatever Dr. Cone told us to do. Then when I got home, Jack told me that he had promised the twins that he and I would build a swimming pool and have it full of water by their next birthday, which was three months away. Ordinarily I might would have felt like killing him—seeing as how he'd done the promising without consulting me. But as Bergin came in and took out of the refrigerator a can of Sprite and popped off its tab, she asked me, "Did he tell you who was going to build it?"

"No. But I'm sure he knows a good company."

She laughed. She took a deep swallow of Sprite while looking at me, smiling, smiling, *smiling*. It was an ironic smile. Clearly she was teasing me, teasing me about something, and then after a good long silence that was filled with her looking at me as her smile went crooked up one side of her face, she said, "He told us all at supper. Went over every step of a plan that he wrote down as he thought it up. *We're* going to do it. You, me, him and the twins. He called tonight and rented Mr. Collins's backhoe. He's going to drive it over here tomorrow."

That was a whole different reason for wanting to kill him. It was proof, as Bergin was wanting to point out, that indeed Jack could be impulsive and nutty, that we were indeed a family that could provide stories for other families to pass around at their dinner tables. But as I thought more fully about all of us digging a deep hole in the ground and then filling it in with bright and sparkling water that we would all get into and cool off in—well, somehow it just totally appealed to me.

THAT WAS last week. Now I am standing here having a Sprite in Jack's and my bedroom, looking out the window at the backyard while rain comes down like the north pole has thawed. The rented backhoe sits stuck in mud halfway up its tires. The blade on our tractor, which is what Jack had me drive, is resting in a puddle beside the hole we have dug—Jack and I—while we kept Kirk and Maggie and Bergin busy and involved by stacking rocks. I don't know when we'll be able to get back to work, the ground is such a soup. The backhoe is costing us by the hour, too, which is making me, if not Jack, a nervous wreck. Not that he's exactly quick when he *is* on it. For he learned to drive heavy equipment during a summer in college, and he likes to show off by making the shovel go up and down, up and down, like it is dancing to the music coming out of the barn. He also plants the backhoe's little metal sucker-like feet, up and down, up and down, too, as if it thinks the ground is hot. The twins, and Bergin at times, have laughed, which only eggs Jack on more. If we don't break ourselves or our digging equipment before this pool is dug, I will be as surprised as Spam when he is asleep under his azalea and the sprinklers come on and spray him.

Today Bergin is staying late at school to tutor somebody in biology. The twins are in the kitchen with Lydia, making cookies. Jack will be here in a minute. The rain here on the bedroom window streams down like braids in hair, and I can see the balsa wood airplane that I brought Kirk stuck in the leaves of a tree where the rain taps it, moves it slightly, but where it seems stuck for good.

The phone rings. I hear Maggie answer it in the kitchen. Now she is calling for me. I pick it up on the bedside table, here on the side where I sleep. "Hello?"

222

"Leslie, it's Doug."

"Are you okay?"

"I'm fine. I'm just calling to ask a favor."

"Sure. Shoot."

"Vicky's got this idea. Well, she's already made reservations. This weekend is our anniversary . . ."

"Congratulations."

"Yeah. Well, it's Dylan's weekend to be with Carl over in Palm Key. And Vicky thinks it'd be okay if he drives over there in her car. He's had his learner's permit for three weeks now. And we were going to have Mrs. Holloway come stay with Dylan, and she could be his designated driver, but then, well . . ."

"I know what you're thinking. Mrs. Holloway's not exactly the person Dylan would want in the front seat. A seventy-year-old babysitter? And besides, what would Carl do with her over in Palm Key?"

"Exactly. So . . ."

"Yeah?"

"Do you think I could ask Bergin to do it—to drive over with Dylan this weekend and stay there Saturday night at Carl's and then drive back with him?"

"I don't see why not. She doesn't have any big plans that I know of."

"Well, will you ask her first then?"

"You mean prime the way?"

"I don't want to ask her if you think it'll upset her, or if she'll really want to say no and feel like she can't. Or . . ."

"Doug, we can't always treat her like she will break."

"Why?"

"Because Dr. Cone says so."

Then Vicky comes on the phone. "Oh, Leslie, thanks so much. This would be so great if Bergin does this. I mean, it will just absolutely make Dylan the happiest boy in the whole world. Can't you just see him driving all the way over to Palm Key in my car, just about like he's on his own? I mean, having Bergin with him will look so cool. Why should I be the only one to be so happy this weekend? Can't you just imagine what this will do for Dylan?"

After saying yeah, sure, and no, not at all, I don't mind a bit, I'll talk to Bergin about it, feel her out. And oh yeah, congratulations on the anniversary, what was it now, the sixth? "No, seventh," Vicky says, then thanks me again and hangs up.

Through the back bedroom window I look out at the rain. I see Bergin's car drive up and pull next to the overhang at the barn—windshield wipers beating like a bird flying hard. Any minute now, she will get out and run to the house, and I am standing here, holding my breath, looking out, wanting that, wanting to see that, wanting to just hold the sight of that up against my chest and breathe it in all through me, so that forever I will have it. Just happy and thankful that I can.

SIXTEEN

Bergin

B abysitting Dylan, as you might say. At least stay with him for pretty much a whole weekend. Be his designated driver, as they call it. Which pretty much boils down to being strapped into the death seat of Miss Vicky LaTour's *for Christ's sakes big as a boat* Lincoln Town Car. Made a lot of sense, when you really thought about it. Seeing as how after my few swing steps with St. Peter, I was the one most likely to be fearless to the bone.

I learned about the whole plan as soon as I'd gotten in the house that day, when my dad—or rather Miss Vicky—had thought it up. My mother met me at the back door and clued me in—how my dad and Miss Vicky were going off on a little happy anniversary weekend. That's what she called it. And would I, what would I think about . . . Sure, I said, which was the truth. Fine and okay, I'd be more than happy to do it. Except I had a soccer team car wash and couldn't leave till in the afternoon.

Truth is, I was figuring if I babysat Dylan, I wouldn't be expected to work all weekend on that mud-hole of a swimming pool. The backhoe is still sunk like a yellow spider sprayed with Raid.

So then my dad calls that night. "Did your mother talk to you about staying with Dylan this weekend?"

"Yeah. Sure. That's fine. I'll do it." I said.

And then him again, "You don't mind?"

"Naw."

"Well, we really appreciate it—Vicky and I." And then Miss Vicky herself got on the phone and pretty much gave me the whole rundown on how the weekend. Every minute. Every movement was supposed to go. Sounded to me like being with Dylan was going to get close to taking care of a high-strung poodle.

She said she'd leave me some written notes and pocket money. In the kitchen by the sink. Emergency phone numbers and all of that.

Already it was 4 P.M. I drove my car over to my dad's after he and Miss Vicky were already gone. I didn't even have to go into the house. The last thing I ever wanted to do was to go into that house. I didn't need the pocket money. And I didn't want to read how-to-take-care-of-the-poodle instructions. I just knocked on the glass back door where I could see Dylan on the couch spread out like a spill, watching MTV and waiting for me.

So Dylan and I got into the Town Car. And I strapped myself into the death seat. The seat belts—both of them. The chest one. And the lap one. Both had dried mustard and catsup on them from I guess Miss Vicky. And Dylan himself on the way to some soccer game or other. Or else one of Miss Vicky's clients, going with her through some drive-thru and eating on the way to some house she was going to decorate to high heaven. "I think your new nose looks nice," Dylan said as he cranked up the car. Dylan backed out of the drive the way Miss Vicky had taught him to—one hand on the back of the front seat, his head turned all the way around like an owl's, and his feet doing a pitty-pat dance on the brake and the accelerator. So we were backing out like the car had a deep hacking cough.

I didn't want to talk about my nose. And his driving style, or rather Miss Vicky's driving style passed on, was indeed holding my attention.

"Does it hurt anymore?" Dylan asked. It was true, my nose was still a little blue at the bridge.

"Naw."

I really wasn't hot on keeping up a conversation. I planned to listen to my Walkman all the way to Palm Key. There must be something the biology books never tell you. Or don't yet know. About the male species and cars. About how their hormones must be connected. Since when a guy gets a driver's license, right away, there's a surge. And it was just like Dylan, too, to think that driving a car big as a boat was cool. Probably he was hoping a whole lot of people he knew would see him. But frankly I was holding my breath and trying to keep my face hidden by the sun visor. And if Dylan wrecked us both, I had my hand ready to pull out of my purse my driver's license and insurance card to show that we really were legal. It was just a crying shame that people like Dylan, fifteen, big as anybody but denser than anyone, could sit behind the wheel of something so almighty powerful as Miss Vicky's Lincoln Town Car, aimed to where it could blast anyone off the highway.

I put a Puff Daddy CD into the slot and plugged myself in.

My nose *had* turned out a little different. I'd been hoping for a hump in it, something that could be a conversation piece. But instead it got shortened.

"Don't turn right on red, here," I said. And then two seconds later, "Don't change lanes, either. Just stay where you are."

I was starting to remind myself of my own mother when she was teaching me. And that's not pretty.

What I remembered about the only other time I'd been to Palm Key. Which was when I was nearly twelve. And my mother had been going out with Jack and they had driven over to the Gulf and had taken me one night there to supper. Fish. All fish. Every restaurant there sells fish. Almost nothing but fish. The drive is so empty of anything but road. Long monotonous, lonely road. On and on, just seemingly forever. Black pavement straight as a rope pulled tight. And ditches on either side, so you pray you do not fall off. With long stretches of no houses, or buildings at all. Just scrub pine and swamp and road and ditches and weeds. The boredom could kill you. Boredom could make you eat the insides of your mouth off. Or lick the window panes. At least if you're a kid and in the back seat.

It is fifty-five minutes of straight-aimed road with those deep ditches on either side. And only two little towns. Well, not really little towns like you might think. One's just a four-way stop with a shutdown filling station on the corner. The other is a crossroads with a post office. So there are miles between anywhere safe to turn around. It is like after you make the decision to go, you can't change your mind until you get there.

It's an easy drive, too. And perfect for Dylan. For if you can aim straight, you're bound to get there.

As soon as we were almost to the highway, Dylan looked over at me and said, "You thirsty?"

"Not especially," I said.

"Well, I am," he announced. Then jerked the car into a filling station that was being turned into half of a grocery. Studs were nailed up to one side. The concrete foundation had been extended to equal more than twice what had been there. Dylan went into the part that was still open. And came out with a bag of chips and a Coke. Miss Vicky had already made sure we'd been tanked up with gas. I think, too, she'd had the car washed. It smelled a little like a vanilla bean spray.

I doubted Dylan could drive and eat at the same time. He made me nervous. The way he put the chips between his legs. And the Coke in the drink holder between us.

By the time we drove through a little town called Archer, the Coke and chips were gone. And we were still alive. Then, "Okay," I said to Dylan. "You can pick it up to fifty-five."

He slouched down and straightened out his leg. Speed was both what he had a crush on and what could scare the bejesus out of him. You could tell. He had on gray Janco jeans and Reeboks the size of rabbits. Over the last month, he'd gotten a new haircut. A bowl. Or a skater, with the sides and back shaved so the rest hangs straight like an orange cut in half. There was a fuzz on his upper lip as if a cat had sat on his face and shed.

I stayed plugged in. And he kept switching stations on the radio. As we moved away from what felt like a little civilization. To the straight flat pavement that we could not see the end of. The four-thirty sky was gray from the showers left from the front that had just come through. The road was every bit of how I remembered it. And then some. Swamps or else walls of woods stretched away on either side of us. Telephone poles on the grass shoulder stretched in a line. The wood of the poles was bleached to the color of light toast. Dylan kept experimenting with his driving stance. First one hand on the top of the wheel while the other played with the radio. Next, one hand on the bottom of the wheel while the other tapped the radio rhythm on his thigh. I felt stuck to the velvet seat. The wind whipped the new leaves on the trees so that their undersides faced the road. Gray-green and thin. Their newness seemed tender. Then I realized the wind was not all that was whipping. "My god, Dylan," I yelled. "Look at the speedometer." He'd gotten us up to eighty without even a clue.

"This thing practically goes by itself, doesn't it?" he asked and looked at me.

"Look at the road," I said.

He held both of his big feet up off the floor. The car then coasted back to fifty. I felt like saying *yeah*. That the car was smarter than he'd ever be. But I'm not usually mean by nature. I prefer premeditated meanness.

We were on the other side of a town called Bronson, in no-man's land. Dylan started complaining that the car was pulling to the right. "Well, hold it to the left," I said. I was sure he was making it all up. Just looking for things to complain about. Something to talk about. Something to drive me nuts about. But then, "Look," he said, after a few more miles, "I'm not kidding." He lifted his hands off the steering wheel. We did a sharp swerve to the right. And if I hadn't grabbed the wheel. I think we'd have ended in the ditch.

"For crying out loud!" I yelled. "Don't do anything that stupid."

"But it's pulling. See. It's pulling to the right. And bad."

"You didn't just make it do that?"

"Hell, no." By then we could hear this *boopety-boop* sound.

"Pull over," I said.

"Where?"

"Anywhere."

"There's nowhere."

It was true. There was only a strip of grass on either side of the pavement that then fell away to a ditch that was full from the recent rain. So there was almost no shoulder. At least no shoulder big enough for Miss Vicky's frigging boat. We maybe could get two of the wheels off, but not all four. And not all four on solid ground.

"There," I said, pointing. Every once in a while a grass road would be cut off into the side of a swamp or woods. A gate and a sign across it. A place where hunters could go during deer season. Or duck season. Hell, *some* season. Hunting camps, I think they're called.

We whizzed by the one I'd pointed to. Or rather, boopety-booped past it. "What're you doing?" I yelled.

"I can't just stop without planning it. I got to know ahead of time."

"Yeah, right," I said. The last thing I thought I could handle would be to be broken down on a road like this with Dylan. Who for God's sakes didn't know his own backside from his front. Much less a tire jack from a spark plug. Not that I did either. And that's what really worried me. I was in charge. I was all we had. I leaned forward, squinting into the setting sun. I was desperate for the next hunting camp road.

"There. See it. There's another one, I think. Stop there. Pull in there."

"Okay. Okay."

By now we were going about two miles per hour, so what did he have to plan for? I guess, though, the boat was hard to steer.

He pulled onto the grass road. A culvert was under us, filled with water. It was a metal pipe big enough for a rhino to walk through. It was sandbagged into place with so many bags it reminded me of army foxholes I'd seen in war movies. Dylan and I both got out at the same time. He walked around to my side, and we looked down at the tire. It was about four inches from being totally flat. It looked to me like the hubcap was bent, too.

I squatted. Dylan did, too. I don't know what for. I don't think either of us really knew what we were looking for. But then Dylan ran his hand over something in the tread. It was a screw. A flat screw head with a slit in it where a screwdriver could go.

Miss Vicky must have picked it up at a building site. Or more likely, Dylan at the filling station crossbred with the grocery where we'd stopped.

"What'da we do now?" he said. "Call the Lincoln dealer?"

"Maybe." I was trying to think this through.

"They're supposed to come get you. Any time. Any place."

I hate to admit he was thinking quicker than me. I opened the car door and pulled out my purse. My mother had given me her cell phone, and insisted I bring it, so I pulled it out now and dialed 411. "Get a pencil and paper, quick," I told Dylan. Then dictated to him the phone number the operator gave me.

But when I called, the Lincoln dealer was closed. By now it was nearly five o'clock on a Saturday afternoon. Then I think it was the way the place got to me. The isolation of it. The occasional car that whizzed by, slowed a minute, then went on with its rubber-tire sound on the flat pavement. It all made me nervous. Nervous as hell. And afraid. Scared shitless, to tell the truth. Maybe my imagination was running away with me. Maybe I'd seen too many movies. But the thought that one of the cars would stop. That there would be some-one mean in it. Someone who looked bred out of the swamps. Or who never appeared otherwise in daylight. And it was dusk now and so time to come out. And they would work us over one way or another.

One way or another, we would not come away from this road the same way we were now. And I didn't want that. I didn't want anyone to stop. I didn't want anything to happen to either of us that I didn't orchestrate. That's the word that came to me, for some strange reason. Some dumb reason I cannot say, it was *orchestrate* that I thought about. So okay, I was going to *orchestrate* getting Dylan and me out of this mess. And the first thing that came to my mind was to look busy. Look like we were okay, and could handle this. We had it under con-trol, so no one would have an excuse to stop. And if they did, we could say *go away*. We were doing fine. Just fine. "So okay, open the trunk and get the jack," I said to Dylan.

I guess I'd seen a tire changed about once in my whole frigging life. And it was Jack who had done it. Once in the last three years when his farm truck blew a tire when we went for hay. And I had sat on the side of the road while he changed it. Sat there and watched him change it.

It was the eeriest feeling in the world, being where we were. Dylan and me. Not a soul around, except for that occasional car that would whiz by. And the ditch on either side of us. And the culvert like a sign of war or a bomb plant under us. The wet sand of where we were parked had clumps of grass in it like unruly hair. Vines climbed a scrawny tree next to the hood of the car. A barbed wire fence separated us from the rest of the swampy woods. The fence posts were like rotten teeth, stumped and leaning. Palmetto and scrub spikes were yellowish green, as ugly as a half-chewed onion. On the side of the ditch was a twelve-pack beer cover faded to a peachy pink. And the chain locked across the side road like a gate had a sign. *No Trespassing. Prohibida La Entrada.*

"Look," Dylan said, pointing to it. "Is that Spanish?"

"No, Polish," I said. He looked at me and sneered. "Just get the jack," I said.

"Sure. I guess you know everything about changing a tire, right?" He said it sarcastic. We had one rhythm now, mean and short.

"No. But I can figure it out."

"Right, Miss Einstein."

"Stuff it and get the jack," I said.

"I think we ought to call a tow truck."

"And wait an hour while it gets here? It's going to be dark in a minute. And I don't want to be here. Do you?"

He was silent. Then punched the keyless entry code on Miss Vicky's door handle that then popped up the trunk. We walked around to the back of the car. The trunk was big enough to stuff a whole little league baseball team into. I'd never seen a trunk that big in my whole life. It had a little shelf up under the back seat, and that's where the spare tire was. I had to crawl into the whale trunk to just

233

reach it. I sat there with the trunk hood popped up over me and Dylan holding it with one hand while an occasional car whizzed by. So I was feeling even more stupid and ridiculous, sitting in that trunk, trying to figure this out. The floor was covered in gray carpet, and the spare tire had even a little circle of carpet over it. And on top of it was a pair of white gloves, great-god-o-mighty I'm not kidding, with blue rubber dots on them that were supposed to help with your grip, I guess. I felt around for the jack and found it wrapped up in a black rubber case, like something a Town Car carried just for looks. It was clear it'd never been used.

Dylan's silence told me he was getting as uneasy as I was. I crawled out of the trunk holding the jack.

He was reading the small print on the sign on the chain-gate. *A conviction can mean a fine and/or prison term.* That was in English, just his speed. A big truck passed with a sound like a *whoosh*, like the sound of a sudden hard rain. The silence it left was more silent than before it had come.

I unwrapped the jack and held it in my hands.

There was this one long crowbar-looking thing with a tag attached, and a heavy-as-hell jack that itself somewhat resembled a grasshopper waiting to hop. "That's a tire iron," Dylan said, pointing to the crowbar thing. And then I saw it was not a tag but a little yellow envelope attached. There were a lot of black smudges across it, so I had to look hard to read it. *Your new vehicle has a locking lug nut feature. Each wheel has one locking nut which requires a special keyed tool for removal. This fool*—which I had to look twice to see was really *tool—is attached to the lug wrench.* On the back of the envelope the same thing was written in French, of all things. Or I guess it was the same thing. But I was, at least, sure it was French.

"So okay. All right." I said to Dylan. "Pop off the hubcap and let's get going."

"We ought to jack it up first," he said.

"Maybe. Maybe not. But okay. Let's do it." Then I saw all this orange writing on the jack.

"Give it here," Dylan said. "I know how to do it."

"How?"

"I've seen people do it."

"Yeah, sure. In the movies?"

He reached for it, but for the life of me I couldn't let go until I read every bit of the orange writing. And since he was waiting now with one leg held at a slant, and a sour twist to his mouth like I was stupid and prim and totally unfit to ever work anywhere outside of a library, I read it out loud. *"To help avoid personal injury, turn off ignition, set parking brake."* I looked up at Dylan. "Well, the engine's off. But set the brake," I said.

He reached inside and did it while I read step two. *"Turn off air suspension switch located in trunk prior to jacking car."* I looked again at Dylan. "So pop the trunk again and let's find it."

"Okay, okay."

I couldn't believe Miss Vicky owned such a complicated car.

"Follow jacking instructions in the Owner's Manual."

"So get it," I said to Dylan. And then I let out a laugh. *Jacking instructions.* God-o-mighty, it sounded like we were getting set to do something outright sexual on the side of the highway. Dylan reached inside the glove compartment and started rooting around. *"Use jack only for lifting this vehicle during wheel change."* Then I added just for the hell of it. "In other words don't use it to smack the driver of the car who ran over the screw that blew your tire in the first place." Dylan looked at me like he could kill me and threw the car manual at my feet. Finally I read the last warning: *"Never get beneath the vehicle when supported by jack.* No problem," I said, then noticed that the exact same warnings were written out on the jack handle in French, too. Either a lot of French people owned cars like Miss Vicky's. Or it was mostly French people who had flats. "Go ahead," I said to Dylan, handing him the jack and then bending under the car with him to see how it would go.

Dylan turned the crank on the jack and the car really did go up in the air. And then for the life of me I never would have said it could happen, but Dylan knew how to get the hubcap off. And the lug nuts. Then he lifted off the bad tire, and I had to help him because it was heavy and wide. We learned it against the car.

I started to roll the spare tire to him. That's when we stopped and stood freaky-still. Both of us. I felt the insides of my stomach start to come up and think that maybe this whole day was a conspiracy or something. Because the spare tire was no bigger than the width of my palm. I'm not kidding. They'd put the wrong frigging tire in the car, I thought. Here it was only a little old tire. A play-like tire. "What is this?" I said.

Dylan measured it, too. It was as high as the others, but only about half as wide. "I guess it's meant to only get you to a filling station," he said.

"Yeah, right." I was disgusted. We'd been just about to handle this whole mess. And no one would ever have known we'd ever even been in a mess. And now this. I leaned the little play-like tire against the car and I reached into the front seat for my purse. I again pulled out my mother's cell phone and handed it to Dylan. "Call your father," I said. "Tell him what's happened. Tell him about this stupid tire and ask him what it means."

Dylan stood up and dialed the number. I didn't want to call anyone in my house. I didn't want to talk to Jack or to my mother or to anyone who thought I was on my way to Palm Key with Dylan so they'd learn I wasn't exactly on my way to Palm Key with Dylan. I didn't want to disturb their swimming-pool making. But even more.

They were already thinking I was one step from having a crippled personality for life. And now. The fact is, I would have been embarrassed to have to ask for help. At least from *them*. Besides, this weekend was between my dad and me and Dylan and Miss Vicky. And now Carl LaTour. It was a matter of my pride, my privacy, I guess you could say. In a nutshell, it felt like my life I was tending to.

"Dad?" Dylan said when someone answered. "We had a flat. We're here on the side of the road. And . . ." I knew Carl LaTour knew who "we" meant. Miss Vicky had filled him in on how the whole weekend was supposed to go.

I watched Dylan turn toward the road while he was telling his father all this. Then Dylan turned to look back at me while he asked, "He wants to know exactly where we are. Have we crossed the Waccassa River yet?"

"I don't think so," I said.

"What about Otter Creek?"

"Does that have a bridge?"

"No. It's a town, he says."

"Well, we haven't passed any towns." I was struck with how dumb Dylan and I sounded. Not knowing for sure what we'd passed. And hadn't passed. Like we could go somewhere and not even know it.

Then Dylan held the phone away from his mouth and looked at me. "He says we aren't anywhere close to Palm Key, and that it's getting so close to dark if we drove to Palm Key more than likely there'd be nowhere open to patch a tire. Or if we need to get a new one, there's no place for that at all in Palm Key. He wants to talk to you." Dylan handed me the phone.

"Hello," I said.

"Bergin?" Mr. LaTour's voice is sort of high and hoarse. I could tell he was standing in the kitchen of his restaurant because I could hear pots and pans being banged. And drink mixers whizzing.

"Yes," I answered like I would answer someone who is a teacher or something. I didn't really know Mr. LaTour. I guess I'd only seen him a handful of times.

"It's best," he said, "if you and Dylan drive back home and get the tire fixed there and then drive over in the morning. Some of those places that sell only tires will stay open tonight. Try one. I'll look one up in the phone book here and give you the address." You could tell he was thinking out loud. "Or probably even Sears will fix this tire for you. Do you have a Visa card you can use? No, call me when you get there and I'll give them my number. " He then read out of the phone book the address of a couple of places back near my dad's house that did nothing but handle tires.

"Okay," I said. "Sure. We'll call you when we get to Sears, or one of those tire places if we come to one first. That's fine. No. I don't mind doing this at all."

I put the cell phone back in my purse while Dylan put the little play-like tire on the car. It was so light and narrow, he could lift it by himself. He tightened the bolts with the lug wrench, then cranked down the jack.

It was close to dark when we got in the car. And Dylan started it. And backed it onto the road and aimed it back toward home.

As soon as we got going good on the pavement, I heard this noise. Dylan heard it, too. It was like something was loose in the trunk. A dull, thumping noise. "Oh, it's just the jack bouncing around," Dylan said. But I knew I'd wrapped the jack back up good. And put it way back up on that little carpeted shelf. It could have fallen down though, I guessed. In fact, I imagined it coming unwrapped and rolling around in the back of that huge trunk. I didn't think about the fact that we weren't turning any corners. We were on that dead-straight road head-ed back home at fifty miles an hour. And if you aren't turning corners, how does something roll? But I didn't think of that. It didn't pass

238

though my mind. We just listened to that thump all the way to the middle of Archer. And then with a loud awful sound and the car pulling like crazy. Then dipping down. Sparks flew up on my side of the car right at the fender. And that front little play-like tire that we'd put on rolled away from us. Crossed under a street light and rolled up into the parking lot of a Handy-Mart. It hit the curb and bounced back and lay down.

Dylan and I sat in the car in the middle of the road. Not quite silent. But not quite able to say anything else, either. Except *god-o-mighty*. And *holy cow*. And two pretty loud *shits*.

We got out. The traffic was backing up behind us. I followed our tire over to the Handy-Mart. Dylan squatted down in the road at the car's front wheel looking for the answer to what had happened.

It was clear to me, though. We—or rather him—he hadn't put the lug nuts back on tight enough.

The woman behind the cash register was pretty nice. Motherly, I guess you could say. She came out onto the sidewalk and looked at me standing there with our tire. And she looked out at Dylan there on the pavement with the car. She had a perm that ran over her head like Chinese noodles. The same color, too. "Y'all are two lucky young'uns," she said, looking out at the car. "It's a wonder you weren't killed, having a wheel roll off like that." Then she looked back at me. She must have seen that I was pretty close to shaking. Or a little undone. Flustered to say the least. She patted me on the shoulder. "Don't you worry, Hon'. I'll call my cousin. He runs a tow truck and he'll get you out of the middle of the street in a heartbeat. Just thank God you had a one-man wreck and didn't hit no one. Otherwise we'd be waiting till midnight for some cop to come and make out a police report. Now just leave that tire there, and go get your brother—is that who that is—is that your brother?"

"In a manner of speaking," I said.

"Well, I'll bet he'd want a Coke. " She opened the Handy-Mart store and went back inside because people were waiting to pay for gas.

It only made sense to tell Carl LaTour what had now happened to us. And that Mrs. Ferguson, who was the Handy-Mart owner, and her cousin, who we now knew was named Leon, were going to dig us out of this most recent trouble. Dylan and I waited in the Handy-Mart while Leon came to pull the Lincoln out of the middle of the road. After he did, he said what I had suspected—that the lug nuts had come off and that's how our tire had rolled off without us. "They's just about impossible to get on tight without a lug gun," Leon said, punching the hydraulic lift on his truck so the Lincoln went up in the air. "Looks, too, like the rim's *ruint*." Apparently we'd skated on it for the few feet after the tire had left us. Leon said there was nothing for us to do now but to deliver the car to the Lincoln dealer come Monday. He offered to keep it on his truck till then. *At least if he didn't have no more emergencies over the weekend*, he told us, and if he did, well, he'd just set the Lincoln down in his own front yard, then load it back up come Monday morning.

Every bit of Leon's plan was fine with me. I handed Dylan my mother's phone again. And made him dial it, then hand it to me. "Mr. LaTour?"

"Yes?"

"This is Bergin again."

"Did you get the tire fixed?"

"Sort of."

"Do you need my Visa?"

"Yeah. We really do. But we need to put a little more on it than we first thought." Then I came right out and told him like I was giving a book report or something that we—and I want you to know I did use the word *we*—hadn't put the lug nuts on tight enough and the tire had come off. I explained how we were standing on Archer Road by a Handy-Mart. And that a tow truck driver named Leon had picked up the car and was going to take it to the Lincoln dealer on Monday.

"My God, Bergin," he said, then added a bunch of other stuff about how it had been a wonder we hadn't had a bad wreck but that it sounded, too, like we'd handled it all well. That we'd done all the right things. He was real nice.

"I guess," I said. Then I put Leon on the phone so Mr. LaTour could give him his Visa number. When Leon was finished, I took back the phone. Dylan was standing by the tow truck with Leon.

"Mr. LaTour," I said.

"Yes?"

"We'll come over in my car right now. I'll let Dylan drive it. He needs to drive something after this."

Real quick, Mr. LaTour said how great he thought that'd be. And how thoughtful of me. Then he asked as an afterthought, what was that law about driver's permits that he'd just read about in the paper? And then, damn, I remembered it, too. That no one with only a permit could drive after dark. And then Mr. LaTour just ran away with my whole plan. "Come here tomorrow," he said. "I don't want you on that road after dark anyway. To tell you the truth, it's gotten pretty busy at the restaurant tonight. It'd be better for me if you waited until tomorrow." He added he'd look for us then. He said he'd take us out fishing. He'd close the restaurant after breakfast and spend the whole day with us.

"Okay." I said, because I couldn't think of anything else to say. And then I added. "We'll be over early. We'll be over at eight."

"And you'll call me if you have any more trouble?"

I don't know, it was like as soon as he said the word *trouble,* there was just this hitch of silence. And then both of us laughed. Each of us and at the same time.

"Yeah, I'll call," I said. "I still have my mother's phone."

LEON DROPPED us off in my father's driveway. As we drove up, that struck me as pretty funny, too, how we rolled up in the driveway in the tow truck with the Lincoln on top. We got out and Dylan went into the house.

I stood in the driveway, though. This was the only part I wasn't sure I could handle. Or ever want to do. To go into my father's house, sleep there, eat there, stay there through a whole night. *The house where I had died.* I looked at my green Celica parked in front of the garage. I could spend the night in my car.

Or I could call someone, someone to come get me. Some friend. But who? What would I say? I could tell about how the car had lost its tire. And that's what I would do. I'd call Simpson. I'd leave Dylan here by himself and come get him in the morning. And then as I was deciding this, Dylan came out of the back door holding a fistful of money. It was what Miss Vicky had told me she'd left in the kitchen by the sink. Dylan grinned, holding it up and looking at me. "Let's get something to eat," he said. "And then, go somewhere. We can stay out all night. Why don't we just . . . you wouldn't tell, would you? Why would they ever have to know?"

I wasn't about to mess up the only perfect plan Dylan had ever thought up.

That's how we found ourselves at Cafe Gardens. And then at a sports bar. And then at The Potted Geranium. Which was the only club we found that was open at 1 A.M. that didn't give us flak about I.D.'s at the door.

We sat at a table in the back with a red and white checkered tablecloth. Until a woman introduced as Mindy Sparks, who was pregnant, in a red tent dress, came out. She sat on a stool and propped a guitar on her stomach. So that all of a sudden Dylan half yelled out, "My God! That's the woman who works in your dad's office." So we skulked out. Didn't have anywhere to go then. Had no choice after that but to go home. At least to Dylan's home. To stay out of sight for the rest of the night.

I stayed out in the backyard for a while. The cat Liposuction came and rubbed against my legs. He nearly gave me a heart attack when he came out of the bushes and up against my legs in the dark, so dark I could see nothing. Almost nothing. I was sitting in a lounge chair on the patio by then. It's amazing how dark a whole neighborhood can get at three in the morning. Only a porch or garage light on. Here or there. And the moon just a thumbnail of pale white light, no bigger.

At about three-thirty, I walked inside the house. I had to go to the bathroom. And I didn't want to just hunker down in the yard. I went through the kitchen. And the family room. The glass walls were like black curtains. Dylan had left just about the whole house lit up. I walked down the back hall to the bathroom. And then when I came out I decided I really ought to check on Dylan. After all, he was my charge. He was spread out, chest down, full length on his bed in his clothes, even his shoes. Asleep. His mouth open. His chest going up and down. He'd left the light on like he didn't want to sleep in this house either, alone, and in all dark. The same posters of motorcycles were on the walls. Nothing had changed. CD's were still stacked to the ceiling. His computer was turned off and sitting quiet. I guess he'd shut it down thinking he'd be away for the whole weekend.

I walked down the hall and looked in at the room that had been mine. It still smelled to me a little like Stella. It was dark. But the hall light was on. And so I could see the pink ruffly curtains that still kissed the pale blue rug. And the dressing table with a mirror big enough to reflect only me. The bed was neatly made. Probably every-thing on it had been washed in scalding water. Probably everything in the whole room had been sprayed with a disinfectant. But I could smell Stella, still. I could still remember me and how I had been in that room and smell the smell of incense and hear the sound of the rain that day. Or the rain I didn't hear that day but should have heard. Could have heard. And the footsteps of Dylan coming to find me that I did not hear. But could hear now because I knew about them now. And that I had lived.

Somebody ought to take it apart. Somebody ought to take the whole room apart and chuck it. Get rid of it somehow.

I went down to the room that was my father's and Miss Vicky's. The place where they spend all their ever-loving. Every day. Whole married life now. The bed was big enough to be a raft. One of those California kings, I think it is called. And I had to laugh. Because Miss Vicky had recently changed the bedspread to a Victorian pink. Raspberry, I think it's called. It didn't have ruffles on it. But it was sure enough pink-to-the-bone in my book. And I was again amazed at the power of love. Or what must be sure-enough-clear-to-the-backbone love. Because I couldn't imagine my father sleeping on pink for any other reason.

I went down the hall that ended in his study. I thought maybe I could sit down there on one of his brown leather chairs and nap. I was so tired my neck felt like a wet weed. The room was done in blue and brown. And there were stripes in the curtains on the windows. The desk was huge and slick. And bookcases went up three walls around it. I sat down behind the desk in his chair that could swirl in any direction.

I leaned back in it. It smelled like a saddle. Like shaving lotion, too, or the skin that I always smelled whenever I hugged my father. Or got close to him. The smell of his skin that I always associated with who he was. The smell that could be on his clothes. Or in his car. Or on a note he had written. And I pulled open one of the drawers and started looking through it. Letting loose the smell that I thought of as him. And then after one drawer, another and another. And then in the bottom deep one, a sketch pad. It was a pad like an art student would use. Or someone like that. And I remembered that my dad did that sometimes. Rarely. But sometimes. Sketched things. Still-lifes mostly. No landscapes. Just still-lifes. Pots. Rocks. Bricks. Hands. He was always big on hands. He used to draw mine when I was little. He would make me hold them still sometimes, so he could draw them, he said. And I would bring him my plaster of Paris hands when we would do them in grade school for Father's Day. Or whatever. I knew he would always like my hands in clay or paint or outlined in only a pencil.

And as I picked up the sketch pad and started looking through it, I was not sure at first of what I was seeing. Because there were hands here, too. And an ear. Several ears, in fact. And an eye. An eye closed. And then an eye half-closed. And an eye with a lid that looked as though it were sewn shut. I kept turning the pages. An arm went down the side of something white and wrinkled. The wrinkles were drawn with the sides of the charcoal pencil, you could tell. They looked smeared. I remembered how my father would sometimes use his finger to smudge a line, to make a shadow, to add depth. And then I turned another page and saw the form of a body under white cloth, the wrinkles holding the form, and covering almost all of it. And there was a profile. The face of someone with eyes shut. And I saw that it was me.

It was in a hospital bed. And a hospital place. You could tell by the outlines in the background. The ears, the eyes, the arms. They had all been me. Parts of me. I remembered how he had sat beside me. And I had thought he had been beside me reading. But instead it had been this. He had been drawing me. At least parts of me. Saving me. At least in this way.

I put the sketch pad back into the desk drawer and closed it. I went out into the backyard. What I had seen was as powerful as what I feared. And being in the house was where it all was. One. And the Other. Death. Life. Loss. Love. I guess you could say, if you really want to name it. And I just wanted to be out here. Be a little distance away.

I lay down on one of the lounge chairs. I must have fallen asleep. Because when I opened my eyes something was heavy on my chest. And one of my arms was numb. It was Liposuction curled up on top of me. He was purring. It's a great sound, when you really think about it. A purr. The way a cat can purr. And I hadn't thought about that before. I'd never really known that. And it's true even when it's a fat ugly cat. And one I've never much liked.

I looked at my watch. It was 6:12. In twenty minutes I was going to wake up Dylan. In twenty minutes, I was going to let him drive me to Palm Key. But over the next twenty minutes, I wanted to do nothing. Not even think. I just wanted to lie here and wait for the sun.

SO THAT'S pretty much how all of yesterday went. And it is over now. And it is 5 P.M. And it is Sunday, and we are in my car. My little green Celica on the way home. Dylan is in the backseat. And I am driving now. Because he is asleep.

It is the same black flat strip of pavement that I have been back and forth on two full. And about one half times. In two days. Straight as a rope pulled tight. Past a whole field of bulldozed pines. Where trees lie upended like a matchbox spilled. And I am past Otter Creek and am nearly to the Waccassa River. Whose Indian sound on my tongue is a dance I want to keep going.

It turned out that when we finally got to Palm Key. Most of the way which I slept, because I couldn't help it. And Mr. LaTour met us in the driveway of his house when we pulled up. Dylan behind the wheel of my Celica like a hired driver who'd done fine. Who'd never run off the road one time. Or over anybody, either. Mr. LaTour hugged us. *Us,* both. And he said it was too darn windy to go out in his boat. But how about we go down to the town pier after a big breakfast.

And so that's where we went. Stuffed with egg omelet and French toast, we carried stuff out onto the big pier in the middle of the town where a lot of people already were. Where the sky was like a sky I had never seen. Like a sky I did not know even existed. Because it circled me. Held me like a glass palm that I could turn all the way around in and never leave. It was like I was inside of the earth itself. And I was looking out. Out at a white-streaked, off-and-on rosy-stained sky so full of clouds I felt dipped in foam. Mr. LaTour was serious about this. He had a wire cart that we could set three poles in and a bucket of bait. Little ol' silver fish the length of a long finger. He put one on a hook for me and handed me the pole. He had on a red cap and a plaid shirt and sunglasses. He handed Dylan a pole beside me. And I sat down on a built-in bench there and propped my pole against my knees.

The water seemed to be dancing with the sun, silver triangles constantly moving. The front that had come in with all its rain had made the water murky, the color of coffee. Beside me a boy dipped a pyramid-shaped crab trap, with a bait fish inside it, up and down in the water. Too impatient to leave it for long. Up and down, up and down, just all morning.

The water murky like that meant the fishing wasn't good. But Dylan and I didn't know that. Didn't know that, till later when I overheard someone on the pier say that. So we were just there on the pier fishing about like we were just pretending to be fishing. Just to be there. And Mr. LaTour surely all along knew this. But didn't say anything about that. And the sun through the fabric on my back was so warm. And the wind kept licking my skin. Palm trees on an island across from us were straight against the horizon like umbrellas. Tiny umbrellas. And the waves came in like pleats in fabric. Or like wrinkles. And the sky changing. Always changing. One minute gray with clouds like a tent over us. Then holes punched in where a sharp blue, lit to the color of a robin's egg, came through. A sailboat was anchored and bobbing near the island. Its triangle sails were as white as bone on the metal-colored water. And the water fabric kept being folded over and over against the shore.

A pelican begged for my bait fish beside me. He came so close he was like a person, like someone who wanted to read something over my shoulder. I turned to looked at him. He looked like an old pelican, or at least one who has seen a lot of weather. He was gray brown with dark wings. Ugly as a thrown-away board. He had a ring on one leg, and his funny deep beak ended like the sharp curved tip of a fingernail. But what tickled me, made me want to laugh out loud—to tell you the truth—was that he blinked. Just like a human. A bored or sleepy human. Every few seconds right on cue his eyelid would close. His eye would open, then shut. Open. Then shut. While the mast of a sailboat tied to the pier made a clinking sound in the wind. And every once in a while a pelican would fly off behind me, its wings flapping in a dull thump of beaten air.

"What are we fishing for?" Dylan asked his father.

"Sheepshead," Mr. LaTour said, just as if we were serious.

Walking back to Mr. LaTour's house, we saw a one-eared dog. He stood in the middle of the street, red-haired and mean-scared. His tail looped over his back like a cocked fist. When the wind stopped, we were bitten by *no-see-em's*. And when we got back to the house we sprayed something on our skins with a spicy smell that was greasy.

Then cleaned our fishing stuff in the outdoor shower there in Mr. LaTour's yard.

AND SO I AM driving back now, Dylan in the backseat like a rag that breathes and snores. He is drooling on the seat, no doubt. But I am looking at the road and watching the rain come onto the windshield, and then I turn on the wipers so that for a moment the glass is smeared with dust and sand. Then clears.

I am past the place now where Dylan and I pulled over after the flat. And I am past where we lost the tire, and it rolled off without us. I am two seconds from dropping Dylan off at my father's house and heading over to the other one where I live. But something inside of me is moving. Something during this last hour, while I have been driving the straight-as-a-rope-pulled-tight road where there is so little to see but scrub and ditches and land laid out where no one lives, is not the same. So that the rain in between the beats of the wipers seems as big as oceans. And I notice the new green on top of the stick-ugly pines like the fingers on hands, in the wind, waving. Cars pass me with their lights on. The rain taps.

And my head is full of one-eared dogs and sky that moves, and fish that we never see but wait for and bait hooks for. And birds that beat the air with wings and blink. And my hands. Pictures of my hands. And ears. And eyes. The whole long length of me with cloth wrinkling over me like the water of the Gulf does day after day, hour after hour, against the shore. Moves before my eyes. So it is like I turn to look at something I did not before see. And I have the funniest feeling. The craziest funniest feeling. Like I have a crush on something. Something like that. That's how it feels. As if I am falling in love. And I can't think of one single god-o-mighty holy-other thing that I could be so hot on except maybe my own, I guess you could say. This. Minute by minute. Anyway, for now. Life. My own, just as it is. And might, in a whole other minute, be.

SEVENTEEN

Leslie

This spring afternoon is one that cannot be described because it is bright beyond bright, with the air holding a moistness in it that seems to wrap around my skin, bathing it. I sit across from Dr. Cone in her office and we talk easily; yet beneath our words, which are a mere top dressing, there is a reality I am not used to. She sits behind her desk, unimposingly, and I am here in the teak armchair across from her. She does not know I know what I do.

Today we are dressed almost alike in gray striped suits—hers a pant suit, mine a mid-calf straight skirt suit, so I can be in court this afternoon. She knows me in ways that no one else ever will, since for months now she has represented me—which sounds like lawyer talk, but I mean in the sense of playing the part of me—to Bergin; I assume that. She has, no doubt, let Bergin bounce her emotions about me off her, become parts of Doug, too, as though turning a kaleidoscope of family members before Bergin's mind and eyes. But most of all, she has taught Bergin to see differently. I know that. I want to thank her for saving my daughter.

For once, I feel a squeezing in my throat, a silence that seems to make me forget words—me, *me,* who has never before been out of touch with a long list of any one of them that would do.

It was last week that I could no longer keep that part of myself unexpressed and under wraps, as you might say: my probing lawyer-self that would not live on the top layer, only, or, more accurately, would not focus on *only* me. I wanted to know her, know her now in something equal to the way she knows me—in fact, all of us—to the core and beyond, you might say. And I wanted to know, too: Why is she so good? Exceptionally good. Unconventional, yes. But beyond adequate; that is clear. Until now I've been content with Jack's assurance: *she's one of the best; don't worry; we're in good hands.* About her professionally was all I'd wanted to know. But now, maybe it was because of the way I am beginning to feel: that after all, all of us are coming to a new place—that we are all feeling differently—that my instincts for digging came fully awake.

For two days, off and on among other things, I made phone calls, and wrote e-mails, and found colleagues of hers in nearby cities. It was a former secretary in Baltimore who had known her a decade before she came here who told me more than the facts.

Now, "None of us is the same," I say to Dr. Cone, as a start.

"How not the same?" She threads her fingers together and props her chin on her hands.

"Clearly things are better," I tell her. "We are all better. And yet, it will never be like it was. Bergin will never be like she once was."

"No. And is that good or bad?"

"Both."

"And you grieve for what is different?"

"Yes. But I celebrate what is new, too."

She smiles at me. "And you won't be the same, either."

"No."

She nods. We are here now in the place of my fears and have to ride that out. Before, I have made stabs at trying to tell her what haunts me, letting her see the depth to which I am afraid to go when I feel again what Bergin has taught me. Of how it was when I thought that I had lost her—not only physically—but in that other way, too. To have thought that I had damaged us so deeply that we could never again trust each other, say what we meant. I knew I could not again survive that. And so I thought about being more careful. I wanted to make us all more careful. We had to tend to what we had with a consciousness that would not let us forget what we could do, unknowingly, impetuously, do. I knew too well that there is never a way to go back and undo what is done. When I first began sharing these fears with her, I thought she couldn't understand. Now, though, I have unearthed the wellspring of her exceptional compassion. And I will never let her know that I know. For the secretary had told me that Dr. Cone had lost a child, years ago—a son who, like Bergin, decided to take his own life, and did. He had been only nineteen.

She nods now. We both smile. She offers me some mixed nuts. "Your fear is in direct proportion to your love," she reminds me, then asks about other things, about other signs.

What I don't tell her are about the things I would never tell her, just as the things she would never tell me. But they are good signs nonetheless. About how the weekend before, when on Saturday Bergin had been with Dylan in Palm Key, Jack and I and the twins had worked on that damn swimming pool hole. We had dug the machines out of the mud and pushed the soft earth around, sometimes with one twin in each of our laps while riding on the tractor and backhoe. So we were ready for bed with bones so tired I felt a century old and barely walking.

Maggie and Kirk fell asleep in front of the TV and we lifted them, one in each of our arms, to carry them to bed. As we closed their bedroom doors, Jack reached for me. He curled his finger under the bracelet that he gave me and that I never take off, so he led me by it as though it were a hook and he had me, totally had me. I tugged back. But he teased. He wouldn't let me go. He led me, took me by the bracelet and his finger into the barn and to the stairs that lead up to the loft. "I want to show you something," he said.

Mutton and Chops were in their stalls stamping, tired of standing in the mud out in the pasture and hoping, at the sound of our footsteps, we would throw them more supper. But I had fed them plenty earlier and vowed not to give in. Besides, I was still mad at Chops for being so damn uncooperative when I wanted to ride him. The dogs followed us, except they couldn't climb the ladder. So they stayed at the bottom and whined. Spam didn't bother, because after the heavy rains he was too happy with his soupy azalea hole.

"What? What?" I kept asking, and half laughing.

"You'll see. You'll see."

He led me up each step of the ladder to the back of the loft where only a few bales of hay were left and where the tapestry luggage that was meant to be Bergin's Christmas present still sits like surreal rectangles meant for what, no one knows. "Look," Jack said, pulling up a bale for us to sit and lean against and pointing out of the high window that is at the back of the loft.

"What?"

"The sky."

"What about the sky?"

"Just look."

"It's so cloudy there's nothing to see."

"Um humm." He leaned against me and stroked my neck with his opened palm. Then he kissed me all the way down it.

"It's just an ordinary cloudy sky," I said.

"Um humm." While he was busy with my buttons, he added, "That's exactly what I wanted you to see."

I started laughing then. "And a little bit more, too, I see," and then found myself responding.

NOW I LOOK at Dr. Cone and ask with all the serenity in the world, because I know there are no answers to anything I want to know, "Is there a chance Bergin will be able to leave next year, as she would have? Do you think she'll be able to go to college? Or what should we be thinking about? Should we be making any plans?"

"Every bit of all of that is possible. But I don't know when."

"This has all been so strange," I say. "So strange. I've never known what it felt like to be so out of control. To have so many mysteries come into my life. To have it be run away with so definitely, so . . . beyond me."

"But not irretrievably."

"No." I smiled, thinking again of Jack and that he seemed to always be able to center my life, bring me back to it, make me feel things I was unaware that I could feel. "I still have to know where she is, though," I tell her. "All the time and in spite of myself. I seem to have to know where she is all the time, every minute. I can't *not* feel in touch."

"That's understandable."

"So it's not crazy?" I realize that when I ask that, I sound like a child myself. Then I say with total self-awareness, "But I can drive her crazy about it, though. I know that. I know what I feel is unreasonable at times."

"But it's okay."

We look at each other silently for a minute. I stand up, mention my court date and that I have to run. It is now that I do what I have come to do: to thank her for saving my daughter. I try to say every-thing I want to. But she brushes me off. She is like me, embarrassed by the fuss. As I leave, I reach for the door handle, take hold of it and turn it, and then I look once more back at her and smile. Funny, she can be as quiet as Doug at times, and yet her silence is swollen with warmth. I do not read into it anything but good things. Good, *good* things.

I walk out toward the parking lot. Every step down the halls and through the glass doors, I feel Jack. This is his place, his home away from home. He is always here in one form or another. And now I think of Bergin here, too, in every step, in every door I go through.

"Hey!" The sound of it startles me, for I have my head down, looking at the concrete walk. But when I look up, I see Hoot squatted down in a dug-up flower bed, putting in rows of tiny geraniums. I stop and greet him, and he stands up and we talk for a minute. He looks well, or as well as Hoot will ever look, considering all he has done to himself in the past. Then I tell him how proud of him I am. I say it twice, and each time he grins but tries not to. He squats back down now, because he can tell I am in a hurry and about to walk off. As he upends another of the little pots to fish out the roots and flower all in one, he calls out to me, "How's your daughter doing?"

I am near the curb now where I will cross into the parking lot. I really am almost late; but then, I don't exactly stop, but I hesitate. I hang at the curb just an extra second, my foot suspended in space those few inches above the pavement, because I can't help myself: I call back with a loud and strong voice, almost singing it, because as I say it, I realize it's the truth, the absolute and ongoing truth. "Well!" I say, "She's doing really, really well, Hoot! And thanks for asking!"

I step down and head for my car, holding onto the sweet sound of nothing else but those simple single words.

EIGHTEEN

Bergin

I was walking down the steps of the school and into the parking lot. And, well, my life is pretty much a funny thing now just about all the time. Like, how at the same minute I was walking out of the school and seeing Luke across the parking lot, the phone was ringing in my purse. And I knew who it was. Didn't even need to answer to know. I was waving at Luke and knowing that if I didn't answer the phone I would not be able to live with knowing I would be pushing a valuable member of society over the edge, if you know what I mean. Because *she* had given the phone to me in the first place. Given it to me to put in my god-o-mighty purse. To be with me every minute of the day. Just all the time. And I don't think I need to even say, *guess who?* So I was letting it ring while I walked to my car. Luke and half the football team were crowded around his car, shooting the bull. Or chewing the fat. Whatever you want to call it.

I yelled, "Hey!" to them, and they waved back. Because I can think about Luke and say *hey* to Luke, and be okay with everything about Luke. Because I know he's as caught in trying to be what he thinks *he* should be as I was caught in trying to be what I figured *I* was supposed to be. And when I wanted to cool things off with us, he just simply hadn't known any other way to respond than to be hurt, to think I didn't care for him at all. So it is the lack of words, of the *right* words, and silence—I know now—that can twist the way a person sees. Can put the whole world under water, so that sounds and sights and thoughts go strange. But I was hearing now only too clearly the phone still ringing in my purse. So I stopped and answered the holy-mama cell phone that was, of course, attached to the holy mama back home. Or at her office in the courthouse. Or wherever.

"Bergin," she said as soon as I said, "Yeah, what?" which is the way I always answer, since 95 percent of the time I know it's going to be her. "Are you coming straight home today? Because I was wondering. You know, it's my night to fix supper and be home early because Jack has that meeting at the hospital. And Lydia is out of town. And I was thinking I'd have homemade pizza. But I really don't know how to pull off the dough. So, would you mind stopping at the Foodway and picking up one of those crusts that hang in bags on a rack somewhere near the meat department?"

"No problem," I said, then flipped down the little lid on the cell phone that she pays for me to carry with me just everywhere, all the time. I slipped it back in my purse.

That's how I found myself standing in the Foodway looking around for the pizza crust, knowing that it wasn't just for pizza crust that she had called me. "Be patient with her," Dr. Cone had told me the last time I had seen her. Then had smiled about like she was singing a country western song. "'Cause as you know, love comes in all shapes and forms."

"Yeah."

"And I think she just wants to hear the sound of your voice."

"I know."

I see her all the time now. Dr. Cone. But not professionally, except if I want to. Because I am volunteering a few afternoons a week in the

Discharge Department at the hospital. I help people pack up their stuff and roll them out in wheelchairs and all of that. And I see Hoot out there all the time working in the flower beds. Sometimes we have a break together. Hoot and I. We go down to the cafeteria for a Coke.

So I stood there in the meat section of the Foodway looking down at my foot in a sandal because the weather has turned warm. Last week we had one of those spring break kind of days when practically the whole senior class at school skipped and went to the beach. But instead I mowed the back pasture on the tractor in my bikini. So I have this strange tan, like the line where my tennis shoe was is now on my feet like I have white fake feet glued on. It was crazy funny and nice how the whole time I was riding the tractor I was happy. Just happy as Spam in slop, if you know what I mean.

And one time I stopped and turned the motor off and let it be quiet. I was just sitting on the tractor seat, not a soul around. The whole place was quiet except for birds. I was sitting there looking crazy funny in my bikini, leaning back in the tractor seat, when somewhere in the woods, the woods down behind the pasture so they are a far distance from where I was, I heard clearly and suddenly a tree fall. Instantly I knew that something powerful—or momentous, I guess you could say, since I might as well put all those SAT words that I have stuffed into my god-o-mighty head over the last four years to some kind of good use—had happened. Anyway, a tree. And falling. The splitting sound of the trunk cracking, then the rustling of leaves as it tore downward through the branches of other trees, then the dull thump on the ground. They do that sometimes. Soaked heavy from rain and the trunks hollow. Especially the sweetgums. So that the rotted wood just gives way. And no one can say when or where. It's sad when you think about it. The loss of a tree. But it was wonderful too, that I was there to hear it. And that's what I was thinking. That I was glad. Glad that, like Dr. Cone had told me, things move. Change. Get better. Or at least different. And that I'd stuck around to know that.

So I took the packaged pizza dough and headed back out to my car. I call Simpson sometimes on my mother's phone while I am driving. She says there is this cute boy in her class at her school who saw me with her last week at the movie we went to. And he wants to call me. Go out with me. I don't know. Sometimes I think I'm sick of cute boys. But I'm thinking about it.

Nothing, though, in this whole crazy funny life of mine can equal now what Miss Vicky did two days ago. That's when she called me and said, "Can I have dinner with you, Bergin?"

Then she added, "It doesn't have to be anything that will take too much of your time. I know you have a lot of things to do at school and all. But a quick supper somewhere where just the two of us can talk, if you know what I mean."

I told her, sure, fine, I knew what she meant.

So she took me to Shoney's. Picked me up in the Lincoln Town Car because she insisted. Didn't even mention the scratches and the bent wheel we'd put on it, when Dylan and I had our little wreck.

So she guided me into a booth in the back. There were all these gray-headed people in there getting the early bird specials. Right after we sat down and ordered, Miss Vicky began giggling. She put a hand over her mouth. Her fingernails were painted a light pink. The pink of a tongue. Or of the inside of Liposuction's ear. Something as rosy-faint as that. Then she just blurted out. "Bergin, honey. You're only the third person besides me in the whole world to know. I'm going to have a baby!"

It took me a minute to digest that. Or at least start to digest that.

Then I started counting. Because if I was only the third other person to know, that meant she'd probably already told my dad and Dylan. And that was it.

But as you might expect, I didn't need to ask about what the rest of us thought, because while our fried chicken dinners were being set down in front of us, Miss Vicky was already going into that. "Your dad, of course, just about fainted when I told him. And the truth is, I just barely know. Just *barely* know. Only about six weeks. I thought it was menopause at first. You know, early onset. But no. The doctor says it's for real. The real thing. And I think your dad really did think I wasn't able. And I guess I *am* pretty close to being a medical miracle. But after he got over the initial shock. Well, he didn't say much. But I could tell. And I can tell every day that he gets up and when he goes to bed and the way he looks. Well, I think he's just tickled pink."

I laughed.

I couldn't help myself. It just all struck me that way. And I'm laughing still. Because the next thing Miss Vicky asked me was would I mind if she redecorated my old room in her and my dad's house and gave it to the new baby?

And then, would I mind that whenever I stayed with them if she put me in the guest room? Or how would I like it if I helped her redecorate the guest room the way I'd like to have it?

So the room with the pink ruffly curtains long enough to kiss the pale blue rug and the dressing table with a mirror big enough to reflect only me is. Get this. Going to be turned into a room for a baby who will be arriving almost exactly seven and a half months to the day from the one when we were sitting in Shoney's planning for it.

No way, I told her. No way would I ever mind.

So the room where I could not bear to ever go again will never even be there ever again for me to try to go into again. Except as a room where someone wholly new and unexpected is going to live.

Miss Vicky then asked me if I would mind if she used my name, too, should it turn out that the baby is a girl. Elizabeth Bergin, she wants to name it. And call it Lizzie B.

Not at all, I told her. Not at all.

Of course we'll know the gender in another few months, because Miss Vicky says she fully intends to have that amniocentesis test, seeing as how she's so old. She invited me to be with her at the hospital when she gets that test, in fact. And when she invited me, I laughed again.

It really is funny, when you think about it. How everything is turning out. It really is nice, too, if you know what I mean.

SO I WALKED in about an hour ago, carrying the pizza dough. I walked by the table in the hall where we put the mail.

I saw three letters there addressed to me. I know what they are. I know now why my mother was calling me. Wanting me to get straight home. The pizza dough was only an excuse.

Because she would not mention what is here. But that the letters are on her mind. All the time, on her mind. And she wants to know what I will do. Will do.

And Kirk and Maggie were whirling around in the kitchen under her feet. And she said *hey* to me. And thanks for the pizza dough, to me. But does not mention what is on the table in the hall addressed to me.

As I passed through the kitchen to drop off the dough, I saw all these pots and pans pulled out like supper is going to be a major deal. Which it always is. And she has on an apron that says on the front, *There are two choices for dinner. Take it. Or Leave it.*

But I am now lying on my bed with Stella beside me. From here I am listening to Kirk and Maggie and my mother banging things around and chattering and trying to get the dough to look like it really is going to be a fit-to-eat pizza.

Probably sooner or later, I'll go out there. All three of those letters are from one college or the other. More than likely one of them will say yes.

Sooner or later, too, I know that one day she will mention what is up in the loft. And she will pretend how she forgot to give it to me for last Christmas. Then we will climb up there and together carry all that luggage down.

What I am sure of, though, is that everything that has happened to us will never ever let us be like we were. I won't ever tell it like this again, either. I don't think we'll ever even talk about it much ever again. If at all. But that's okay. Every bit of that is fine.

I can live with that. In fact, that's how I want to live with that.

But for now, I don't know how else anything will be fit to eat, if I don't take a part in it. Only just a second ago I heard a jar of something, probably tomato sauce, bang onto the floor, and Maggie scream.

And now my mother is starting to cuss in her made-up no-sense language. I guess I better get up.

Like I said, it's pretty crazy funny, when you think about it. Pretty nice, too, if you also know what I mean. How everything is turning out. And I probably ought to go on in there, because I have just now heard another pot crash.

It's clear. They need me.

THE END

ABOUT THE AUTHOR

SHELLEY FRASER MICKLE is an energetic, modest person who sees the good in the world and tries to make it even better.

A commentator for Florida Public Radio since 1995, she has read many humorous essays on NPR's *Morning Edition*, which have been published in a collection titled *The Kids Are Gone, the Dog Is Depressed, and Mom's on the Loose*. Many other essays of hers have been published in the *Orlando Sentinel*.

She is the author of two previous novels: *The Queen of October*, which was a *New York Times* Notable Book, and *Replacing Dad*, which was made into a CBS television movie.

Mickle is the mother of two grown children and lives on a farm in Alachua County, Florida. Her web site is www.shelleymickle.com.

Mickle, Shelley
Fraser

The turning hour